Jordan Bryant

LISKA JACOBS

Catalina

Liska Jacobs is a Los Angeles native. She holds an MFA from the University of California, Riverside–Palm Desert. Her essays and short fiction have appeared in *The Rumpus, The Los Angeles Review of Books, Literary Hub, The Millions,* and *The Hairpin,* among other publications. *Catalina* is her first novel.

CATALINA

CATALINA

LISKA JACOBS

MCD × FSG Originals · New York

MCD × FSG Originals
Farrar, Straus and Giroux
175 Varick Street, New York 10014

Library of Congress Cataloging-in-Publication Data
Names: Jacobs, Liska, 1983– author.
Title: Catalina / Liska Jacobs.
Description: First edition. | New York : MCD / Farrar, Straus and Giroux, 2017.
Identifiers: LCCN 2017001263 | ISBN 9780374119751 (pbk.) |
  ISBN 9780374716721 (ebook)
Subjects: LCSH: Young women—Fiction. | Self-destructive behavior—Fiction. |
  GSAFD: Psychological fiction.
Classification: LCC PS3610.A356446 C38 2017 | DDC 813/.6—dc23
LC record available at https://lccn.loc.gov/2017001263

Designed by Abby Kagan

Our books may be purchased in bulk for promotional, educational, or business
use. Please contact your local bookseller or the Macmillan Corporate and
Premium Sales Department at 1-800-221-7945, extension 5442, or by e-mail at
MacmillanSpecialMarkets@macmillan.com.

www.fsgoriginals.com • www.fsgbooks.com
Follow us on Twitter, Facebook, and Instagram at @fsgoriginals

1   3   5   7   9   10   8   6   4   2

For Stephanie

CATALINA

1

It's just past breakfast so I order up a pitcher of Bloody Marys and a bagel. I dash off a text to Mother: *I've landed safely, sorry I couldn't stay longer.* The phone is a slick new thing, touch screen with buttons too small for my fingers but still they make a satisfying *click click.* Before I left New York I bought a Gucci case for it—alligator skin, because it was gaudy and expensive, and because I liked the idea of a decorative predator. I turn the ringer off and slip the phone into one of the dresser drawers.

The Miramar is a bougainvillea-and-jasmine hotel—cobblestone circular drive, name in cursive on a black iron gate, golden California light spilling everywhere. My room faces the pier, and when I'm out on the balcony it's like walking on the giant banyan and jumble of palm trees below.

All the cocktails here are named after celebrities: the Capote is a mess of bourbon and mint, the Marilyn has gin and a cherry. The Bloody Mary is the only one named for what it is, and after the last two days, it's exactly what I need.

I had gone to Bakersfield because New York had turned on me. It felt treacherous, everywhere reminders of *him*. I wanted somewhere I would feel safe, somewhere familiar. Instead, almost as soon as I got off the plane I remembered why I left Bakersfield in the first place. Mother, with her thin lipstick smile. How she reached out for my shoulder, but took my bag instead. How she never asked how I was feeling, only said how thin I was, how great my skin looked. By the time she invited my older brothers over for Sunday dinner—something that never happened when I was around, but apparently became a tradition once they bought houses in the area—I was already looking up flights to Los Angeles.

They showed up with their perky, two-of-a-kind wives and their darling, demonic children. At first they feigned surprise at seeing me, but then one did his best Donald Trump: *You're fired*, he said, pushing his thinning hair to one side and pointing at me. His wife pinched him, saying, *Don't listen to him, hun, it's happening everywhere*, while her boys tugged at her jeans, chanting *Mom, Mom, Mom*. In the kitchen, Mother wasn't just holding down the button on the blender, she was pulsing it—the ice for her margaritas *crunch-crunching* between the kids' chanting, *Mom, Mom*.

I took the first flight out this morning. Then it was just a short cab ride to Santa Monica. I try not to imagine the face Mother will make once she realizes I've left.

I hang my dresses and blouses and slacks, calling up for more hangers. I arrange my shoes in the closet as if I am moving in. I read over the dry cleaning services and note that they will press your socks free of charge.

The bed is wide, a California king, with a down comforter that puffs up around me like a hug, saying, *just wait, just wait*.

I try not to think of how few options I have left. How being laid off feels like an end that rings on and on. How Eric did not ask me to stay—how in that last moment, in his office, he did not stand up and say anything. Just sat there, hand beside mine, close but not touching, until the human resources woman coughed politely and he moved it away.

But let's not think of that.

I look up at the ceiling, where a fan made to look like palm fronds turns in quiet arcs. Just beyond the eggshell walls is a bustling little beach city—my college town. Those days seem so long ago. Charly and Jared are living in Santa Monica now. Southern California homeowners, for God's sake.

Their wedding, more than six years ago, was the last time we were all together. Charly, lovely in white lace, already making excuses for Jared, with his sweaty upper lip, still hungover from his bachelor party.

At the reception, a DJ announced Mr. and Mrs. Jared Brownstone to a cheering room, and Robby stood, whistling and clapping. Jared raised his arms above his head, a victorious gladiator, and the crowd ate it up, their cheering thunderous. Someone stood on a chair and shouted into a megaphone. Others used the toy hand clappers with the bride's and groom's names written in white paint. I took a Xanax with champagne, telling myself to be quiet—to ignore that nervous flutter, silence that inner alarm. *Just be content. Drink and be content. This can be enough for you too. You are married to your own college sweetheart. It has not even been a year. Give it time, just wait.* Charly beaming—*beaming*—as she looked at me from across the room. A look of cul-de-sac contentment, a future filled with barbeques, pool parties, and playdates. *This is enough for her,* I thought. *It is enough for them all.* And then there was Robby, frowning at me because I asked the waiter for another glass of champagne. Because lately I'd been taking Xanax like Tic Tacs. *But Robby,* I thought, *don't you want a happy little wife?*

I started looking for jobs in New York the next day.

Our little clique has kept in touch since then, mostly online. I know all about Jared's promotions, Charly's new job at the elementary school, how they began renovations on their house, and how a few months ago when they were in New York we somehow did not

5

find the time to see each other. And Robby too—his new job working for Jared, and dating a woman who takes a lot of selfies, all outdoors, usually summiting some peak.

Should I call them? I'm not ready to hear Robby's voice—still tense and hurt, waiting to be let back in. Charly? She will definitely want to go shopping. And we will get Frappuccinos with skim milk, and try on dresses, and talk about whatever argument she and Jared are currently in the middle of. God, how exhausting to be back.

I can almost feel my old self, that girl who loved art—museums especially—who dreamed of a career far from here. Poor girl, joke's on you. You're back. Your old life just waiting for you, like a second skin.

When I called Charly from Bakersfield, she whooped: *Elsa's finally coming home!* She chattered on about planning a trip for us. Robby wanted to see a jazz festival happening on Catalina Island. A friend of Jared's had a sailboat. *It'll be perfect,* she said. *It'll be just like old times.*

And that second skin goes *zip.*

In eighth grade, Charly's parents divorced and her mother took her to Southern California, to Simi Valley. We reconnected at UCLA years later. We fell back into it easily, discovering that whatever made our childhood friendship necessary was still there. Then, sometime after my divorce with Robby, as she settled into a life that consisted mostly of pleasing Jared and I was occupied with a new job, we let our friendship lag. It was easy to do. I urged it along, letting weeks go by before returning phone calls or answering emails, intentionally keeping my New York life separate. Private. But Charly is loyal to a fault. Like a good soldier. Or a dog.

This is when being sober is the worst. I call to check on my room-service order, asking them to bring extra pillows and Advil too. The room-service boy lingers, saying he thinks redheads are pretty. He's young and breakable and it would feel so goddamn good to break something. He's cute, with a cleft in his chin, but I'm way too tired to do anything about it.

I shower with my drink and take one of Mother's Vicodins. *Let it begin*, I think, rolling myself into one of the hotel bathrobes, the fabric soft and vibrantly white, wonderfully impersonal. *Let it begin.*

2

Only a week ago, I'm in my tiny New York apartment, thinking about what will happen if I flee. Beside the set of Alvar Aalto vases is a file box, heavy with pens, papers, and an automatic stapler I took from the museum supply closet. I'm thinking about what it will be like to go home. How in Bakersfield Mother and I will barbeque pork chops and chicken breasts and rosemary potatoes, getting drunk on cheap chardonnay that will coat my tongue like a lump of butter. How at the salon I'll catch her frowning at my reflection, *too pale, too brassy.* We'll talk about my brothers' kids, the Lakers, whether or not she should buy an electric car, but not about New York. Not about *him.* And I'll be nearly bursting with it. She'll smile when I say I miss him—a polite smile that isn't really at me but at the red bell pepper she's chopping for the grill. And she'll say, *Try this, it's from the farmers' market. It has so much flavor.*

So I will not call her. Not yet.

I spend the rest of the week organizing things in my apartment. I think Eric will call but he doesn't. I rearrange furniture, I dust, I scrub, I throw away papers. I wait for the severance package to hit my bank account, and when it does I spend a day at the department stores near MoMA—the ones where I used to shop with Eric. I do not see him. I avoid calls from Mother and coworkers—I practice saying *ex*-coworkers. My studio apartment starts to feel claustrophobic—the box with all my museum stuff still sits untouched in the center of the room.

I buy a package of yoga classes, but after one session I instead go to the bar across the street. I call a friend or two from the museum. They do not call back. I develop a taste for whiskey old-fashioneds, which the bartender shows me how to make. He's Cuban, and I let him make out with me one afternoon, both of us whiskey drunk, our breath tasting exactly the same. He doesn't kiss anything like Eric, who had not been properly kissed in a long time—always trembling, his lips a little too wet, whispering against me, *Elsa, Elsa, oh God*.

The Cuban wants to go into the back, but who will watch the bar? So we lie on one of the black leather booths, my hands in his hair, which is soft and yielding like animal fur, and I dig my nails into his scalp when I come.

Then I'm without a bar, drinking at home, and that's when I decide the girl in the mirror isn't a blonde. Her skin is too wan, too freckled. She looks soft, vulnerable. Like someone you might give an Indian burn to on the playground, just to see her cry. She should be a redhead. Light auburn, I decide. Something that says I have some spunk, a bit of backbone. So I dye my hair one night, and the girl in the mirror, wearing Eric's favorite blue dress, looks all these things and more. She is mysterious, keen, sharp—touch her and you'll get cut.

One morning I'm up, or maybe I never really slept, either way I'm walking through Central Park, making my post-layoff pilgrimage to MoMA. I've started early, when the city isn't exactly quiet, but it's quieter than later in the day and everything is blue, blue, blue. There are personal trainers in shorts and sweatbands, shoulders defined, foreheads pinched in hurried lines, shouting at their clients,

"Let's go! Let's go!" Across the lawn, sleepy women practice tai chi, their walkers and canes resting against a tree where someone's dog dozes, yawning without opening his doggy eyes. Dragonflies dart toward the pond, their wings like shiny plastic wrap. The smell of onions on a fryer, coffee roasting, and, somewhere not too far off, that animal smell drifting up from the zoo, sharp and earthy.

Then I'm in front of MoMA buying iced tea because the heat has already settled thick and hot across Manhattan. This is when I see her, Eric's wife. She's coming out of the employee entrance, a to-go coffee in her hand. And there's Eric behind her, a similar cup in his. It's almost painful to look at them together, stopped in front of the Picasso exhibition banner. Eric in a dark tailored jacket, collar unbuttoned, with just a shadow of gray beard. Such serious eyes. From here they look almost black, but in certain kinds of light—the cool morning of a hotel room, that ashen white light of a blank exhibition space—they flash green. Mary in her Vince sheath and silk scarf. Her dark hair against his silver. *Complementary.* A masterpiece in form and color. I swallow a sharp lump. He leans down and kisses her on the cheek. She's very petite; he has to stoop to reach her. No other parts of their bodies touch, just his lips to her upturned face. How sweet.

They've been together for twenty-eight years. I'd been with MoMA for the last five. My first year, as executive assistant to the world-renowned curator Eric Reinhardt, I managed his professional life. Phone calls, meetings, interviews—travel to Paris, Rome, Berlin, Chicago. How thrilling it was to always be at Eric's side, to be part of such exalted glamour. And how this accomplished man marveled at *me*—my enthusiasm, my desire to learn, my eagerness to please. *You have promise,* he said. *I need you.* And so that second year I became his personal assistant too. It wasn't long before I started scheduling myself in. *You have to eat too,* he'd say. Then there were the long conversations at rooftop restaurants or tiny bistros, Eric telling me how he met Mary in college, how he had been a painter—she was studying art history. *She came to one of my shows,* he says with a slight smile. *She thought my work was terribly important.* When he remembers what it was like to be young, dreaming of a different life and still thinking anything is possible, his eyes become cloudy with longing. Those green eyes, bright against his olive skin, appraising me. His hand on the table, close to mine, but he does not touch me. Not yet. *Yes,* I think. *The answer is yes.* But nothing. He moves on to something else, and I pull my hand away. Is this how it started? Or was it further back, in my interview, when he first shook my hand and my name rolled around in his mouth and came out like something blooming—*Elsa.*

Mary and Eric part ways at the bottom of the steps and I watch him disappear back into the museum. She turns to watch him too. Poor lovely Mary. A typical museum wife, all silk scarves and bold prints, chunky jewelry and German-made shoes. The scarf is a nice touch, it waves from behind her—*Catch me,* it says. *Come and get me.*

So I follow her.

We go up Fifth Avenue back to Central Park. I'd have lost her if it hadn't been for that beautiful scarf taunting me. At the Plaza she turns and enters, saluting the doorman with a sweet little wave. I can't see her face but I can see everyone else's as she walks by: the mustached old man at the front desk, his eyes crinkling at the corners, his face saying, *What a lady.* And the plump women beside him smile, their teeth flashing like tiny paparazzi.

In the Palm Court she speaks quietly to the hostess, who stands a little taller. It occurs to me now that I'm not dressed for the Plaza. I look down at my shorts: they're pre-ripped and cost almost two hundred dollars, but I don't think that matters to anyone here. I'm wearing a tank top with a built-in shelf bra and running shoes. The mustached man from the front desk brushes past me. He doesn't speak but I see him eye me, mustache shifting from side to side.

I wait until Mary is seated, at a table alone and out of the way.

I sit behind her, two tables and a fan palm between us, so that I'm looking at her back. What is she doing, eating lunch alone? Had she gone to take Eric out and he declined?

I watch her order and think about when their only son was killed in Afghanistan. It must have been two years ago now. Eric and I were working late, just beginning our research for the Picasso exhibition. We'd pulled out some line drawings from MoMA's collection—of donkeys in flagrante, of large women, their legs spread wide—the paper yellowed, a smudge of a fingerprint in one corner. *Picasso*, Eric was saying, *always leaves you feeling seduced, a bit abandoned*. I watched his face, how he frowns a little and sucks lightly at his bottom lip when he's really focused. *But then he's got you by the scruff of your instinctual being, and you can't help but return to him again and again*. His eyes were dark then—as black as green can get. We were so close I could smell his breath. I remember wanting to climb right in there and taste it.

The city noise rushed up from below: a siren, a car horn, meeting the sound of a helicopter above. The women with their naked breasts and crooked eyes stared at us, and Eric's phone rang, too loud, and then he was crouching down, hands on the floor, vibrating with a primal pain.

How vulnerable he looked at that moment, all balled up. I had to kneel to hold him. I covered him with every part of me until he wasn't crying. Until he turned to me, mouth on mine—hot and searching—hands at my breasts. He was shaking. *You are so beautiful*, he said. *Oh God. Oh God*. It was the first time I had sex with a man who needed me. So different from mere wanting.

He bought me the Alvar Aalto vases when he came back from his bereavement period. *To thank you*, he said. Their curving converging lines still make me blush.

A plump waiter, clean-shaven with sagging cheeks, brings Mary sparkling water and a bowl of sliced lemons. I can tell her chin is propped up by her hands. She might be looking out at those clouds and sighing. I look too and we stay that way for a moment.

Then the same waiter comes over to my table. He's very good at pretending. He doesn't even let his eyes slip to my clothes, just beams and asks if I'd like still or sparkling water. I order from the breakfast menu, and when he opens his mouth to say it's past noon I give him a look that shuts him right up. It's a good look. I use it on babies or noisy couples in movie theaters.

I order eggs Benedict and a Belgian waffle.

Mary takes the scarf from around her neck and puts it over the back of her chair. It's from MoMA's gift shop. I recognize the silk, the strange orange color.

The waiter brings her a salad, a bowl of rolls, and balled butter in a shallow dish. I watch her smear the butter—well, really I watch her elbow and shoulder work at what I can only guess is smearing butter. I think about how Eric told me she likes to garden, how she loves a good nursery and could spend a whole day deciding between types of hydrangeas. How her favorite place is the Catskills because of the fall foliage. He tells me she describes the colors as Froot Loops. This makes me like her more than I probably should. And for a moment I think we can be friends.

When my food comes Mary gets up. I look down at my plate, then out the window. I feel the wind her body creates when she passes by. My mind goes completely blank—an excuse would be impossible. I have a strong urge to vomit. When I look up she's not in the room. I call the waiter over and ask where the woman went. I'm almost shaking.

"What woman?" he asks.

"The one eating a salad right over there, where did she go?"

He leans in. "To the bathroom, miss."

I push my credit card in his hand and say if he's fast I'll tip him in cash. I put two twenties on the table so he knows I mean business.

When he's gone I can feel the hair on my forearms, how it runs up along my shoulders and neck. I'm holding my breath.

It's just the scarf and me now. It's draped over the chair like a silk refugee, trembling under the ceiling vent. Outside in the hall I can hear the hotel staff and customers, phones ringing, elevator doors opening and shutting, the satisfying click of heels on marble.

I'm very quick about it. I cross the room and shove the scarf into my purse. I meet the waiter at the hostess stand and sign there. He offers to-go boxes.

"Not hungry," I say, and head for the door.

Outside the humidity beats down. I'm fingering the scarf and breathing hard. It's exactly how I thought it would feel—stiff, smooth, and sturdy. Once in Central Park I examine it closely. It fits perfectly across my shoulders, a shawl really. Creased from where Mary had knotted it around her neck. I can smell her perfume now, Dior Diorissimo. I had bought it for her on Eric's behalf many times before, a floral scent that tickles my nose. I have several thoughts at once: turn it in to a lost and found; rip it to pieces; keep it for myself.

3

There are large glossy photos of Santa Monica in dark frames just above the hotel bathroom toilet: the Ferris wheel at night, slightly blurred and out of focus, and seashells shot in the style of Edward Weston. I remove them, pausing to consider launching them over the balcony, but instead hide them in the closet.

I'm feeling refreshed from my nap and I finish unpacking my duffel bag: hair products, a towel, several bathing suits, and a beauty bag that contains, along with makeup, various prescription pills stolen from Mother.

I line the pill bottles in a neat little row on the countertop. Some are from last year, the labels worn. Thank God Mother is a vain, nervous woman. She keeps a collection of doctors. It makes her feel good, I think, to have someone to call, someone paid to listen. *And where does it hurt, Mrs. Fisher?* She amasses pills in great quantities, but rarely takes them—it's a comfort just to have them on hand. This one for nerves, this one for energy, these for arthritic pain, migraines, sleep deprivation, sluggishness. They are flat, pale colors in odd shapes—like wedding sweets or old-timey valentines.

To keep them from rolling around in my duffel I had wrapped them in the scarf. I should use her name: I wrapped Mother's pills in *Mary's* scarf.

There are many bottles. *Probably too many*, I think. So I combine a few that look similar. Who cares? I definitely do not. After all, I'm doing what Eric suggested on that last day: *Go home. See your mother in Bakersfield. Be open to possibility.* Fine, a blue one if the mood strikes, or maybe a white, or seafoam green. So many possibilities.

I tuck the scarf into the bedside drawer, pausing to rub the silk between my fingers. It really is beautiful, the fabric heavy and light at once.

I picture Mary coming back from the Plaza bathroom, the Palm Court empty, her scarf gone. She'd ask the waiter, and what would keep him from describing me? Jesus, would they try to hunt me down? Would Mary know me by description? Would they have video?

It's one of the few gifts I did not help pick for her. I consider calling Eric, but I've never called him at home. I'm not even sure I can find the number. Instead I call room service and order another Bloody Mary, which, I tell myself, is basically a salad.

An older man delivers room service this time. Gray whiskers, a wrinkled uniform, and judgment in his eye. He tells me he's never delivered just one drink to a room before. The drink is perfectly cold, though, and has the right kind of garnish: two olives and celery that goes *crunch*.

It's just before sunset when I decide a jog is a good idea. Maybe because the sky is the perfect mix of light, that time of day when you can't help but want to be outside. Unless you are afraid of the raccoons living in the Santa Monica sewers. They love dusk too. Two of the little hoodlums are pillaging the dumpsters behind Third

Street and Broadway. Two more appear on the bluff, tackling trash cans as I jog by. Their black-masked faces pause when I pass. I think I hear one hiss, so I pick up my pace.

The Bloody Mary is doing me no favors. I'm slow, barely able to walk fast, and with each block I taste tomato and cracked pepper.

By the time I reach the end of the bluff, I'm sweating and my right calf is screaming. I stop to sit, the bench wet from the marine layer. They call this June Gloom, the ocean and sky the same matte gray, the horizon one big wash. I take out the Vicodin I had tucked into my pocket. There isn't a water fountain so I bite the sides of my tongue to produce enough saliva. The pill catches a little so I taste bitter chalk but then I settle in, waiting for that smoothness to wash over me, the weightlessness. I can see the Ferris wheel from here, jutting out at the end of the pier, its lights flashing in the twilight.

When I was five, Mother took my brothers and me here, almost to this exact spot. It was the first time I'd seen the ocean. We didn't come to tan, or swim, or eat corn dogs. We lined up with everyone else in Palisades Park to watch a winter storm finish off what was left of the Santa Monica Pier. The lower half had crumbled in January, and just when they started to rebuild, another storm had come. Mother was upset she had missed the first spectacle, scouring newspapers and magazines for photos and taking them to show her friends at the salon.

I remember how crowded it was, how we were bundled up like babushkas and how the man next to me had a tripod and scowled whenever I tried to look at it. The storm was furious: I remember being scared at how the palm trees bent, as if they might snap off and impale us. I cried, and Mother said I'd have to wait in the car if I was going to be a baby. Then the ocean shrank back, but only for a moment, before it came crashing forward. The crane being used to repair the damage caused by the first storm was swept into the water and everyone pushed against one another to get a better look, shouting. My brothers hollered like beasts—rain pelting them—and Mother smiled. She *smiled*. And the crane beat with the waves against the pier until it cracked and gave way and everyone yelled into the storm to congratulate it.

I don't remember my next trip to Santa Monica. Probably when a friend got a car and we explored the beaches for ourselves. How it seemed like you had to trek across the sand forever until you finally reached the water. How if you drove north to Malibu, to the cliffs and mountains, you could tan and swim and explore tide pools. How farther south there were even sandier beaches—and bonfires, and boys whose schools had stables, and who might sneak you in to see their horses. But once there, they always, always, wanted something in return.

Near where I'm sitting, a group of homeless men stir. I can hear one of them smacking his lips together in an exaggerated yawn.

I take the long way back to the hotel through the manicured neighborhoods behind Palisades Park. It smells better back here, less like piss and more like the flowering magnolia trees that line the sidewalks. People are jogging in beautiful, athletic pairs. A flock of cyclists pedal by and I catch words from them shouting at one another as they ride. A group of stroller-toting mamas speed-walk across a four-way stop. Finches and crows hang out on a park lawn together, a screeching racket.

Have I moved back to this place?

It's too soon to be thinking that. I still half expect Eric to show up and—I don't know what. Leave his wife? Give me my job back? This afternoon, when I woke up from my nap, I lay in bed with the sheet over my face, eyes open so everything was soft and warm, and I thought of him. That full bottom lip, that intense stare. Just when it was getting good—Eric's hand exactly where I needed it to be, my face uncovered for air, and because I wanted to have my eyes open for this part, always open for this part—the maid walked in. Standing at the end of the bed in her little white uniform, her creased face looking at me with horror, which she buttoned up real quick, mumbling, *Excuse me, I come back, I come back* as she backed out of the room, picking up one of the Bloody Mary glasses lying empty on the floor.

4

I decide not to call Charly just yet. It's been too long, and a girl has to acclimate. I rent a car and drive Pacific Coast Highway with all the windows down.

My favorite beach to sunbathe is private and just behind Malibu Colony. I haven't been in years, but if there's anywhere I can be alone and content, it's this beach. The only way to get to it is by scaling large boulders and then ducking through an abandoned beach house that burned down years ago.

It's a Tuesday, so the roads are clear, and when I get there the place is totally empty. No surfers, no one sitting out on their decks, nothing. The burned-down beach house is exactly where I left it.

How does anyone go to the beach and not want to be naked? The sun glints off the rolling waves, the palm tree tops flutter as if they had tinsel hair, and the sand is almost scalding. I find my spot, tucked behind a boulder on a gentle slope, so even if someone walks by I'm hidden from view. I leave my clothes and bikini in a neat pile and lie on my towel. I want to roast.

I hear gulls in the distance. The waves. A breeze makes the palm trunks creak softly. Somewhere, a wasp. No city noises. No cars, no horns, no talking and shouting—gone are those sounds that make a place familiar. It hits hard: *I am alone.* A vicious little shiver crawls up my back.

I'm about to put my clothes back on when a figure blocks the sun.

He's tall, athletic, and whistling a tune I can't quite place.

I grow indignant under his gaze, a little nervous. *Why doesn't he walk on?* He kneels down, tilting his head, watching me.

"The water is warm," he says with an accent.

I push myself up on my elbows. "What song were you whistling?" He has very dark eyes and a shock of black hair.

"That?" he says, and sits as if the question were an invitation. "A very old Mexican song about lost love—*que tengo miedo a perderte, perderte después.*"

"Tragic," I say without moving.

He continues to study me. The tilt of his mouth suggests he likes what he sees.

Fine, I think. *Let him look.* I'm looking too. Broad chest, carefully groomed hair—modeling comes to mind. Sharp jaw, thrust in profile so I can admire it. Diamond in his ear, catching the sun. Who doesn't love a man who needs female validation? Gives you a fighting chance. I realize he's dug his feet into the sand. I look out to the ocean; he follows my gaze and we stay that way for a few minutes.

"Do you plan on swimming?" he asks without looking away from the water.

I shrug.

He laughs—a beautiful, rehearsed laugh, and holds out his hand. "Come."

I take my time with my suit. When I'm done he's waiting by the water. I can see now he's already been in. His trunks—which are European and small—are wet and clinging to his thighs.

The water *is* warm, and he swims with powerful strokes. I can make out his arms slicing through the waves as if they were small mountains and he a giant dividing them in two.

Past the wave breaks we float on our backs. He laughs and says, "I don't usually see anyone on *my* beach."

"Is this yours, then?"

He smiles, very good teeth, and takes my wrist gently.

"Come, I'll show you how to bodysurf tandem."

We do this a few times, him beneath me, the water pulling us toward the beach. Then we're tumbling, falling beneath a wave. My legs shake from the effort. When he notices he says he'll massage them, holding them tight and rubbing with his thumbs.

We go up to his house—the light beige one that I've walked past so many times. It's funny where you can end up, the places that become center stage.

He lets me shower and change and asks if I'm hungry. We walk down to the cafés and other women look at him, pretending not to but catching him whenever they can. I see men look too. He orders us sandwiches and buys two bottles of wine. We hold hands now and he strokes my forearms and talks about his job producing Latino television programs.

None of this matters to me, frankly. I'm just glad not to be alone. I need noise to drown out that inner ringing, that pulse of anxiety before it goes full pitch. I ask about his life, and can't tell if he's telling the truth. I suspect he's lying. I don't care either way. Back at his house he says he'd like to see me naked again.

"American women are always nervous about their bodies, but you're different. You're something else."

Whatever, I think, but I play along and undress for him.

"Radiant," he says. "But ah, a sunburn! Lie down, Mama, I'll be back."

I'm obedient, and when he returns it's with a bottle of cold aloe, which he rubs on every single part of me.

That familiar boil starts at my knees, and then I'm at the mercy of my body, panting and sighing, and asking him to come in me. I do not think of Eric. Except sometimes. When I slide into pleasure looking up at the skylight swimming far above us, and when I'm on my stomach and the sheets smell like the hotel where Eric and I used to meet. It does not take either of us long to finish.

After, he asks my name and if he can see me again. Not this weekend, I say. This weekend I'll be in Catalina with friends.

I give him a fake name. And yes he can call—here is a fake number to go with "Susanna," the girl from San Diego County visiting her ailing grandparents in the city.

He gets up then, to pour us more wine.

Back at the hotel the wine has worn off and I'm sore and my head hurts. The room seems smaller now, and the smell of cologne is stronger on me than the smell of the beach, so I shower and take two little white pills that might be Xanax or possibly Percocets. I let them dissolve under my tongue. Such bitterness.

I've left Mary's scarf draped over the back of a chair near the open window so that it tangles a bit in the breeze. No matter how much I air it out, it still smells like her. I'm afraid it will look awful on me, so I've resisted trying it on in front of a mirror. It's a burnt dusky orange, similar to the color of the prescription bottles, only darker, and when the breeze lifts it up the light catches the underbelly and it's two-toned—bright and dark.

Looking at it depresses me, so I decide to leave it and people-watch in the lobby. The hotel boy—the one with the cleft chin—rides down with me in the elevator. He chews his lip and then says, "Are you enjoying your stay, everything in your room all right?"

"The toiletries are shit," I tell him seriously.

The lights on the elevator buttons blink gold at each floor. I can see his throat working. He's very young. His mouth opens and closes; there's a blemish above his lip like a beauty mark.

"But I'm probably taking too many showers." I give him my slow smile. And when the elevator doors open with a polite *ding*, he's smiling too. I read his badge. "Bye, *Rex*."

I walk through the open lobby, the breezy sunlit lounge. There are potted ferns and mirrored walls so that the light slants every which way. Outside there's a group of women sitting together, drinking white wine and eating oysters. It's late in the day, the sunlight warm and thin. They laugh and wave long, manicured nails. I wonder if they go together to get them done. This kind of sisterhood makes me want to cry, but instead I sit at a table beside them and order a bottle of pinot grigio. The waiter eyes me, his expression saying *Lush*.

Don't judge me, old man—just bring me my bottle.

The biggest woman of the group, her turquoise earrings brushing the tops of her bare shoulders, says to her girlfriends, "Well, if he can't satisfy me, I'll get a piece on the side who can."

The other women laugh into their hands, rocking back and forth over their table of shells, saying "You're terrible" and wiping at their eyes.

I try to be okay with sitting by myself. I take out my phone and scroll through it, pausing on Robby's number—is it ever a good idea to call your ex-husband? The answer is always no. I move on to Charly's. I should let her know I'm here.

An older couple, retirement age, seat themselves across from me. His shirt is unbuttoned way too low; I can see his stomach hair. Her face is bloated, painted up like a marionette. They order a cheese platter and he sends his drink back twice. I hear him say, "Babe, get *anything* you want."

The waiter brings my bill and stays to turn the empty bottle of pinot grigio upside down in its bucket of ice. I say a little too loudly, "Charge it to my room." The wine has gotten me drunk quickly, and I stumble when I stand. I can feel everyone looking at me; there's really no one else to look at. The raucous ladies are suddenly regal, their mouths shut up tight, and that retired guy is squinting at me. There's always so much in *that* look. I've seen it often, and always at some exhibition. Deciding whether something is beautiful or hideous, and *it is such a fine line.*

It's not very late, and back in my hotel room everything is spotless, the bed made, my breakfast tray removed. On the writing desk is a travel-size kit of facial creams from the hotel spa. I think of the room-service boy, Rex, how he has stolen this for me, and out comes a laugh so brusque and strange that I jump.

I decide then there is really no avoiding it. Plus, I'm drunk. And those pills were most likely opioids. So I sit on the balcony facing the beach.

Jared answers. I hear Charly in the background ask who it is. "Hey!" Jared shouts into the phone. "Long time no talk, let me get Charly. She'll squeal." I listen as a kitchen sink shuts off, the phone muffled against something. I imagine Charly wiping her hands on a dish towel, fixing her hair. It's a funny image, the domesticated Charly. It shouldn't surprise me, since taking care of Jared seems to be her life's work, but there was a time when she claimed she wouldn't marry until she had done three feature films and a sitcom, and written a book. Now she's Mrs. Jared Brownstone.

Down on the pier someone lights a sparkler, electric red against black.

"Oh my God," Charly says breathless into the phone. "Are you here?"

A breeze picks up. It's cold and wet and the sparkler dies out. I'm suddenly sure she can hear the waves, smell the Pacific through the phone.

"No," I lie. I tiptoe back inside, stretching out on the bed with the facial-cream kit beside me. "Not yet. I'm at JFK." It's one of those expensive kits, where everything is organic: shea butter and lavender and sweet almond oil. The ingredients written first in French and then in English.

"Oh," Charly says, sounding disappointed. "But you are coming?"

"Yes, of course, just some last-minute stuff with work."

She sounds reassured. "You know you can stay with us. We've had the place remodeled."

"Come stay with us!" I hear Jared shout.

"Thanks, but I'm treating myself to the Miramar."

"Ooh, very nice! Remember how we used to sneak into the pool at night, hoping someone would buy us fancy drinks? They always had such funny names."

"I think they've redone the bar since we were last there. It's a whiskey bar now." I rub a little of one of the creams into the backs of my hands. It smells powdery and expensive.

"Babe," she calls to Jared. "The Miramar has a whiskey bar now." She pauses; I can tell she's smiling. "Jared says we'll come to you, then. You know how he loves his whiskey. How's tomorrow?"

This other Elsa can't stay in the airport forever, so I agree. "Works for me."

She's thrilled. "This is really happening! I can't believe you'll be here after so long." There's a moment of awkward silence.

"Have you told Robby?" I ask, and barely resist laughing. I think of that hotel boy, Rex, how breakable he is, how the smell of the facial lotions makes me almost giddy and I want to just cackle, cackle, cackle.

"Yes," Charly says simply. "Robby and Jane will want to come for drinks too. Have you met Jane?"

"Briefly last year," I say, spreading the lotion across my chest and neck so that the expensive smell is everywhere. "They were in New York for a restaurant convention. She seems nice enough."

Robby is hopeless. Wants all his womenfolk to be friends. When they were in New York, I had been busy with work and there was only time for a quick chat over bagels and espresso at the museum coffee cart. I remember she went on and on about some athletic endeavor she was hooked on while Robby listened, interested and sincere. I remember him doting on her, asking if her coffee was sweet enough, making sure to get the sweetener she liked from the barista. I remember how reserved he was with me, vaguely polite, his hand always touching her, and when we parted, how triumphant he looked when Jane hugged me. I can see them, arm in arm, leaving the coffee cart for one of the galleries, both fit and tan and good-looking. Jane with her short pixie hair, her sculpted shoulders, and Robby with that mop of messy curls. I remember thinking what a perfect little homecoming couple—king and queen of their California lives.

"She's a sweetheart," Charly says cheerfully. "And she's invited you and me to lunch at her Brentwood restaurant. She manages Sycamore Kitchen."

I wonder for a moment what Charly and Jane must be like together—their adventures—wonder who is the instigator, who wants to get away, who wants everything to stay the same.

"You'll love it," Charly is saying to me, to her old best friend. "All the waiters are adorable. Oh, Elsa!" she cries. "I'm so glad you're coming home."

And that *home* hangs between us. I don't know what to say, so I agree and we say our goodbyes and hang up. The silence in the room is overwhelming—the flowery scent of lotion everywhere.

5

When I arrive, I see the old gang before they see me. I hang back a bit to steady myself. Robby's listening to his girlfriend talk—his chin tilted down, curls brushed back. He's wearing swim trunks and a button-down shirt. I can't see his feet but I'm sure he's in flip-flops. I wish I felt more than this faint sadness whenever I see him. It's really more for him than for me; I never had much to lose. I remember when he asked me to marry him. After finals, on our way to the desert, the sky clear, taillights pulsing up and down the 10 freeway, and Robby looking at me, a little breathless. His prize.

Jane's very animated. Her arms and hands wave as if she were an instructor worried about losing Robby's interest. I can only see the back of her, her bare, ropy arms flexing as she raises them above her head, fingers gesticulating under the soft hotel lights. And there's Jared, short and muscular, in tight trousers, the bottoms rolled up to show off expensive loafers. Flirting with everyone while poor Charly looks on. I think, not for the first time, *If only she understood how fragile men like Jared are. How easy they are to bend. Even easier to break.* But there she stands, as usual, her face a little pinched, watching him entertain the pretty bartender.

Charly sees me first and runs up to me with a huge hug, pressing my body against hers. I feel tiny in her arms even though we are about the same height—her breasts and stomach pushed against me, pliable and warm. It's an intimacy I'm not prepared for—not just that heat, but the familiar smell of my best friend. The same L'Oréal shampoo, the cucumber body lotion, and something that is entirely Charlotte. She pulls away from me, smiling. Her face is how I remembered it too. The same small features, the same plump, freckled cheeks and pert little chin. I have a dizzying sensation of déjà vu. But then creases around her mouth and eyes give away how much time has passed, and her hair, instead of a rich brown, is a faded muddy color, and rigorously flat-ironed. It makes her look mousy. I don't remember mousy.

"Elsa," she squeaks.

I'm relieved when Robby's girlfriend steps between us. "How are you?" she asks. We hug as if we had small bug arms. She has the same pixie cut from when we met in New York, only a bit longer now. Her hair is the color of hay, almost yellow, with bangs swept to the side. I remember the hair, and that she insisted on paying, but I don't remember her smile being so full, so bright.

"Elsa," Robby says, and he tucks me in the crook of his arm. "You remember Jane?" Now that I'm closer, I can smell cigarettes on him. This surprises me. Robby smokes only when he's stressed.

But Jane's looking directly at me, as if we were once sisters blown miles apart, only to be reunited at this moment in the Miramar hotel bar. "I was just telling them about the hotel," she says gesturing. "Did you know they just finished a multimillion-dollar renovation?" Her arms raise again, her fingers stiff like conductor wands at the ready.

"Yes," I say, hoping to deflate her. "The rooms are lovely. Have you stayed?"

Her arms lower. "No," she says, and she reaches awkwardly to touch my dress. "I love this."

I'm wearing the blue one with the open back, Eric's favorite because he can trace my shoulder blades, travel down my spine, caress each vertebra.

"Elsa, you're a redhead!" Jared says, lifting me up. We laugh when he sets me down.

"Auburn," I correct him. "And thank you for noticing."

"The red suits you," Charly says, patting the empty stool beside her. "Sit with me, sit with me."

"So what's everyone drinking?" I perch on the stool. The pill I took in the room has reached from behind and smoothed out my head. "I'll buy the next round," I tell them.

"I'll have a whiskey," Jane says, holding Robby's sleeve.

"My kind of girl. Let's all have whiskey," I say.

"This is *my* treat," Jared says, waving a finger at me. "Drinks are on me." He nods his head at the cocktail waitress, asks what Japanese whiskies they have, whether he can buy a bottle, never mind the price.

I had forgotten this about Jared, with his J.Crew looks, Cole Haan sneakers, and the latest Apple watch on his wrist—the rich, all-American man-boy, with his flashy displays of generosity, so eager to buy his worth.

"They have Ohishi whisky," Jared says to no one in particular. "Apparently they use koi carp for weed control."

Charly is looking at her husband. "Soda with lime for me, please."

"Oh, have something stronger," he says.

Robby's brought the drink menu from the bar. "Want to drink poolside?"

I'm happy to flaunt a group on the hotel grounds, so I lead them outside. The pool is shaped like a jelly bean, the bottom teal-colored, so the water looks very dark. There is no one in it, but beneath a cluster of palms a mother rubs sunscreen vigorously onto two children, never mind that the sun is low in the summer sky. The little girl looks over at us, clutching a towel across her body. The boy picks his nose. Across from them, near trellised bougainvillea, the Miami couple sits, the man shirtless, paunchy, his chest dotted with coiled black hair, except for a patch of white around his belly button. His girlfriend rests a manicured hand in that tuft of hair, her thumb stroking.

We take over the chaise lounges at the opposite end.

"Did you guys bring your bathing suits?" I ask, slipping out of my dress.

"Ohh! That's a cute bikini," Charly says. She's perched at the edge of the pool. The wine Jared ordered for her sits untouched on the patio table. "You always did have the best suits. I couldn't find mine this morning." She rolls up her pants, and dips her legs into the water.

"You found it, but you hated it," Jared says, winking at me. He's a gym guy, quick to take his shirt off but slow to get in. He stands near Charly, chest flexing.

"What about you, Jane?"

She's put on sunglasses, so I can't see her eyes.

"I came from work," she says.

"I have an extra in my room," I offer, but she shakes her head.

Robby leans over so his chin is resting on the arm of her chaise lounge. I can't hear what he's saying over Charly, who's shouting at Jared for splashing her pants when he dived in, but then Jane is saying, "No, babe, really, I don't mind. Go in." And she kisses him sweetly on the nose. Robby pulls his T-shirt over his head, throwing it playfully at her; she whistles softly.

I dive in and swim from one side to the other in one breath. When I surface, the children have splashed into the shallow end, their fluorescent arm floaties bobbing gently around them. The little girl jumps from the step into her mother's arms. I can't see her mother's face, her floppy hat is pulled down low, but the kid is enraptured. Total delight. Her little body glides through the water, held afloat by her mother and those pink floaties. The boy stands at the step now, holding his arms out, shouting, "I'm next! I'm next! My turn!"

"So how long do we have you?" Charly says to me from the pool's edge. "I was starting to think we'd lost you to MoMA forever."

I'm still watching the two children. The boy whoops each time he jumps toward his mother, splashing the little girl, who watches from the pool steps. She is maybe four years old, but already wearing a miniature pink bikini. The boy, a few years older, is in bright red trunks that hang below his knees. Spider-Man peeks out from one of the pockets.

"Oh, I haven't taken a real vacation in ages. I thought I'd stick around for another couple of weeks."

"And MoMA can spare you?" Jane asks, so politely that I think maybe she isn't so nice after all. She isn't looking at me, though; she's sipping her drink and watching Robby over the rim of her sunglasses.

"The show is practically done, and Eric"—God, it feels good to say his name out loud—"Eric," I say again, "thought I deserved a vacation. He insisted, really."

"Who's Eric?" Robby asks.

"My boss, Eric Reinhardt."

Jane raises her brows. "Eric Reinhardt is your boss?" She turns to look at the others. Jane is the type of girl who loves to know the answer—to everything—and she brightens up a bit, becomes more animated. "He did the extended Mike Kelley retrospective. I read about him in *Artforum*. He must be fascinating to work with. What do you do for him?"

I can almost feel Eric touching me, in his office, in a hotel room, beneath the table at dinner—in the dress I just slipped out of, which still smells like him. "I'm his executive assistant, so what don't I do?"

They laugh.

"Oh, let's not talk about work," Charly says. "I'm so excited about Catalina! And Tom's great, his boat is so, so gorgeous."

"It's a Morris Yacht Ocean Series," Jane adds. She's on a roll now. "A friend of my father's used to build them in Maine back in the 1970s."

"Who's Tom?" I interrupt.

Jared smirks, draining his whiskey. "You'll love him. Or he'll love you. Just your type, practically royalty. His family owns a potato chip company, real American money." He wades over to me and squeezes my shoulders.

"How do you know this guy?"

Robby answers, "We did some design work for one of his companies. Took a real liking to Jared."

Jared is proud, though it's clear Robby meant it as a slight. There's a harshness about Robby for a moment, a sneer hidden by the tip of his drink. This surprises me. I swim closer to him but Jared catches me underwater.

"You should stay at the house," he says.

I motion to the hotel grounds. "It's not too bad here." Just then the little girl in pink floaties starts shrieking. Jared lets go and puts his fingers in his ears. The mother's holding the girl's pudgy arm now, and talking to her in a sharp voice.

"Come stay with us!" Charly begs over the noise. "You haven't seen the renovation yet. Did you see the pictures I posted?"

"I saw them; it looks beautiful."

"There's a big jazz festival on the island," Robby says. He's floating on his back. I forgot how nice he looks in swim trunks. He used to swim competitively, has broad shoulders and a long torso. He says, "Buddy Guy, Boney James, George Duke. It'll be bitchin'."

"Bitchin'?" I laugh because this reminds me of young Robby, and I can see gray in his chest hair.

Jane tilts her chin at me, and I sober up for a moment.

"Jane," I call. "Have you been sailing before?" It wouldn't surprise me if she had raced sailboats professionally.

"I've always wanted to learn." She pauses for a moment, looking at her feet. "Tom says he'll teach me."

The mother climbs out of the water. She's in a sensible one-piece. Her thighs are dimpled. The skin around her arms looks soft until she picks up the boy and then her muscles tense, sinewy and firm. She wraps him in a towel as if he were a giant burrito and carts him off, the little girl trailing behind. "Come here," the mother commands, taking the girl by the hand and giving us an apologetic wave as they walk by.

"As soon as you called I made up the spare bedroom," Charly says, her eyes following the mother. "So you must stay with us—at least the night before we set sail. It'll make things easier."

Jared massages my shoulders. "Keep my little wifey company," he says near my ear. "I'm at work all day and she's on summer break." I can smell him, the spice of his cologne, the perfume of his shampoo. The oil streaks on the water must be from him.

"Don't forget about dinner on the pier," Jane adds from her chaise.

Now that the family is gone, it's just the Miami couple. They've ordered drinks poolside, and when the man sits up he has to work to get a gold chain out from between his stomach folds. He winces and cusses. The girlfriend rolls over then, the backs of her calves pink. She fusses over him, trying to get the chain untangled. "It's stuck in the hair," I hear him say. "You're making it worse," she says. His face has grown red beneath his tan.

Charly gets up to lie beside Jane. "Oh yes, dinner with Tom. Elsa, you'll come too? Are we totally overwhelming you?"

I assure her she's not, even though yes, I am overwhelmed. But that's what the pills are for. "Of course I'll come."

She looks relieved, lies back on her elbows, and kicks her feet out in front of her.

"He'll probably buy us all dinner, the guy's a real asshole like that," Robby says.

Jane frowns. She looks like she might object but instead asks Charly about the restaurant's vegetarian options.

Robby splashes me. "Hey, want to race?"

"I don't want to upset your girlfriend," I say, still watching the Miami couple. The woman has left. It's just the man now. He looks small by himself. He slowly collects their towels and deposits them in a bin. When he walks by he's holding his shirt against his body, eyes averted.

"Jane?" Robby says, as if the thought never crossed his mind. "She's not like that." He's smiling at me like he used to.

"Is she anything like a woman?" I ask.

"Jane's one of those cool girls."

I laugh. "Am I one of those cool girls?" I swim around him so he has to turn to talk to me. Now that his hair is wet, I can tell it's starting to thin. A pity. He had such great hair.

His blue eyes flash.

"We'd better not race," I say. "I've had too much to drink."

I retire to my room after another round of whiskey cocktails, when our talk begins to go circular, with Jared repeating the same old stories. *Remember when Charly's mother remarried at the Beverly Hills Hotel?* Back when Trader Vic's was still a tiki bar and restaurant, and it was like being in the hull of a ship—all wooden gods, and ferns, and strong mai tais. Such a grand old hotel, like stepping back in time. *Remember the parties at Jared's place near campus?* The wicked punch, the music, the awkwardness of partying in such a tiny apartment. His roommate So-and-So now in Texas crunching numbers, bald but drives a Maserati. What's His Name lives in Silverlake, married with two kids and a dog. Charly and Jared saw them last October. They had their own little Oktoberfest. Barbequed alligator and rabbit-and-fennel sausages, homemade sauerkraut, pale ales and Belgian darks. The little kids eating

Hebrew Nationals and drinking apple juice in tiny plastic beer mugs. Cheers, they'd said, crashing them together. *It was the cutest thing,* Charly assures me.

I nearly push them out the hotel doors when I say goodbye.

It's quiet in my room, and my head is swimming with their voices. Robby saying *It's good to see you* and Charly pushing her breasts against me in one last hug, *I missed you* in my ear. Jane waiting, sober and patient, by the door.

I call room service, and when Rex appears—looking smart in his hotel uniform, a bottle of sparkling water in hand, and his young face irresistibly eager—I smile and ask which bathing suit I should wear for a sailing trip.

"What's your name?" he asks, a little short of breath. He's the type that would need an inhaler.

I give him a fake name—Ingrid, a wine rep from Portland in town for a trade show.

"All the good wine is from Oregon," I say. He nods yes, yes.

I make him wait while I try each bikini on. I like the look of oxygen stuck in his chest. He keeps glancing at the door as if someone might come in.

I rattle a prescription bottle like a tambourine and offer him some. I ask if he can get coke, he says he thinks so, the waiters do it in the hotel restaurant, he'll be right back. But I make him stay and have his waiter friend bring it up. His name is Austin—the one with the coke. He shows up, wearing sunglasses on the back of his head, baggie in hand, crushing Altoids between his teeth. He eats several at once, holding my hair back—a tight ponytail in his fist—so I can lean into the coke easier. His menthol breath cold on my neck.

Austin wants to help pick out a bikini too, but I don't like the way he clenches his jaw at me, how when he talks to Rex he nearly barks. I put on music, and laugh sharply when Austin suggests we rent porn.

"Not that type of party, sweetheart," I say, and hold the door for him. "I'm going to bed and you should get back to work. Thanks for the coke." He stalks out, knocking over an open bottle of zinfandel.

Rex won't stop apologizing. I help him put down towels, which doesn't help at all, and for some reason this makes us laugh. And then the boy is just looking at me, full in the face, eyes nearly black. I'm reminded of Robby's face all those years ago—on that desert highway, all astonished wonder.

I tip him outrageously but he refuses to take it. I push the bills into his hands. "You have a nice smile," I say, my voice shaking.

His cheeks are red when he leaves. I feel better and fall asleep in a gold-and-turquoise bandeau bikini.

And there is young Robby, schoolboy Robby, with thick dark hair and a sparkle. It's after finals, a trip planned to Joshua Tree for the two of you because he knows how you like to fuck under the stars and the night sky in LA is flat gray and dull. He asks you again in the car, this time with a small gold band. You're in the passenger seat and there's traffic and he slips the ring on your finger and you betray yourself. You say yes, believing you love him because you want to love him. And so you head down the freeway, out of town, listening to Big Mama Thornton with Robby's hot hand on your leg, his face bright because you've finally said yes.

At the hotel he's giddy. His hands tremble when he takes off his Hanes, he's breathing hard as if this were your first time together. *It is*, he insists. It is the first time you make love as an engaged couple, and it *means something*. He says *make love* as if what you did before was for animals. But you *are* an animal—you know this much about yourself, God help him.

You fake your orgasm. He doesn't. He tells you he loves you.

When he falls asleep you go outside. There are so many stars. Too many. It's overwhelming. It could be a blanket with pinholes stuck up into it, suffocating you.

In the morning he makes you both coffee, kisses you and wants to go back to bed. You insist on a hike and wait outside while he showers.

That's when you realize it. You do not love him. Outside you watch two teenagers playing in the pool. One is dark, the other fair. They're athletic with well-carved shoulders, tight from roughhousing, forearms forceful and unapologetic—all defined jaws and almost manly chins. You wonder what they taste like and you join Robby in the shower.

6

The hotel phone is ringing. It is an ungodly piercing noise, making my head rattle. I refuse to answer it. I'm convinced it's Robby asking why I've come back. I could see it in his face last night, the way he looked from Jane to me, and then the more he drank, the less he looked back and forth. That question just getting bigger and bigger: *Why are you here?*

My hangover is wicked, everything fuzzy, somewhere between memory and dream. Robby and me under the nighttime sky, speeding down the freeway. That hot hand on my leg, blues roaring. Am I remembering it right? The phone stops ringing. I watch for the red light to blink, telling me I have a message from my ex-husband. Sure enough there it is, more maroon than red.

Beside me is a stack of untouched pillows, as if the maid snuck in and plumped them, arranging them perfectly, to emphasize how empty that side of the bed is. I reach over them to find a pill bottle.

I'm not sure exactly when, but sometime in third grade I suspected my father was coming home only to kiss us good night, leaving the house after we were asleep. It was his side of the bed that gave it away. In the morning it had the same untouched look, the pillows all neatly stacked.

I let the pills dissolve under my tongue and wait for the covers to creep up around me, the promise of hotel sheets—starchy, stiff like beaten egg whites. The air conditioner clicks on, a hum you could drown in.

When Mother leaves to pick the boys up from summer camp I sneak into her bathroom. I expect my father will come home now that the boys are coming home too. It's been a long summer of just Mother and me—phone calls from my father to say good night, cereal with coffee creamer because the milk's gone bad. The house smelling like lavender and bleach, because even if she wears pajamas all day and can't get to the grocery store, Mother will still clean the house.

Her bathroom has stone gray shag carpet and a mirror over the sink that faces a full-length mirror, so if you stand in front of it there are many yous walking down many halls. She collects things, my mother. Jars of eye creams, tubes of face serums and oils, bottles of perfume that look like tiny glass sculptures. She keeps the empty ones beneath the sink, each haunted by its own scent—honeysuckle and geranium, amber and oak moss, rose and musk. I like to hold them up to the skylight and peer out through the brilliant crystal world. My favorite, though, is her collection of lipsticks. Not just reds and pinks, but Lovers Coral, Blushing Pearl, Plum Velour, Crimson Night. A different shade for every day. *You've got to wear it like armor,* I heard a woman at the salon say. *Like you're going into battle.*

Mother gave me a case of colored Lip Smackers because I'm not supposed to use her lipsticks—they are expensive. But I want to look nice for my father, so I steal one called Party Pink, my favorite because it smells like My Little Ponies.

Then suddenly my brothers are home, rambunctious teenagers eager to put me in my place, to let me know I am still a child, just their eight-year-old little sister. The house is loud and filled with their boy scent. We have pizza for dinner and then my brothers make Mother and me laugh with stories of camp—I can smell the mountain air, feel the icy streams, and those stars! They charted the sky and show us their sky maps: Pegasus, Orion, Hydra with its deep-sky galaxies, so filled with mystery. They punch and nudge over new secrets. Their faces look older; could that be possible? Yes, change could be like that—sudden and infinite. I stare at them in wonder.

My father doesn't show, the boys do not ask why. Or maybe they do but no one asks in front of me. They go to bed still rowdy, filled with their stories, the smell of campfires stuck against their skin, their faces bright. Mother goes out back for a cigarette and to finish the bottle of wine she opened at dinner.

I don't like to go to bed until everyone else is safely tucked in, so I take a book to the pantry, which is large and has its own light. I keep the door cracked because small spaces scare me a little.

Hours pass. Or at least I think they do. I'm deeply engrossed in my book, a collection of fairy tales—enchanted spindles and apples and straw woven into gold.

The television clicks on in the living room, and I realize how late it must be. A game show tells me it's Mother. I'm glad I stayed up; neither of us is alone now. I think, *This must be what it's like to share a room*, how my brothers must feel, comforted by the soft sounds of someone beside them.

I hear a key in the lock. The television is muted. I listen closely, concentrating on the bit of white lace the pony on my sweater is wearing. I watch it rise and fall on my stomach and try to make it completely still. Outside big rigs roll down the main highway like waves. A bird calls softly, as if the sun has already risen.

The familiar drop of keys, the soft pulling off of his shoes, the way the floorboard creaks under his weight. I think, *I'll wait until Mother has hugged him and then when he walks in, reaching for the warm beer that's just above where I'm lying, I'll pretend to be asleep.* A pretty picture for my father. So I spread my hair across the pantry floor; it smells like Dove shampoo and is long and light brown and very soft. I think of sleeping princesses, the kind I've been reading about in my book. I take out the Party Pink lipstick and apply it to my lips.

But neither parent comes into the kitchen. I can hear their hushed angry whispers. I hold my book in my hands, thinking I should throw it against the floor and shout, "I'm here!" And they'll have to stop. But I do nothing. I stay silent and listen. *Don't you dare*, comes my mother. She says this again and again—*I said no*—until his voice grows tall and desperate. The sounds heighten, the couch thuds, clothing tears, the sounds of physical violence—skin against skin, and then, for a moment, nothing. Then sounds worse than before. His grating moans, her breath deep and loud, a voice of its own.

I would search her face later, search for signs of what those sounds meant. But she never gave anything away. They got back together after that night, stayed that way for several years, long enough for the boys to go off to college. Then they separated for good.

I wake to laughter and shouting and bicycle bells. The air salty and warm.

I check the message when I'm fully awake. It's Charly, not Robby. She wants to go to Jane's restaurant for lunch. I call back and say I'll be ready in twenty minutes. I don't invite her up. There's a small bag of coke on the counter next to a cluster of Mother's prescription pill bottles. Austin's left an empty Altoids tin, the mint dust spilled onto the sink. Crumpled over the wine stain is Mary's scarf. There's a dark violet patch across the raw silk from where the wine seeped in, and a piece of its knotted fringe has twisted right off. It's still beautiful, though, perhaps more so. I wring it out in soapy water and hang it over the shower.

Down in the lobby Charly's in jeans and sensible walking shoes. We hug again, and I pull away awkwardly to wave at Rex, who blushes a little and turns back to help an elderly couple with their bags. Charly watches me do this but she doesn't say anything, just rushes me out of the hotel and into the bright blue. Santa Monica is jamming today, people on bikes, wearing bikinis and swim trunks, groups of women pushing heavy-duty strollers, their wheels kicking up dust and little rocks. I walk a little behind Charly as we step onto the crowded sidewalk and cut through the park. Her gait has changed or maybe mine has, either way we can't seem to get in step. She marches past the panhandlers sitting in a small circle, their arms outstretched. She's talking about her new teaching job, how she loves being around the children. At first I think she's joking—she was always the first to throw a look at an annoying child—but she's serious.

"The principal asked me to start assisting in the Studio Lab too," she's saying. I try to catch up. Her pace is breakneck, and the pill I took before leaving the hotel hasn't helped my hangover. "Which is really great because it means more face time with my students. You'd think six hours a day would be enough, but no one understands that these kids need more guidance than that. Especially the boys." She smiles to herself. "There's one boy in my class who is such a sweetheart, Elsa. He told me I was his best friend. Isn't that the sweetest? He calls me Mrs. B." She sidesteps a group of picnicking moms, all of whom are breast-feeding, which puts us back in step with each other.

"Soooo, have you booked any gigs lately?" I ask.

She waves her hand dismissively, smiling at one of the mothers. "Oh that's all in the past. The money was too inconsistent, I needed a real job. But I am thinking of talking to the parents at the school about starting a theater program."

One of the feeding babies lets out a shrill whine. Charly slows down to look.

"How's Jared's job?" I ask, because she's gotten a faraway look about her. She's almost completely stopped walking. The mother with the crying baby successfully latches him on, and the park is quiet again.

"Oh, it's fantastic," she says, resuming her pace. "He was able to get Robby some work—he's been struggling financially. We even lent him some money. I don't think Jane knows about that. They've moved in together." She's paused to watch me, anxious, ready to comfort if necessary.

I laugh. "Really, Robby and I are old news."

She sniffs and starts walking again. "I always thought you guys would get back together. Don't get me wrong, I like Jane, but she's always doing some marathon or on a new diet." She hangs on to my arm. "They came over last month for a barbeque and she was suddenly vegetarian, when just the month before she was on a high-fat, high-protein kick, eating bacon and putting butter in her coffee. She spent the whole barbeque telling Robby they had to get to bed early because they were planning a pre-dawn summit of Mount Baldy. Can you imagine?" Charly shakes her head. "We just don't have that much in common."

I almost say *We don't have that much in common either*, but the pill finally kicks in and everything's softer—my headache, my stiff body, even my sudden sadness over walking beside a stranger.

We turn onto Montana Avenue and there's the rich, heady smell of the magnolia trees, and the California sunlight is golden, syrupy; my limbs feel pleasantly heavy.

"I missed the weather," I manage.

7

I wonder if Jane greets every customer with the same blank, brilliant smile. She looks amped up, supercharged, ready to go. It's exhausting just looking at her. I imagine her in Charly and Jared's backyard, pushing grilled corn and summer squash salad around her paper plate, waiting out the long summer twilight with that insistent electric smile plastered on her thin hard lips. She's ultrafit, like Eric's wife. Like some retired long-distance runners, all severe lines and angles. Barely a curve on them.

I met Mary at the close of my first exhibition as Eric's assistant. We were celebrating at a dive bar, drinking with colleagues. Eric, his short silver hair brushed forward as if he were some Brooklyn hipster instead of an almost fifty uptown transplant from Chicago, is smiling at me over his beer. It's the smile that gets me; it's everywhere in his face, even those serious eyes. He's looking at me as if I were the only person in the world who could make him smile like that. We are huddled in a corner and I'm on my second drink. This one is much stronger—a gin and tonic or maybe a vodka soda. There's a shuffleboard table in another corner. The assistant curators are playing, all loosened ties and rolled-up shirtsleeves. I'm feeling light-headed and lovely, excited to be alone with Eric in a dark corner of a bar. I want to touch the back of his hand. Painter's hands. Strong, with long fingers and round, knotted knuckles; I can track a vein up and over the forearm, disappearing beneath his shirt. Is *this* when it starts? Maybe.

His wife comes in then, not smiling but pleasant enough. Eric and I play a game of shuffleboard, his wife hovering at a barstool and flicking pretzel crumbs from the counter. I ask her about Santa Monica because Eric's told me she's from there. He also told me how she played softball, and was state champion her junior year, and how she likes her eggs at Balthazar on Sunday mornings. But still I ask questions, nodding politely when she answers in short, clipped sentences while fingering a silk neckerchief and looking toward the door with increasing impatience. When our shuffleboard game ends her purse strap is already over her shoulder. Eric holds the door open for her when they leave. I remember him glancing back—that funny little wave.

Do you miss me? I want to know.

Sycamore Kitchen is a sparse modern restaurant with an exposed kitchen and blond wood floors. The bar is crowded with business suits and girls in wedge heels, the backs of their slim calves the color of milky coffee. Jane seats us outside on the patio.

I order a bottle of champagne. I ask for a bucket too. Jane, with authority, directs a busser to angle a large white umbrella over us.

"Join us," I tell her, and when she objects I'm reminded again of Mary, the cool tilt of her head, the polite, immovable smile. "You have to, I'm making you," I say. "I want to hear all about this restaurant. I want to hear all about you."

She relents when Charly joins in, even laughing at herself when the cork pops and she jumps. The pills start to really do their work now. I can feel my shoulders drop, like a warm liquid is smoothing out all the ligaments. I get Jane talking about herself. I want her to let down her guard, wash away that Mary exterior. *Why this restaurant? What do you really want to be doing?* The pills have me now, and the wine helps. The blush-colored bubbles are sharp, exhilarating. I look through my glass and the sky is rose gold. *And how long have you been working here?* She starts telling us about the art on the walls, which is so pedestrian, so Los Angeles, I want to laugh.

"They're Julius Shulman prints," she's assuring me. "Have you been to the Stahl House?" I nod, momentarily distracted by the breeze. There's a great sycamore growing over the roof and I'm watching the leaves nod too.

And how long have you been with Robby? Are you planning to get married? Her eyes get large, she might even be blushing—or could it be a flush from the champagne? There's a second bottle now.

"Relax," I'm saying. "If I cared I wouldn't have divorced him."

Have some more champagne, and I'm refilling our glasses. The little bubbles racing to the top. *Do you have oysters?* I want a pile of those opalescent shells surrounding us. She looks at me strangely and I quickly bring the conversation back to Robby.

We laugh about his snoring, how he loves slapstick and stand-up, how he has to be up and outside before seven in the morning. I don't allow her to do anything except laugh when I make little jabs about his inability to understand most politics, his prejudice against money. I even make her laugh about how he orgasms. *Isn't it always the same?* I am cackling.

We make eyes at the young waiters.

Jane is laughing, tears in her eyes. She's saying, "You're such a bad influence!"

Charly is delighted. She's looking back and forth between Jane and me, as if to tell Jane, *See? See? Didn't I tell you?*

"How old is he really, Jane?" I say, pointing.

The waiter in question knows we're talking about him. He's made sure to be very attentive. Tight jeans, young, with a thin mustache, his hair pushed back in a severe pomp.

"Shhh," Jane says. "I'm the restaurant manager—I have to work here."

"You're the *boss*."

She bites her lip, leans in. "He's twenty-one, from Indiana, wants to be an actor."

"Poor guy," Charly says. "He has such a long way to go. He's so young. Doesn't he look so *young*?"

"We hired a host the other day who still has braces."

"I think they are delicious," I say with moxy. "I've picked one up at my hotel."

The two women look at me, waiting for the joke.

I raise my glass to the young waiter. "Salud."

"What do you mean you've picked one up at your hotel?" Charly asks, her voice so low I almost laugh in her face. "Do you mean a prostitute, Elsa?"

"Don't be ridiculous. One of the room-service boys has a crush on me, you saw him this morning—tall and clumsy. He brings me treats." I enjoy the look on their faces. Jane has the same expression Mary had when I told her I was divorced and single.

So I add, "I modeled bathing suits for him."

Charly's mouth is in a small *o*. Then she laughs so loud and sudden that the table next to us looks over.

Jane hides her mouth behind her napkin, and then all three of us are laughing.

When we've recovered, Jane says, "Robby must have had his hands full with you."

"Well, he's a man, isn't he?" I drawl. "They love to be miserable." The alcohol and pills have lessened their hold. I have a headache right behind the eyes, and there's a cool drip of desperation down my back.

"A scary thought," Jane says, frowning.

I refuse to let them pay the bill. I hear myself saying I've just gotten a raise and that this is celebratory. We toast to old times, and new. My hand trembling only a little.

When Charly walks me back to my hotel, I'm already replaying the afternoon. *Was I too loud? Did I laugh too much, or just enough?* I can feel the heat in my face. When we hug goodbye Charly says, "I missed you, Elsa. You were always so carefree—nothing ever touches you."

8

Back at the hotel my room is clean again. A dress that slipped from the chair onto the floor is now folded on the bed. The sheets and comforter have been plumped and smoothed over like a layer of fondant. Someone has removed the rug with the wine stain and replaced it with a different one, the same pattern but a different color. There's a clean stack of towels; my makeup and pills and Austin's Altoids tin are lined up in a neat row; the end of the toilet paper has been folded into a point.

And Mary's scarf is gone. It's not folded with the dress or the towels. No one's hung it in the closet or placed it back in my duffel bag.

Something climbs into the back of my throat, sour and swollen. I've thrown off the bed pillows and sheets, and I'm rummaging through the couch when there's a knock at the door.

Rex is there, his hand behind his back. I'm telling myself to calm down. "Look," I say. "Help me look—the fucking maid stole my scarf."

"Oh no, I—" A smile twitches at his lips. His hands fidget behind his back.

I'm breathing heavily, and for a moment I want to smack him. Really hurt him. If he were any closer I'd swallow him whole and spit his little pearlescent uniform buttons back to his mother in Idaho or Iowa or wherever.

"Give it to me." I can feel the wet on my upper lip. He brings out his hands. On his right there's a class ring. He spreads his fingers wide and empty.

"I thought you'd be happy. I sent it to dry cleaning. It won't be charged to your room." He's backed away from me, still holding his hands out.

I touch his class ring gently. It's very cold, compared with his hand, which is soft and warm. I can almost twist the ring clean off. It's only his knuckle that keeps it on.

"Can you get it back?"

"They won't have cleaned it yet. I just took it down an hour ago. There was a wine stain."

I shake my head. "I don't care about that. I just want it back."

He looks at me.

"Wine stain and all," I say. "Can you get it for me?"

He nods and leaves and I'm suddenly exhausted. I crash down onto the rumpled bed, the pulled-apart sheets, and stretch out. I push my face into the only remaining pillow, breathing in that blank hotel linen scent. I think of Jane's and Charly's faces when I said *I modeled bathing suits for him*. How had they looked at me? Was it with envy or alarm?

When I wake it's dark and the curtains are drawn. My bedside clock is blinking. The power in the hotel must have gone off sometime in the night. I get up and pull the curtains back. The scarf is near where I had been lying. I pick it up, fingering the stiff silk. It's hardened where the wine stain has dried. The smell is comforting. No, more than comforting. It's reminiscent of some memory, teasing me: a floral smell that is half Mary and half her perfume. I take what I hope is a sleeping pill and a little pink pill too, because

51

the light in the room is slanted and spooky. A note on the floor reads:

INGRID, I'M SORRY—REX

It's in a neat, almost girly hand—the g is a fancy loop, the rest of the letters evenly spaced. What a nice, capable name. At the window I can see the tiny lights on a buoy out in the bay. It must be early still because the sky is soft and gray. I can just make out Catalina Island on the other side. It's a looming lump of land right on the horizon. It seems indifferent, a little judgmental.

I've been only once, when I was eleven. I did not like it. Avalon's a terrible, touristy town with families and couples spilling out of golf carts because there are no cars allowed, and the boardwalk is barely a mile, which I guess is too far for most tourists to walk. The Catalina Express is a great big bucket of a boat that crashes head-long into swells rather than riding with them. It just plunges right in, launching deck trash cans at the crowd of summer camp kids who are goofing off, daring one another to walk up and down the stairs without holding the rails. A chubby blond boy falls, skidding a little across the deck so that his knees get cut up and bloodied. His father saying *Good* and his mother giving him a look that says *We will not be having any fun.*

All the summer camp families are there for the day. My parents are in much better moods now that they can talk about their boys with the others, Mother beaming. *This year they learned to scuba dive!* My father telling a man and his wife, *They'll be better off for it, of course.*

And there's a dusty bus ride to the boys' camp, eucalyptus trees and someone peeling an orange. She's a teenager, probably not yet fifteen. An attractive girl with dark hair, she puts her finger to her lips and winks. The bright orange peel flies off, disappearing into the dust kicked up by the van.

The boys are tan and smiling a secret joy. They show us the kay-aks they used to paddle into coves where they learned about sea-weed and ocean currents. One of them saw a leopard shark, the other a sea turtle. We must have stayed until dinner. I remember coming back to Avalon at night, to the Hotel Atwater, an aging Victorian-style building with sloping floors. I make my parents laugh by showing them if you place a marble on one side of the room it rolls easily to the other side.

How clever, Mother is saying.

There's a bar on the ground floor that has all-night karaoke, and I dance in our hotel room to someone's dramatic rendition of Journey's "Don't Stop Believin'."

Such a silly girl, my father says, hugging me tight.

We play cards. I pretend the stick pretzels are cigarettes and talk with what I imagine is a mobster accent. But then they start to fight, about something, anything, and my father leaves for the bar, and Mother tells me to get to bed.

A great baritone wakes me. It's coming from the bar below. It's my father, his singing slurred.

I call into the darkness, but no one answers. The room is strange at night, with its sloping floors and peeling pink walls.

In the morning my parents take me out for waffles and buy me a hot pink hat that says "Island Style." They buy me a caramel apple too and let me play games in the arcade.

And then I'm at the stern of the boat. It's loud from the thun-dering engine, the fierce beating wind. My parents are below, where it's warm. I have the hat in my hands and I'm thinking of that older girl with her dark hair, how the orange peel looked when it sailed out the window—her one finger pressed against her lips. How beau-tiful and mysterious she was, with that secret hush, that wink meant just for me.

The pink "Island Style" hat is flapping wildly in my hands. I watch, transfixed. Then, one finger at a time, starting with my pinky, I let go. It billows out like a handkerchief and then whips up violently, shooting out, up against the sky—for a moment I think it might fly on forever—but then it dives down, down, crashing into the boat's wake.

9

I read and reread the email: *I still think about you when I touch myself —Elsa.*

I've slept through the morning and into the afternoon. The television is on, and everything seems to take place in New York. Reality TV shows, police procedurals, music videos. There's Central Park, the Flatiron Building, ferries coasting back and forth to Ellis Island. I almost see MoMA a handful of times.

Why not send this to him? It says everything. Only, I've never been this blunt before. Is it sexy or desperate? Something would have to give; he'd have to write back if I sent this, wouldn't he? I let my finger hover over the SEND button until I'm almost sweating. Instead I turn the television off and send this: *Hey you, I'm in Los Angeles—on vacation. I miss everyone, though. Write me back when you can —Elsa.*

I remember at the last Christmas party, the curators saying *Things are changing*, only I did not believe them. *What silly spoiled children,* I thought. Because there is only wine and beer, not a full bar, they think the world is ending. Eric telling them *It will be okay,* and then leading me by the hand, away from the party, down to the vaults below, to the soft-lit corridors, the blue shadows, the art-works packed away in their housing. That dazzling smile and those dark eyes, the smell of his cologne—and then the pretense drops, and there's just the sound of my breath and his, hot and labored against my neck.

I take two white pills and shower for dinner. The restaurant where we're meeting the potato chip heir is on the pier, one of those commercial places where the fish is flown in frozen and they use the cheapest liquor in their drinks, but I don't mind because there's a gift shop, and someone might come around to sing or do card tricks at your table.

I wear sandals and a linen sundress that would make Eric stare at my shoulders, his eyes saying *Yes, yes, yes.*

The streets let off heat, the sun slants over the Pacific, the hotel thermometer reads 85°. When I step into the lobby young Rex is talking to a valet. He waves when he sees me. It's a small gesture, full of innocence, and I can barely smile in return. I refuse to feel guilty, though—I haven't done anything.

Outside there are people everywhere. A young French family argues on the corner, the son crying, "Papa! Papa!" His pale, freckled face is sunburned. The pregnant mother holds her stomach and looks away from them both, out toward that lovely orange-pink sky. Couples are sprawled on blankets along the grassy bluff, care-takers push despondent elders in wheelchairs, pigeons and gulls waddle among debris from an overturned trash can. There are dogs on leashes: fat ones, skinny ones, shaggy ones; some so ugly I want to kick.

At the beginning of the pier the air is different. It smells saltier, a little sour, nasty. I hear a lifeguard tell a couple in bathing suits that blue algae bloomed recently, and is now dying. The surf is pea-soup green.

"The water's too warm," he's saying. "But don't worry, it won't hurt you." The couple look disgusted. They turn away from the water. Down at the end of the pier old men cast lines and gut fish. The wooden pier groans from the weight. There are tourists in flip-flops with sunburned thighs buying cotton candy and corn dogs and tickets for the roller coaster. There are babies crying over sand in their diapers; the older kids cry too, they want a picture drawn by the cartoonist. Children know that life is incredibly unfair.

The Klonopin—or whatever it was—puts all that noise at a distance. I feel loose, my limbs, my ligaments, down to the blood and bone. There's a lightness in my chest, not quite giddiness, but I could see how it might get there. Even that feels far away, though, a healthy, breathable distance. I suck in that rotting sea air, feel my chest expand—exhale slowly, a gentle wind, just light enough to puff along those tiny sailboats out in the bay.

The restaurant is a cluster of Budweiser posters and cowboy hats, bearded men all greeting, *Howdy little miss.* So I sit at the bar to wait for Charly and the gang. In the corner a woman laughs with her friend, beside me two men hold hands and speak in quiet voices, every table has tourists and out-of-towners. A man asks my name. I think of telling him Susanna from San Diego, or Ingrid the wine rep, or somebody else entirely, but something about him seems to be daring me to lie. So I give my real name.

"Thought so. Jared described you to a tee. I'm Tom," he says, smiling, but I can see his jaw clenching, biting that smile in half. He gives me a firm, lingering handshake before touching my bare shoulders. "What a beautiful dress."

Tom Cooper should be unattractive—hooked nose, small eyes and chin, and completely bald, smooth and shiny. But he has an aristocratic air about him. He's older, almost forty, tall, broad, athletic. He tells me about windsurfing, how he scuba dives, rock climbs, and sails. He's an excellent horseman; his uncle has a horse ranch in Wyoming, and he invites me up sometime. He's well-groomed, scrubbed clean, and absolutely menacing.

"And how do you know Jared?" I ask. I can tell he's enjoying talking about himself.

"He did a bit of design work for one of my companies—real good guy. We flew down to Baja a few summers back. That wife doesn't let him get out much. Got the guy on a tight leash."

"I don't think Charly could leash a dog."

The side of his mouth tilts up, more of a smirk than a smile.

Just then Jared and Charly arrive. Jared bounds over to clap Tom in a big embrace, but Charly hangs back a bit. I can tell they're fighting. She's withdrawn, icy. She apologizes for being late but won't say why. This I remember. And for a moment I'm relieved at how familiar this is.

Jared orders two double Cadillac margaritas and a shot of tequila, which means the fight must have been a doozy. "Enjoy your marg," he says to his wife.

Charly gives him her back and turns to me with an artificial smile. "Sorry we're late," she says.

"It's okay, Robby and Jane aren't here yet."

She doesn't touch the drink, just fiddles with the straw. "The valet took forever too," she says before giving me her drink and asking the bartender for a club soda.

Then Robby is there with Jane, who's all happy liquid energy.

"We ordered at the bar," Tom says, pointing at Jared. "This guy couldn't wait." He kisses Jane on the cheek, shakes Robby's hand.

"Hey, man, I'm on vacation as of today." Jared tosses back his shot and orders another.

The six of us squeeze into a booth. I'm between Tom and Jared. I can smell Tom's aftershave; even this smells expensive. He rests his thigh next to mine, all coiled muscle. He smiles that same biting smile at me.

"You okay, Jared?" I ask. "You're already on shot number two."

"*El numero dos*," he says, sucking up the last of his margarita and putting an arm around me. "Aw, Elsie. What happened to you? Where'd you go? Remember the fun times we had? Remember those desert trips? Coachella in its early days?" His mouth slants.

"Before it got filled with shitty hipsters," Robby says from over his drink.

"Yeah, man! We used to pack up my Jeep and smoke pot the whole way." Jared leans his head back, his eyes slits.

"You were all at UCLA together?" Tom asks.

"Except for Jane," Robby says, bumping her playfully.

Jared, still with his head tilted back, says, "Seems like forever ago."

"Remember that highway patrolman?" I say to Charly, who laughs.

"I thought we were done for!" she says.

Robby has his face in his hands now, but he's smiling. "It was my fault. I shouldn't have been driving."

"What happened?" Jane asks politely. She's scooping salsa with a chip and watching Robby.

"I think that cop gave me a free pass. He saw that shit-heap I was driving—"

"Hey!" Jared interjects. "That was my baby!"

"It was a crap car. The seat belts didn't even work in the back."

"But it was roomy," Jared says, and he nudges Charly, who smiles at the napkin in her lap.

We're quiet for a moment, the past kicked up like pleasant dust.

The bartenders with their perfectly groomed beards are doing tricks with tequila bottles, throwing them back and forth between each other. It's like an Old West show. When they finish, one pretends to fire a pistol, blowing his index finger as if it were smoking.

Jared still has his arm around me. "What does New York have that we don't?"

"Money, jobs, art, culture," Jane says, counting on her fingers. I can tell she's relieved to finally join in.

"Hey, Los Angeles has culture," Jared interjects.

Jane sits up straight. "I'm not saying we don't have culture, but look at our publishing industry. The *Los Angeles Times* is a joke compared with *The New York Times*, and LA doesn't have anything equivalent to *The New Yorker.*"

"Who reads *The New Yorker* anymore?" Tom says. He has a drawl I can't place. "Even *Harper's* sounds old-fashioned. I've been thinking of going into the magazine business—print is dead and all, but I think it just needs the right kind of digital experience. You wait and see. After my next trip."

"Where are you going next?" Charly asks him. She's perked up a bit since Jared teased her about the backseat.

Tom makes a show of thinking about it. He stretches back against the crusty leather booth. I can feel his leg push into mine, but I refuse to move.

"Don't tell me," I say. "You haven't decided."

He arches his eyebrows in my direction.

"Maybe you can help me," he says in his lazy drawl. His eyes are a peculiar blue almost-gray, and they catch the restaurant light, flashing with amusement.

The waiter comes over then, spreads a bounty of guacamole, fish tacos, grilled yucca, and a pitcher of margaritas.

Instead of eating, I check my email. Still nothing from Eric. Only a couple of spam emails for Viagra, a monthly email from a power yoga studio in Greenwich Village, and an email from the Democratic Party urging me to contribute.

The group is talking about sailing to Hawaii versus Mexico as I rummage through my purse and find two pills. They've been crushed a bit; I have to wet my finger to get all the pieces.

Robby catches me taking them. I pantomime a toast to him with my water.

"How many cabins are on your boat?" I ask Tom.

"Three, but sleeping on deck is half the fun."

"Should we bring sleeping bags?" Jane asks. She's practically climbing up Robby's shoulder in excitement.

"The boat's got everything you need. If you forget your swimsuits, I have extras on board."

"Bikinis too?" I say.

I sense the wink before it actually happens. "They get left behind."

Charly makes a face. "Do you clean them?"

"We'll bring our own suits," Robby says.

Jared leans his head on my shoulder. "I'm going to sleep here, if that's okay."

"Okay!" Robby says, patting Jane so he can get out of the booth. "Jared's done. We better get him home before he pukes. How many margaritas did he have?"

"I don't know. Maybe three?" I say. "Can he still not handle tequila?"

"No," Charly says with a sigh.

Tom and Robby help Jared outside, with Jane guiding.

"Everything okay with you guys?" I ask when it's just the two of us.

Charly nods, handing her keys to the valet. "He doesn't like the backsplash tile I put in the kitchen." She turns and looks at me. Her eyes are very dark brown, and under the pier lights they shine. In junior high she outlined them in black eyeliner, giving them a bruised look. It was her signature style; I remembered it long after she left for Southern California when her mom divorced her dad. I doubt she's even wearing mascara now.

"I'm really glad you're coming to stay with us," she says, and I realize those dark eyes are shining from tears. But then the valet is back, handing her the keys to a Prius wagon.

"Whose car is this?" I ask.

"Ours," Charly says, and she climbs behind the wheel. "The gas mileage is great."

I can see a baby seat perfectly for a second, bright yellow with white trim, eerie in its emptiness. Then Jared is shoved in front of it.

Charly leans out the window and yells, "See you tomorrow, Elsa!" And they drive off, the Prius falling into traffic on Ocean Avenue.

I look to Robby and Jane, to see if they saw the baby seat too, but Robby is shaking Tom's hand. They're making a joke I don't hear. I laugh anyway. Then Robby hugs me with one arm, climbs into a sports coupe. Jane smiles from the driver's seat and gives Tom and me a wave.

I'd shiver if it weren't such a peaceful night. It's warm enough to be in a dress, drunk and feeling the breeze. I can smell fried food and the Ferris wheel is lit up, a bright spot against the black sky.

"Can I walk you back to your hotel?" Tom asks from somewhere in the darkness.

"You didn't drive?"

He moves farther from the streetlight, and I can't make out his face at all. "No, my boat's in the marina," he says. "I took a cab here." That drawl really is something else—like syrup, thick and marinating everything.

"Well," I say, reaching into the dark to find his arm. "What's the name of your boat?"

10

Morning is thick in my mouth. I slept in my dress; it smells like cigarettes and Tom Cooper's cologne. I roll onto my back. My jaw hurts from his kissing.

At the hotel bar he ordered White Russians. Insisted I drink one, saying, *You need a proper cocktail.*

Then it's up to my room, *Let me escort you, Elsa.* Stopping in the hallway, an arm on one side, his free hand clasping my head, turning it this way and that as if to examine it. *Such a pretty pout*, he said. *Are you very high, very drunk, or both?* And that smug, grating smile, those perfectly bleached teeth. He's the pain-builds-character type. Every kiss practically suffocating, hands digging into my waist. I was working hard to keep him out of my room when suddenly Rex was there, all cleft chin and puppy paws, saying something about management needing to speak to me about property destruction. That got Tom leaving real fast.

I remember Rex helping me into my room, unlocking the door with my weight against him, and me asking *Is management really mad at me?*

No, he's saying, *they aren't, it's okay.*

Rex watches from the doorway while I rinse until the travel-size mouthwash is empty. I want to ask if he'll hold me, but don't. Instead I ask if he'll check my email. Everything's a bit fuzzy, the room spinning. *No new messages.* I feel sick and want to wrap myself in something—in anyone. I touch Rex's face, somewhere near his lips—or maybe it is his lips. Can I pretend Rex is him? If I blur my eyes, let that liquid wave of pills and booze wash completely over me. *Eric, Eric.* But it's no use. They don't smell the same, they aren't the same height. I tell him he should leave, but first—*but first, help me from this dress. No, wait, don't. It's better if you don't. Good night, good night, good night.*

This morning is too bright, each part of the room clean and perfectly arranged: the polished writing table by the window, the mid-century chairs and couch in the small living room, glass table-tops with glossy magazines stacked in tiny spires, a dresser cabinet where the TV is on but muted. The air conditioner clicks on, rattling the sliding glass door. Too clean, too empty.

I try to remember how I got here, lying here in this room, surrounded by things I won't even be able to afford in a month—two months if I max out my credit cards. There is someone in the hotel room next to me; I can hear their shower turn on and off, the sound of their television. I shut my eyes and imagine moving through the building, down to the street below, out to the city in the distance, beyond, to New York and Eric.

I imagine this other Elsa who's still with him. She'd be at work already, by his side. They'd find ways to get close during the day. For a moment I can't recall his voice and I panic. So I drum up his voice from that day but pretend things were different—*Don't go,* he says. *I'm sorry HR is here, watching us. If she wasn't, I'd hold you, I wouldn't let you leave.*

I check my messages. There's an email from Eric: *Had coffee with the new interns this morning, they all look terribly young and incompetent. Take care of yourself, Eric*

I imagine him writing this at his desk, his office door closed, the cursor blinking. What could we really say to each other? I want to cry. Instead I take a little pink pill and two oblong ones and call down to room service.

It isn't Rex today but a woman my age who brings a bottle of champagne and a carafe of orange juice. I tip her more than I should because I'm horrified this might be my future.

My phone rings while I'm packing. It's Robby.

"Hey, crazy night last night, huh? It's funny Jared still can't handle tequila," I say, packing my toiletries. I combine some of the pills, tossing out the prescription bottles with Mother's name worn off.

"Yeah, about that, what were you taking?"

"I'm proud of you, Robby, just coming out and asking like that." I rinse the Altoids tin Austin left behind, drying it with a towel. "Those were pain pills. I'm also taking Xanax again and possibly Klonopin or maybe they're Percocets. I'm not sure—there's pink pills, tiny white ones, and blue too." The champagne has hit me hard.

"Jesus, Elsa, is everything okay?"

"Don't worry about me, darling," I say, shooting for fabulous, but even I can hear the edge in my voice. I try again. "I'm on vacation. Just blowing off steam." The pills I like to dissolve under my tongue I put in the tin, hoping they'll taste minty now. I slip the tin into my purse.

"Maybe Catalina isn't a good idea."

Rather than folding my clothes, I wrestle them in and zip the case. I sit on top of it drinking my mimosa, the scarf wrapped around me like a shawl. I think about our wedding in the desert, that convertible Mustang—black and tan—how the wind changed once we hit Joshua Tree, all sun-baked earth and desert flowers. Mrs. Robby Bishop. Were those happy days? What a blur that year turned into. Some three hundred days drilled down to one sentence: *They divorced in 2010.*

"Don't be like that. I wouldn't have told you—and please God, keep it to yourself. I'm fine. Like I said, just unwinding a bit—you don't know what New York's like. Very high stress. Now, be a good boy and push some pixels around. That's what you're doing these days, right?"

"I do UX design."

"Great, buy Jane something nice. I'll see you tomorrow at the marina. Okay?"

"Elsa, I'm worried about you."

There's a knock at the door.

"Wonderful, honey, you and me both. We were always such a good team. I have to go, someone's here. Goodbye, Robby, see you tomorrow."

I hang up before he can say anything else.

It's Rex. I hardly recognize him without his hotel uniform. He's wearing a hoodie and shorts and the same black Converse as when he's working. Seeing his bare legs is shocking: they look too exposed, pale and hairy, with pink knobby knees.

"Here's my number." He thrusts his hand out. His face is very red. He's taken one of the hotel cloth napkins he brings with breakfast and written his number in marker across the bottom.

"It's just in case you don't want to go home yet. I live with a couple guys on campus, but you can stay with us for as long as you want. You can even have my room. I'll sleep on the couch. If you don't mind parties and dude stuff everywhere, it's not too bad." He smiles. He must have recently gotten his braces off; it's an uneasy smile, his lips creeping back over his teeth, which are perfectly straight, perfectly white. *Gleaming.*

"You're very sweet, Rex. Thank you," I manage.

But he's already cleared the tray of champagne and walked out the door.

11

Charly and Jared's house is in Ocean Park, a part
of West Los Angeles that sits on top of a hill, beneath the Santa
Monica Airport. It's a modern house, slate blue with huge sky-
lights and a slanted tin roof that makes the place look like a space-
age barn.

The last time I saw it was at their housewarming party soon
after Charly and Jared returned from their honeymoon—when
Robby managed to hold it together long enough for me to feel okay
about leaving. The party was set in their backyard, Aperol and
Campari spritzes under newly planted California sycamores and
trained bougainvillea, tiny white lights along paths of white stone.
I remember watching them, the newlyweds, play host and hostess. Charly comfortable and relaxed, arm in arm with her husband.
And I remember Robby, now my ex-husband, how he sat and looked
at me from across the patio, all sad, sappy eyes. I thought I'd
crumble and give in again if he cried, but he didn't that time. We
even danced and toasted Charly and Jared. We were very grown-up.
I left for New York soon after.

The house looks the same. Except for the Prius wagon parked in the driveway with that baby seat in the back. It looks well used too, as if Jared and Charly had a baby and it grew up and moved away and someone had forgotten to take the car seat out.

Charly answers the door barefoot and dressed in a flannel shirt and cuffed jeans. "Sorry I'm a mess. I just got home from my therapist." She hugs me and takes one of my bags. "I don't know why you didn't stay with us from the beginning. The Miramar must have cost a peach." Her face looks a little pale, even with the smattering of freckles across her nose. "I'm sure you can afford it, I'm not saying that. We have a Jacuzzi in the back! I've turned it on. Jared had to go into work. It's *so nice* to have company. Usually it's just Sibley and me." She pauses. "Sibley's our cat."

I don't ask about the baby seat in the back of the Prius. The house is too spotless for a baby to be living here. Too cold, with its shining stainless-steel appliances.

I think of her Internet posts, all the cat photos. Here's Sibley on the bed; here's Sibley looking bored; Sibley and me at Christmas; Sibley looking out the window. There are no babies in those pictures.

"Just Charly the cat lady," I mumble, forgetting I've already had a bottle of champagne at the hotel. Thankfully she hasn't heard me.

"Here's the guest room. Do you recognize the curtains? You gave them to us as a wedding present."

"Your house is really beautiful, Charly."

She grins, turns on her heels. "You haven't even seen the remodel!"

I follow her through the house. They've redone the kitchen, added a modest library, and extended the master bedroom to include a deck.

"It's weird to plan where your reading chair will be in forty years—but that's what we did. I'll be here and Jared will be there."

I can see them suddenly in their seventies, in their respective reading chairs, Jared complaining just so Charly will fuss over him, which of course she will. A hot water bottle if he's too cold, a damp cloth if he's warm. What should she make for dinner? What should they do tomorrow in the garden? Fuss, fuss, fuss.

She slips on a pair of bright yellow Crocs. When I stare, she says, "My gardening shoes. They're hideous, I know. But super comfy."

The backyard is lovely, with jasmine and honeysuckle and a tall sycamore hanging low enough to climb. They've added a bird-bath and a family of gnomes. A jet takes off overhead, rattling the windows.

"We're trying to get the airport shut down, there's been such gruesome crashes," she tells me. "Just last month one went nose-first right into the golf course. That's a mile away from my elementary school—*a mile*. Can you imagine?"

Champagne is lovely but it's quick to give you a headache. I ask for water.

"Of course. Sit here, you can watch the black phoebes hop around in the sycamore tree. They're my favorite. Jared prefers the blue jays—did you know they aren't really blue jays at all?" She presses her hands together, a nervous tick that I recognize. She goes on chattering. "Jared got me a bird guide last Christmas. What we call blue jays out here are actually scrub jays. Not as good a name, I know." She stands for a moment, exhales. "I'll throw something together for lunch."

We sit on the backyard deck, eating pasta with basil pesto and cherry tomatoes, watching black phoebes dart and flick their tails. They're rather dashing birds, with their sooty black bodies and crisp white bellies. We laugh when one scares a squirrel from the bird feeder.

"Jared and I grew the basil and tomatoes ourselves," she tells me. Sibley, a fat British shorthair, is on her lap.

"You guys are doing really well," I say, but it comes out sounding flat and insincere. I try again. "I love how the landscaping has grown in, and the Jacuzzi is a nice touch too." We look at it, the steam working up, bubbles swirling.

Charly shrugs, pleased with herself. "It's no MoMA, I'm sure."

Even the wine is good. She brings it out in a bucket of ice but pours only one glass.

"You're not drinking?" I say.

She shrugs and sips her iced tea. "I'm nervous about wearing a bikini. I feel so bloated."

"We'll end up skinny-dipping drunk anyway, so what's the point?"

This makes her laugh and she tells me again that she's missed me. We finish with lunch and move into the living room, where she's pulled out photo albums. "Remember this?" Charly asks shyly, flipping one open to a page that shows us much younger, standing in front of the Metropolitan Museum in New York.

"Jesus," I say, touching the photograph. I had forgotten my first trip to New York City was actually *with* Charly.

She's excited now, tucks her feet and watches me closely. "Remember?" she prompts. "There were fifteen of us. We stayed in a hotel that had kitchenettes."

"In the lobby we could buy gumballs and press-on tattoos from a vending machine," I say, still touching the photo.

"Yep." She smiles and points to the plump, enthusiastic woman standing with us in the photo. "She insisted we call her by her first name, Sandy."

"*Miss* Sandy."

"That's right," Charly says, laughing. "Like kindergartners instead of seventh graders. We felt very grown-up by then."

"Hadn't we wanted a summer trip to Italy?"

Charly nods. "But we failed to raise the funds."

"And New York City was the consolation prize. I forgot about that."

"Look at our clothes," Charly says, and she leans closer to the page.

I'm starting to remember—that we went to some exhibition, that we were learning about Greek gods and goddesses. *Had they removed part of an ancient city and reassembled it in the Met—could that be right?*

Charly doesn't remember, but I can picture myself walking through ancient stone arches, able to reach out and touch them. The signs say "Please Do Not Touch," but there aren't any ropes or glass. I can stroke the face of Medusa, tickle a lion's tongue, his nose slightly rubbed off so he looks friendly—the snakes around Medusa's head are worn too. She looks like those women in hair commercials, all wild-eyed and free. It's fuzzy, part memory, part dream. Possibly all imagined.

And there is Miss Sandy leaning toward me, saying, *Can you imagine working here? Surrounded by all this history?* I think there might be tears in her eyes. And I'm thinking *Yes, yes.* Only I don't see history, I see beauty—in the coolness of the marble floors, the stately columns and pillars, the museum staff who come from the restricted-access floors with their flashy suits and funky dresses and jewelry, talking with easy confidence, their voices bouncing off the walls and floors. The art was a footnote, not the main attraction. It was the museum itself, the *institution*, that hooked me.

"I don't remember an ancient city," Charly is telling me. "But oh my God do you remember when the Jenner brothers stuck gum on the boobs of Central Park Alice so it looked like she had two pink gummy nipples? I had a crush on the taller one, but they both liked you. Wasn't that always the case." She's laughing, so I don't think anything of it. "Poor Miss Sandy," she's saying. "And when one of the girls—was it Magda? Or Mimi? Whichever, one of them wandered off to buy an ice cream and got lost and it was absolute chaos finding her."

I'm surprised Charly can recall all this so clearly. It sounds faintly familiar, but it's murky, like a film I once saw but can barely remember now. The only thing clear is Miss Sandy, who I remember perfectly. A plump high school art teacher who asked for Diet Coke on the plane ride back, reading *Aperture* and petting the pictures with longing.

Charly lightly strokes her own image with her forefinger. "We were so young. I almost put this one up online, but I didn't want to share it. You know?"

"Then it wouldn't be yours."

"Exactly." She looks at me with her dark eyes, crow's feet just beginning at the corners. She looks so sad suddenly. I take her hand. It's warm, a little damp, but soft like a child's.

She looks at our hands, clasped together, one tawny and freckled with a wedding ring, the other willowy and smooth.

"Even your hand is prettier than mine," she says, and moves away.

When Jared gets home with pizza and beer, we're in our suits, about to get in the Jacuzzi. He smiles, kisses my cheek, tells me I look wonderful.

"Have you been working out?" he asks. I tell him the most exercise I get is lifting a wineglass to my mouth or opening a prescription bottle. This enthralls him.

He drinks whiskey and smokes a joint on the edge of the Jacuzzi, half in shadow, watching me. Charly is trying to tell us about how the real blue jay is native to the eastern United States, but Jared speaks over her. He tells me some story that implies he's brilliant at his job.

This too is familiar, and I start to get uneasy. Then Jared's in the water. He swims around his wife to get to me, to ask if I want to share a joint.

Charly gets out. "I'm tired." Her voice is snappy.

"Come on," Jared slurs. "It's not even midnight." He puts an arm around me. "Oh!" he says. "Better yet, bring out more drinks."

I can smell him, a sharp scent of juniper and cedar that isn't unpleasant but is very strong. His arm is hairy, and I can feel it like a wet Brillo pad against my neck.

"Get it yourself," she says, and shuts the door with a heavy thump.

In the dark with Charly gone, I feel edgy. *Why doesn't he go after her?*

I say good night and move away from him. He hesitates. I can't see him in the darkness, but there's splashing and for a moment I hold my breath. Then there's the thump of the door again and I'm alone. I shiver. The water level is much lower when it's just one person.

12

Sleeping has become treacherous. In dreams everything converges, what's real and what's not. You linger at the beginning of sleep, or maybe it's the end. Everything's just about to happen. The lines almost touch—if you imagine hard enough maybe they will. That curve of her hip, how the buttock and thigh almost share a line with that other hip, that other leg—everything bestial. Picasso was a madman.

You hear Sibley's collar, or maybe it's the elevator, the one just down the hall from his office. Everything hovers at that moment of anticipation, when you know he will cross that space, flushed and demanding, pull up your dress and enter you—one quick thrust so that you always gasp—only now *you* are the one who needs it, that sense of urgency, one hand pushing you onto the desk, the other searching for your breast, your throat, your mouth. *But wait, wait*—you exist in that moment of suspension for as long as you can because it will be too short, it will never be enough. It is gone already.

I jerk awake. It's like waking up in a bed of molasses, everything sticky with leftover dream. *Are my eyes even open?* The problem with drinking and pills is that at some point you wake up like this. After the moon sets but before the sun rises, when it's completely dark. *Have I died? Has the world whisked me away?* And then it hits you all at once: *This is my life.*

Back at the hotel I could cry and no one would hear me. But at Jared and Charly's, with the curtains Robby and I picked out for them as a wedding present hanging above me, and Jared's snoring vibrating across the hall, I'm trapped. I can't cry here.

I stumble into the kitchen and gulp down a glass of water as if I've never learned to drink from a cup. I get the water everywhere, on my nightgown, the floor, the cat.

In the black morning the chrome kitchen is even more unwelcoming. I take the water to my room. It's already morning in New York, so I text Eric:

What are you doing?

I pull the sheets up to my chin, waiting.

Nothing.

I want to text something else, but don't. It would be too pathetic. I wish I hadn't turned Mary's scarf in to the hotel's lost and found. I'd sleep better if I had it. I'd curl up like a child with a binky. But I handed it to the girl at the front desk, told her I found it by the pool, *I'm sure the owner is missing it.* It pleases me to think Mary considers it lost on the east coast when really it's on the west coast in a bin with sunglasses, hats, and fanny packs.

The curtains glow softly. There's a knock at the door.

"I thought I heard you in the kitchen," Charly says. "Is everything all right?"

She's wearing an oversized man's robe. She sits on the end of the bed.

"I think I might still be a little drunk." I can barely make out her face; the light in the room is so pale, so delicate.

She's quiet. I wonder if I spoke out loud or only thought I did. She's looking around the room, sort of staring off.

"I think I'm going to lose Jared."

"Oh, stop it."

"It's true." She puts her head in her hands.

I reach out but hesitate.

"You saw the way he was with you last night. And you're our *friend*. How do you think he is with all the other girls? The ones at work or the gym? I can't compete with gym girls."

I tell her to hush; I say he loves her. "He's always been that way with me—it doesn't mean anything."

"I can't give him children. We've been trying."

"There's ways around that now," I say.

She sits up, her long hair stuck against wet cheeks. "We're doing another IUI next month. That's why I shouldn't be drinking—but I already know it won't work. None of them have."

She isn't facing me, but looking out at the room. My hand is still hanging in midair between us.

"This was supposed to be a nursery."

The morning is brighter now, as if to prove that this is indeed not a nursery, only a sparsely furnished guest room with my clothes thrown around it.

My mouth is dry. I don't think she can hear me when I say *I'm sorry*. It sounds like I'm whispering it to myself.

"We got the Prius for family trips. One of the moms at the school gave me their car seat last summer. What am I supposed to do? I can't take it out—I won't take it out. The day I do is the day I give up trying."

I jump when she makes a half-choked sob. She holds her head in her hand, with a low moan. Then she's looking up toward the window and I can just make out her face in the soft light now—jaw trembling, brown eyes watery.

I'm about to say something, anything to comfort her but feel so horribly unprepared. Inadequate. She inhales sharply.

"The worst part? We have no one here. I mean, Jared has Robby, but who knows what they talk about. I doubt it's this kind of stuff. Who do I have? Jane?" She lets out a huff, wipes her nose with the back of her robe sleeve. "You know what she said to me? When they were over for a barbeque, Jane and I were by ourselves in the kitchen and she went to pour me wine and I reminded her I couldn't drink—we were right in the middle of a cycle—and she said, *Are you guys still doing that?* She said it just like that, like it was some kind of fad. I haven't invited them over since. If it wasn't for your visit I probably wouldn't have invited them out with us again."

I laugh lightly. "I'm sure she didn't mean anything by it. Jane strikes me as a bit out of touch."

"You sound like Jared now. *Don't be so dramatic, Charlotte*, he says." She pushes herself up. "Why am I telling you this? You've been home for five minutes and I'm crying all over you." She turns in the doorway, the early-morning light making her look squat and soggy in her robe. I can tell she's still waiting for me to say or do something comforting, and when I don't she pushes her hands together nervously. "I'm making blueberry pancakes for breakfast," she finally says. "Be ready to go by nine."

13

Jane and Robby arrive an hour later, all eagerness and well-slept energy. I get the feeling they've been over before for what Charly calls her *farmer's market breakfast*. You wouldn't know she had just been saying how close she was to writing them off; they're talking excitedly about the trip with Robby, who throws me inclusive looks every so often.

"I can't wait to get sailing," Jane says, squeezing her coffee mug. Charly offers her a top up, and they share a look of glee over the pot.

Jared stays in bed until it's just about time to leave, then surfaces in his pajamas, calling for Charly from the living room couch so he can lie across her lap. "Will you make me a cappuccino?" he asks, pushing his head against her so she pets him. "You make them better than I do."

We get to the marina late. It's overcast and the gulls and sea lions are crying, the water like glass. Tom's waiting at the slip entrance looking smug, wearing expensive sunglasses and a baseball cap.

"Hiya, landlubbers," he says, and swings the gate wide so we can walk down the dock.

Jane is giddy. She's the first on the boat, first to exclaim how beautiful it is—and it is *gorgeous*. Tom gives us the grand tour: fifty-two feet long, handmade in Maine with three cabins, a pullout settee, varnished teak deck, cherrywood trim—and a saloon with not one but two wine coolers.

"Do you like it, Elsa?" Tom asks me.

"You can sail this by yourself?"

He smiles, puts a leg up on the U-shaped seat. "I sailed it down from San Francisco—no island trip, let me tell you. The wind was brutal. At night the fog was so thick you couldn't tell whether light on land was a fog light or a headlight. But I did it."

"It sounds so exciting!" Jane exclaims. She and Robby have already chosen the second cabin, a cozy two-person tucked in the port side of the boat, directly opposite the one-person berth I'll be in.

Jane is looking out at the harbor, the various masts and flags and usual marina litter blocking the horizon. "You'll teach me how to sail, right?"

Tom laughs, a big august sound. "Sure. Come up to the cockpit with me. I'll show you all the goods. Jared, you want to cast off?"

"Righto, Captain. Robby can help."

"What should I do?" I ask.

Tom takes hold of my arm, steering me. "You can be in charge of the *booze*, Elsa. You'd like that, wouldn't you?" He has that same look from the other night. Angry and turned on. A little shiver crawls over me. He releases my arm and says casually, "Choose something good. The coolers are stocked."

I try to smile at him, but those blueberry pancakes did me no favors. I can feel them like one big lump. I'm relieved when Jane calls for him and he turns to go.

Charly is rubbing sunscreen onto her face downstairs.

"I'm feeling a little woozy already," she says.

"That's just nerves, I'm excited too." I pat her arm lightly.

"Don't be gentle with me, Elsa. I don't want your pity." She plops on an oversized hat, one with flaps that tie under her chin. She ties it tight, hands me the sunscreen. "Don't want to age any quicker, do we?"

I shake my head no, and she ducks back out to the deck.

Robby comes down, hands in his pockets, pretending to inspect the cabins. The rumbling of the engine's loud, so he has to shout, "Nice piece of craftsmanship!"

"Could you imagine living on one of these things?" I wait for him to mention our phone call. "What a life."

He comes close so we don't have to yell over the engine.

"If you like that kind of thing." He shrugs. "I prefer a real job. These guys that inherit never have any authenticity. They're all pretense."

"Dial it back, Robby, we haven't even left the marina."

The boat bounces gently off one of the buoys tied to the slip.

"Sorry!" Jane shouts down to us.

I busy myself with looking in Tom's wine storage. He has a good selection. There's champagne and prosecco, three or four different kinds of white, not one of them a California chardonnay. The labels are all smooth and exotic, and several still have price stickers— in a foreign currency, of course. I choose a bottle that makes me think of country estates and powdered wigs. The label is in French, but the price sticker is in rupees.

"Elsa." I can feel Robby looking at me.

"Who wants wine?" I shout from the base of the stairs.

"I do!" Jane says. She's standing at the wheel, with Tom behind her. Jared is sitting just beside them looking miserable and hungover.

"Jared, hair of the dog?" I yell. He shakes his head no.

Tom smacks him on the back. "The Pepto-Bismol will kick in soon. Then I'll break out the scotch."

Jared seems less than convinced. The engine kicks up a notch as we make our way through the harbor.

"I'll bring up some sparkling water," I shout to him. I can feel Robby waiting for me. Whatever he wants to say, ignoring him will not prevent it. He's standing in front of the wineglasses, cupping one in each hand, waiting patiently.

"Robby, what would you like to drink? Wine?" I hold the bottle up.

"Sure," he says, trying to catch my eye.

My cheeks burn. I think maybe I'm sick. This isn't a hangover; I'm actually sick. Something serious and old-fashioned, like tuberculosis. God, does that sound nice. I'll go to the hospital and be diagnosed: *This is the reason. It's because of this.* And I'll lie in a hospital bed looking out a hospital window. Don't they always have a window looking out onto a garden or a busy street or maybe even an ocean? I'll watch the clouds and listen to the murmuring between the nurses and doctors, all of them confirming there is something wrong. *She's ill*, they'll say. *She needs rest*, the room smelling of antiseptic and new carpets. A diagnosis. What a luxury.

"Raising sails," Tom shouts, and there's commotion above, a great vibration when the motor shuts off followed by a lurch and thrust forward.

The room spins, the bile threatening to come up.

"Oh Jesus," I say, and turn for the bathroom. "Where's the toilet in this place?"

But Robby is there, steadying me as the boat rocks violently. The bile recedes, leaving an acidic aftertaste.

"I'm fine—I just don't have my sea legs yet." I try to swat him away but he grips me tighter.

We were together for three years before that wedding in the desert, married less than a year. Even those first years dragged—we took the same route home from UCLA every day, and if there was traffic we'd just sit there, all the way down Wilshire, slowly inching forward. Our whole life together stretched out like that. And that inner ringing beat-beating until I thought I might burst. Funny how what seemed never ending feels like a blip now.

Robby pulls me to him. "Come on, girl, you're gonna be okay," he says into my hair. I remember the intimate smell of him, the taste. It's thick in my mouth, and in the hull of the boat it's suffocating.

"I'd be fine if you wouldn't hug me."

"Maybe you should go up, get some air. I can bring the drinks."

He looks at me for a moment. I can feel him studying my face. I'm sorry I couldn't love him.

"How many have you taken today?" he asks.

I pull away. "Let's not start the trip that way. If we start out badly, I don't know where we'll go from there."

"What happened in New York?"

I busy myself with finding the wine opener. Thoughts of Eric already invading—the smell of him, so different than Robby's, and they do not mix. The hull of a boat cannot contain them both.

"Elsa, tell me."

I've found the wine opener, but it's the expensive kind that injects air into the cork. I'm struggling with it and thinking of Eric, and his office overlooking Fifty-third Street, and how when I'm called in a woman from HR is there too. She's the one who asks me to sit. Talks about cutbacks—that assistants, sadly, are the first to go. *But Eric can't do this job without me*, I'm thinking. *I've made myself indispensable, right?*

Eric chimes in too. Saying how he fought for me but in the end it wasn't up to him. I don't understand anything they're saying. Then they are both standing, both talking about things that don't matter and in the same voice, as if they both know me in equally intimate ways. My face must concern the HR woman, because she's repeating herself, saying the severance package is *quite generous*. The lights are on in the building across the street, and I can make out people standing and talking together, their backs turned to me. Eric's hands are in his lap, tender as bird wings. *Did you hear us, Elsa?*

I'm thinking, *Who is this Elsa? Her name is so sterile and dead. It's not me.*

He puts his hand near mine.

It's better this way. You see, don't you? And his hand just sits there, so close I can feel its heat—he is on fire.

Then Eric suggests the vacation. *Make the time off a good thing, go see your mother. Go back to Los Angeles and see your friends. It's been years, hasn't it?* You nod your head yes, it's been more than five years.

The city swallows us up, the HR woman says.

And then Eric says, *It's really a generous severance package.*

And you're thinking, *Haven't they already told me that part?*

And they're sharing a look, and saying, *I know, I know.*

And he moves his hand farther away . . .

"Nothing," I say to Robby, who is standing with the bottle open now. I shake my head. "Nothing happened. Work has just been stressful."

He sighs. "I always knew New York was a terrible idea. Didn't I say?"

"I remember something about it."

"Los Angeles is the last frontier for the American dream. If you can't make it here, you can't make it anywhere." He hands me a glass of wine.

"Still a good speech," I say. "Even if it is complete bullshit."

He looks embarrassed. "Yeah, I hope so."

"I thought the new job was going great? That's what Charly said anyway."

He shrugs, uncomfortable. "I'm lucky to have a job, everyone's fucking coding these days. You don't know what it's like competing with these twenty-year-old kids—they're hungry, really fucking hungry, and they all went to Cal Arts or RISD. I'll be thirty-five this year, and it's someone else's game out there, a young guy's game, and there aren't enough jobs for us all."

"But you've got Jared—isn't he the boss?"

"And he still likes to do keg stands." His face is strained. He suddenly looks old. "He's *my* boss."

We drink. The silence is deafening. "I give that speech to the interns sometimes—the one about this being the final frontier. They always seem to be from the Midwest, and I like to scare them a little."

Jane shouts down to us, "Prepare to tack!"

I take the bottle and wineglasses.

Robby stops me. "I think the original speech ended with: *Please don't go, Elsa.*"

His eyes are sad, clouded with an expression that makes me wonder if there's still time to swim back to shore.

I take the wine and glasses to the cockpit.

Jane is at the wheel. She's a natural. I thought I had her figured out. Early thirties, with a zest for life that is maybe a little too consuming. Maybe she has competitive older sisters and has to be the best at everything. But then Charly tells me she's from Palos Verdes, her parents are pilots, and her younger sister is an engineering PhD student at Berkeley. In her family Jane is the black sheep. She went to Santa Monica College, got her associate's degree, and then started managing a restaurant on the pier. She competes in ultramarathons, actually won one last year. She met Robby online. *She was lonely*, Charly says. They moved in together quickly. *They make a good partnership, everyone needs companionship*, she says. This legitimately bums me out. Jane does not strike me as a woman willing to exchange love for solace.

Even now as she stands fierce and unflinching at the boat's helm, facing the horizon with the Los Angeles coastline disappearing behind her, a big toothy grin at the open sea in front of her, I cannot accept it. *How could she settle?* Her short hair flaps beneath her hat and for a full minute she does not blink. I think I see tears at the corners of her eyes.

"From the wind," she tells Robby. She wipes them away with the back of her hand.

Tom sits beside her with a gadget in his lap, but he's looking at her with something like awe.

"I brought drinks," I say a bit too loudly because his expression worries me.

"Ah, you found the Chateau Smith-Haut-Lafitte," Tom says in perfect French. "I knew you'd pick an expensive bottle." He pours a glass for Charly and Jane.

Robby returns from below deck with an Alka-Seltzer for Jared, who laughs.

"Thanks, buddy, I've got it bad today."

"You'll be okay," Robby tells him.

"Once we break open the scotch," Tom says with satisfaction. "It's twenty-five years old. It fixes everything."

"Let's get to it, then!" Jared says, brightening. "To a grand weekend!" We all hoot, and he downs the seltzer.

The wine is delicious; it settles right behind the eyes and loosens things up back there. The sun comes out. The swells are gentle and occasional ocean spray cools us. Once the city is out of sight the wind picks up. We travel at six knots, making a steady slice across the bay. The sky is huge, the clouds moving across like giant graceful elephants, but then they're morphing, shifting into something else. The wind must be fierce up there.

A pod of dolphins trails in our wake, and we scramble to take pictures, Jane leaning over the line, dipping her fingers into the sea and laughing into the wind. They glide easily to the bow of the boat, with Jane following, her shoes slipping on the deck. The pod takes off, leaving her at the bow to stare after them. Against the horizon her silhouette looks boyish and solitary, and she doesn't answer when Robby calls out for her to be careful.

Before we reach open water I've vomited. Everyone on deck is pointing and yelling at a sea lion and her cub, and I'm chucking up blueberry pancakes and expensive French wine into the toilet. I rinse my mouth and take my medicine: two pinks and an oblong white. The boat jerks and the open pill bottle goes crashing to the floor.

"You okay?" Robby calls from up top.

I hastily pick up the pills. The bottle's cracked, the lid won't click into place.

"Elsa," he says, popping his head in. "You okay?"

I shove the pills into the Altoids tin. "Fine, Robby, fine," I tell him, and give one of my slow-burn smiles. Dazzle a man and you blind him.

14

The trip across the bay on the Catalina Express takes about an hour; sailing the twenty-two miles takes half a day. The excitement of being out at sea wears off about halfway there. Charly catalogs the kitchen's contents, getting excited when she finds it's fully stocked. Robby lies out at the front of the boat, yawning and flipping through a book. Even Jared and Tom look a little bored. But not Jane, at the wheel, lips set in content determination. I see her breathe deeply every once in a while, puffing her chest out like a proud animal. The wind picks up, rocking the boat so that most of us are sitting with one hand holding on to something.

Charly says to Jared, the wind beating the words back, "I packed lunch!"

We tack with Jane steering and Tom pulling ropes. Charly repeats herself now that the wind is with us. "Tuna sandwiches," she says.

"You didn't have to do that," Jared says, embarrassed. He looks at Tom, who has climbed back behind Jane, his perch since we left the marina. "Tom has plenty on the boat," he says.

The sun glints purple off Tom's polarized sunglasses so that I can't read him. He smiles, though. "We're camping the first night, so any extra food is great," he says, taking a sandwich. "Thank you, Charly." He looks at her softly so that she blushes a little.

"I put red bell pepper in it," she says.

Tom offers Jane a sandwich.

"No, thanks," she says. "Where are we anchoring?" Her gaze does not waver from the horizon, where the island is growing larger, more defined. She takes a PowerBar from her jacket pocket.

"Paradise Cove," Tom says, taking a bite of his sandwich.

"Is that on the east side of the island?" Now that the swells have quieted, Jared has brought up the bottle of scotch.

Tom nods. "It's a sandy cove, you have to boat in to camp. If we're lucky we'll be the only people there."

"Sounds like heaven," I say.

Tom looks at me, pushing the last bite into his mouth with his thumb. "It is."

The trip up the east side of the island is gorgeous. The cliffs are dramatic, their exposed earth dark red. The wind brushes the long grasses along the bluff, and at the top of one of the cliffs a herd of bison stands in profile. The ocean here is unlike any water I've seen off the California coast, so dark it's almost cobalt, and electric blue in the shallows. It's clear too, and cold. I run a foot in the wake of the boat as we pass an old quarry, even its "Keep Out" sign seeming picturesque with its weather-beaten rust. I laugh when flying fish jump nearby.

Maybe it's the scotch, or the sun, or the wildness of the cliffs, but we all seem to get a little slaphappy, more adventurous.

Jared is drunk, shirtless, and telling Tom and Robby how much he appreciates them.

"Seriously, you guys," he says, hugging Robby. "Seriously."

Charly calls me to the bow, where a school of garibaldi swim, bright orange and curious. She seems to have forgiven my inadequate comforting from this morning, and forgotten about last night.

"Like *Finding Nemo*," she says, pointing.

Jane has stripped down to her bikini and given the wheel back to Tom. She joins us at the bow of the boat, squealing, "Little Nemos! Did you know they're California's state fish?"

She snaps pictures of them, and then turns to me. "Will you take one of me and Charly?"

I watch from behind the camera as these two women, one in a baseball cap and sports bikini, the other wearing a ridiculous bonnet, sunburned where her jacket has exposed her neck, pose for me. They face away from the water so that the ocean is behind them, pushing their cheeks together with unnatural, flirty smiles. I take the shot.

"Let's get one of the three of us," Charly says.

I hand the camera back. "Maybe when we dock. I'm getting a drink. Do you ladies want anything?"

"We'll be mooring in ten minutes and then we can break out the blender," Tom says to me.

"There's a blender on this thing?" Robby has that lazy look he gets when he's been drinking in the sun.

Tom nods. "Tequila and limes too."

"WE ARE KINGS!" Jared yells from the boat's stern. "KINGS!" His chest is puffed up and he shouts again, but Tom has turned on the motor, drowning out his voice.

Robby gets up and yells with him, his face pink from the exertion. They chant together, and Tom too. "KINGS."

When the boat motors into Paradise Cove the sun is low. There are no other boats, and no one is on the beach. Once we've moored, Tom shuts off the engine and we hear the lapping of water against the hull, the ravens on the beach.

"How do we get over?" Jane asks.

"Do we have to swim?" Charly looks at the water, disappointed.

Tom laughs. "You're welcome to swim. I'll take the dinghy."

Jared lets out a whoop, throwing an arm over Tom's shoulders. "This guy," he says, pointing with his beer bottle.

The girls busy themselves with sunscreen and packing the beach towels. Jane brings hiking boots and a backpack with a first-aid kit. The boys do push-ups on the deck. We drive the dinghy right onto the sand, laughing when Charly tumbles into the water.

"But I haven't changed into my bathing suit yet!" she says good-humoredly.

"I told you to wear it under your clothes," Jared says, helping her up.

"Ow, look out," Jane says, hopping off the boat. "There's rocks."

Robby picks her up, throwing her over a shoulder. "I got you, babe!"

"Robby!" She looks relieved when he puts her down again. She has her arms around him, though—her face freckled from the sun, red on either cheek. She kisses him, a dainty peck. He rests his hands on her hips, swaying them gently.

"Oh, get a room," Jared says, and plops on the blanket Charly has laid out. "Who wants a beer?"

"Me," Tom says. "The first thing I do after sailing is drink a beer, maybe smoke a joint."

The beer is cold, the bottles already sandy. We sit so we're facing the boat, looking out at the ocean we've just crossed.

"Look at that," Tom says, pointing. "Out there is Los Angeles."

Across the bay is a silhouette of a coastline familiar to us all, and yet from this angle completely foreign.

"You can barely see it," Jane says, taking a beer from him.

"Out there is the empire," Robby says, holding his arms wide.

I squint to try to make out where the pier should be, where the Miramar is, where the airport and Charly and Jared's house should be. Bakersfield just north and inland—New York and Eric a few thousand miles beyond that. It's there, I'm sure. That whole life of mine. I suddenly feel light-headed. Strange. Like catching your reflection, that moment just before recognition, when you are a stranger to yourself. I pull my sweater tighter.

Jared moves so he can put an arm around me. "I'll keep you warm," he says. His breath could be flammable.

I get up to put my feet in the water.

"Is it cold?" Jane asks.

It is. Very, very cold. My feet go numb, and for a moment it takes the air right out of me.

"Can you even feel it?" Robby slurs from behind me.

I slip my dress off. I'm wearing the bandeau bikini I tried on for Rex.

"It's freezing," I say, and do my very best to kick water on all of them.

Charly and Jane shriek and jump up. They are out of their clothes and chasing me on the beach. Whatever pills and booze I've mixed has made this a dizzying day. My chest is tight, but light like a bird's. And the more I run, the lighter I feel. I might just fly away.

I run into the water, but the girls chase after me, their shrieks growing louder at just how cold the water really is.

It doesn't take long for our bodies to warm, though. The water is salty, we can taste it on our lips. It feels good to be we—*we* smell of the sea and sunscreen and something sweet. Look at our fingers: *we* lace them together; look at our bodies: *we* float on our backs. I think of those women back at the Miramar, eating oysters and drinking white wine.

Jane wraps her arms around my waist underwater. Charly puts a strand of seaweed around my neck.

"Beautiful," she says.

The boys watch us from the beach. "Come in, scaredy-cats!" Jane calls to Robby and Jared and Tom. She swims over to a cluster of rocks. "I'm going to be king of the hill!"

Robby stays on the beach but Tom and Jared splash in, whooping and daring each other to go farther. Tom dives headfirst, leaving Jared knee-deep in the water. Tom swims very well—long, smooth strides—and when he surfaces, it's beside Jane at the bigger of the rocks. We can hear them laughing as they struggle to reach the top.

"Oh, come in!" Charly calls to Jared, waving her hand at him. "It isn't that bad." We're treading water, watching Jared pace back and forth, the water barely wetting his trunks. "He's always peacocking around you," she says to me. "But when it comes down to it, no follow-through."

"I'm sorry about last night, Charly."

She shakes her head again at Jared, who throws up his arms. "I know," she says. She floats on her back, stretching her legs. "I think this is the most gorgeous place I've ever seen." Her eyes glitter.

We swim together to the rocks where Jane and Tom are, helping each other out of the water. Tom has started heckling Jared from the top of his rock. Jane is perched on one of the smaller rocks, her knees tucked to her chin. She's waving to Robby.

"Come in!" she yells.

"I'm good here," Robby shouts back. "It's getting dark, I'll work on a fire."

"I'll help with that," Jared says, joining Robby, who's already trucking up the trail.

Tom yells after them, "There's a locker at the top of the campsite with wood in it for us."

"That's lucky," Charly says to Tom.

"I never rely on luck. I called ahead and had the rangers put a couple bundles in there for us. There should be fresh water too."

He pinches her chin between his thumb and forefinger as if she were a child and dives back into the water.

We watch him swim to shore, us girls, with the wind picking up so that the salt water on our shoulders and mouths dries like a second skin.

"He's fantastic," Charly says before following him in.

"He scares me a little," I say to Jane.

"Me too," she says.

We build a massive fire and eat black beans and avocado and grilled skirt steak with onions and potatoes that we've rolled in tinfoil and roasted in the fire. It takes a while for the island to get dark, but suddenly there are thousands of stars, and across the bay the soft glittering light of a city. I try to make out where the Miramar might be. I wonder if Rex is working, if someone has claimed Mary's scarf, if a version of me exists there too.

Tom produces Irish coffees, which are very strong. Everyone is sleepy, like tuckered-out children, each of us taking our drink as if it were a warmed milk bottle.

Charly has wrapped herself in a blanket, Jared nodding off, his head in her lap. She rouses him and helps him into a sweater.

"Don't get cold," she says.

He smacks his lips together. "I'm definitely sunburned."

"SPF seventy for you tomorrow, buddy," Robby says.

"Shut up." Jared throws an empty water bottle at him.

Robby has his arm around Jane, who moves to protect him with her body. The water bottle bounces gently off her side.

"Did you just throw something at Jane?" Robby says, pushing himself up. But then he reaches out for Jane to steady him before flopping back down. "I should've passed on the Irish coffee, I drank way too much today," he says, pushing his palms into his eyes. "I haven't drunk like this in a long time."

I struggle to pay attention, to maintain a guarded expression. I look at Tom, who's sitting with his legs sprawled out in front of him. He's watching me, one hand behind his head, the other holding his drink. He looks away from me then, toward Robby and Jane.

"How long have you been together?" he asks.

"Jane and Robby?" Jared asks, pointing at them with the sleeve of the sweater. "Almost a year, right?"

Robby has his arm around Jane again. He's looking at her quizzically.

When she doesn't answer, he says, "A year and four months. I thought you'd have kept track by now."

I can see her shrug in the firelight. She wraps her arms around his side, tucking her face into his chest. He puts a hand in her hair.

"When were you and Elsa . . ." Tom motions to the two of us.

"Oh, that's ancient history," Charly says. "Elsa left Los Angeles more than five years ago. Gosh, can you believe it's been that long?"

"Were they still married?" Tom asks as if Robby and I were not here.

She nods. Jared points his sleeve at me. "No, they got divorced while we were on our honeymoon," he says.

"The papers weren't turned in yet when she left for New York," Charly tells him. "Robby had to do it alone."

"Let's go look at the moonlight on the water," Jane says to Robby.

"But I'm comfortable," he whines, but she's already walking off.

Tom has pushed himself up on his elbows. He watches them walk into the darkness.

"Why the sudden interest in our sordid past?" I whisper.

He leans toward me. I can feel the heat from his skin. It's oppressive, like a furnace in a crawl space. He refills my drink from his thermos.

"I'm just trying to figure out why you're here. Are you back for Robby? Is that it?" His teeth are very white. I can see him biting his tongue a little.

"I care about Robby, but that was a long time ago."

"Just out to cause trouble?"

I shake my head, which is swimming, and watch Jared and Charly, who have moved on to arguing over their kitchen remodel.

"I hate when you're this drunk," she hisses. "We can't discuss anything."

"And I hate when you're the sober martyr," he says, getting up. She follows him, leaving Tom and me alone.

"I didn't want to be in New York anymore," I tell him. I can hear the waves at the shore. The tiredness has settled in my chest like a weight.

Tom throws water on the fire. "You remind me of my first wife," he says, holding a hand out to me. "Hot as shit, but absolutely bonkers." He pulls me upright, holds my arm at my side. I can feel the bones in his hand. "She was a pill popper too—don't think I haven't noticed. I can hear them rattling around in your purse."

"Come on, guys," Charly calls out to us from beside the dinghy. "Before Jared and Robby pass out."

But Tom is still holding me; the smoke from the extinguished fire stings my eyes.

"This coffee is bitter," I say, dumping the last of my drink into the fire pit. My legs feel rubbery. I'm wind chapped and sunburned and completely exhausted.

He lets go of my arm. "Like life, baby, just like life."

15

The morning is quiet, drifting. The water barely taps at the hull; the grass up on the cliffs is still. There are no seagulls, only ravens so large they look like patches of black cloud high in the sky. Even the seals dive in and out of the water in silence.

I ask Charly and Jared if I can help in the kitchen. The others are already snorkeling.

She laughs. "I like my toast toasty, not burned."

"I'm not that terrible at cooking."

"Aw, poor Elsa. You can help make the orange juice," Jared says, handing me a mechanical juicer. Charly's in an apron and humming along with a song on the boat's radio. She tells me she's making an omelet Española, pronouncing it with a Spanish accent. Jared smiles from over the bowl of oranges. There's the sound of his knife against the cutting board.

"I feel so domesticated with the two of you," I say.

"I've never cooked on a boat," Charly says with satisfaction.

Jared hands me an orange half. "Nothing like fresh-squeezed OJ in the morning."

"As long as we can spike it with vodka." I push the fruit hard against the juicer, which vibrates and hisses and sends pulp everywhere.

Jared pulls down a bottle of vodka from a cupboard, waving it at me.

"Leave some unspiked," Charly says. She's greasing an earthenware bowl and reading a recipe from her iPhone.

"Poor wifey, back to being sober—and while on a trip with Elsa. Must be torture, huh?" He gives her a quick kiss on the nose.

"I don't mind one bit. Alcohol is just empty calories," she says, pouring the egg mixture into the bowl.

He grabs her bottom, a firm smack. "And you don't need any extra of those." He laughs lightly and hands me the last orange half. "There. All done. Do you need me for anything else or can I join the others for a swim?" He doesn't wait for an answer, just gives Charly another quick slap on the behind and heads for the deck.

"Elsa, you coming?"

"I'll stay here. I don't think my hangover can handle swimming just yet."

He shrugs and disappears up top.

Charly has her back to me, the ties of her apron are coming undone.

"You okay?" I ask.

When she turns, her cheeks are flushed. "Perfectly fine. He knows I can't drink if I've taken my hormones."

The omelet goes into the oven and she slams the oven door. "I think I'll take some of that OJ—the spiked stuff—please."

"Are you sure?"

Her face takes on a hysterical slant. She makes her fist into little balls and slams them onto the counter, hard enough to send the salt and pepper onto their sides. "It's just not fucking fair!"

There's egg on her front, a bit of yolk, smeared. I want to point out the metaphor; maybe she'll laugh.

"You know I do hormone injections in my ass?"

I shake my head.

"That's what I got up to do this morning: stick a needle in my ass. He doesn't even help with that—I do the injections myself." She motions to the deck, where Jared has gone. "And I can't go drink a bottle of whiskey to cope."

I still haven't moved to comfort her, but I know I should. Eric would ask occasionally, usually while we were a tangle of hotel sheets and limbs, *Do you want children?* And I'd think about saying the truth, *No, I do not.* But something about his face, about anyone's face when they mention babies, as if being a woman renders me defenseless to motherhood—as if my life has not had meaning, and won't, until a baby comes along. So I would lie. *Yes, oh yes, babies, babies. Yes, please.*

"We've been trying for two years," she says, looking at me, her cheeks wet.

"It'll happen," I say lamely.

"But when? I'm almost thirty-two."

"That really isn't that old."

She looks at me as if seeing me for the first time. "You don't want children, do you?" I think I see her lip tremble.

I turn and pour a large spiked orange juice. I can still feel her looking at me like that, even with my back to her.

"Babies are adorable, don't get me wrong," I say, taking a drink. I can feel the vodka in my sinuses, making me momentarily light-headed. "Let's talk about something else," I say, looking at her. "You've got egg on you. Let me get it." I take a damp cloth but she's crying now, great big heaves, shoulders shaking as if she's having a small seizure.

"Charlotte, please."

"I'm okay . . . I'm okay. It's just the hormones." She stops crying and looks at me with those dark, twinkling eyes. "Maybe, instead of drinking, maybe one of those little white pills you've been carrying around—they're Xanax, aren't they? Can I have one?"

"I'm not fooling anyone, am I?" I kiss her forehead, relieved I can comfort her in some way. "If you think they'll help, of course." I pull out the Altoids tin.

"What's their milligram?"

I don't want to tell her that I have no idea, so I say, "Point five."

She takes two and sets them beneath her tongue. "Thank you," she says.

During breakfast Charly is pliant and hospitable, carving out generous portions of her steaming egg dish. I watch her carefully now, or at least I do at first. Then I catch the way Robby looks at me from the water, as he emerges triumphant with a whole sand dollar in his grasp, offering it up to me. Tom catches it too, and looks at me with a wolfish grin—eyebrow raised, earpiece of his aviators between his teeth—then I'm back downstairs, back to my duffel bag, searching for medicine of my own.

16

It's a short sail from Paradise Cove to the village of Two Harbors. Jane barely has time to get the sails up before she has to pull them back down. It's a small village. Tom tells us there is one general store and one bar, which is inside the only restaurant.

"Don't worry," he says to me with a smirk, "they make a killer cocktail."

There are more than a dozen other boats already moored, and at the water's edge is a small group of men and women in summer dresses and island shirts. It's almost four in the afternoon and the light in the harbor turns the water turquoise and lapis. Palm trees line the shore, tall and bent in lazy halos of shimmering light. Drifting from the shore is the sound of a ukulele.

"Is there a festival this weekend?" Charly asks sleepily.

Tom shrugs. "There's always something going on."

"As long as it isn't pirate-themed," Robby says. "That would be so cheesy."

"It could be fun," Jane says to him. "Silly but fun."

"I don't think it's got anything to do with pirates." Charly points to a figure dressed in white, walking down the stone path to the beach. The ukulele is clearer now, joined by a melodica and a hand drum.

"It's a wedding," Jane says softly.

"Well, we'll have to wait to go to shore now," Tom says with a pout.

"Do you recognize that song?" I ask. It's the same melody the Latino producer was whistling on the beach.

We stand for a moment, listening.

"'Besame Mucho,'" Tom says. "You know it?"

"I've heard it before is all."

We watch the bride walk across the sand and join the groom. Cameras flash. The ukulele stops. A man in a straw hat—the kind you can get away with wearing only on an island—reads from a book. The bride faces us; she's wiping at her eyes.

"I bet they aren't even in their mid-twenties," Robby says tersely.

"How can you tell?" Jane is holding her hand to her forehead, squinting.

He shrugs and sits with his arms across his chest.

"Why do you think her dad didn't walk her down the aisle?" Charly asks.

Jared sits beside Robby. "Maybe he wasn't invited."

"Oh. I think that's him standing right there, he's got a cane. Maybe it would have been too difficult to do in the sand."

"Shitty thing to do, have a wedding in the sand when your dad is handicapped," Robby says. He points with his chin, his arms still crossed. "He probably paid for the whole damn thing, too."

Jane sighs. "She's a beautiful bride."

"How can you tell from here?" he asks, shaking his head. "She could be a Cyclops."

Tom goes below deck and comes back with a bottle of champagne.

"Oh, yes!" Jane cries. "That's just the thing, we'll toast them."

"Wait until they pronounce them man and wife first," he says, handing her the glasses.

Robby slouches further in his seat. "How would we know when that is?"

"You're quite the sourpuss," I say. "They'll cheer, of course."

Robby drops his sunglasses over his eyes. "Wake me when that happens."

The groom takes the bride's hand. He's a tall, thin man, and from here he looks completely capable of being someone's husband. Rigid spine, his feet firmly planted in the sand—ready. But then he fidgets, moves from one leg to the other, scratches his lower back, tugs on his earlobe, and I think, *Oh God, he isn't sure about anything.*

The man in the straw hat takes both their hands and the crowd erupts into cheers. We pop the champagne and Tom blares the boat's horn, which makes the crowd erupt again and wave at us. We hold up our glasses and shout, "Congratulations!"

We motor in on the dinghy soon after, each of us packing a small day bag. The wedding party has moved into the restaurant; we can hear their plates and silverware and glasses when we pass by.

Behind the restaurant is the one road, unpaved, cutting through a dry open field, sloping mountains on either side. No golf carts anywhere. This is a different Catalina than the one I visited with my parents. Wild. The conservancy rangers drive trucks with heavy wheels. There is one red schoolhouse that looks out onto a rusting playground, no hotels, only a campsite down a steep hiking trail. Kayaks rest on the beach, ready to be rented, snorkeling gear too. Behind the schoolhouse, rope swings hang from a cluster of eucalyptus trees. Charly and I play on those first. We laugh like we did when we were kids. From here we can see the second harbor, across the isthmus—a turquoise so languid and calm it could be some exotic lagoon.

"It's like Neverland," Charly says.

We watch Jared and Robby play disc golf with Tom and Jane. Jared is being ultracompetitive, which is making the others laugh.

"It's a serious game," we can hear him shout at them. "Take it seriously!"

But Robby picks up Jane, who has the disc in her hand, and runs her to the basket.

"GOAAAAL!" Tom shouts.

"That isn't proper play," Jared yells, pointing. "And that isn't proper terminology, there's no goals in disc golf."

Charly asks if she can push me on the swing. She pulls me way back until I'm shouting *Not any higher!* then she lets go and I'm flying forward so low to the ground I let out a whoop. I tell her to do it again and again until we are both out of breath.

"I could've done that all day," I say when we're walking to rejoin the group.

"You weren't doing the heavy lifting," she says, squeezing my arm.

"Hey! Be nice."

We loop arms and walk side by side. I think of our childhood sleepovers at her house, a grapefruit orchard at the edge of town. Charly's parents were older, in their fifties, more like grandparents, and when I spent the night, we were *free*—we watched whatever we wanted, and ran around with an old airsoft gun, shooting at rocks and empty soda cans. On hot summer days we caught lizards, letting their mouths snap onto our ears, wearing them as earrings until they wiggled too much and we were forced to let them go.

The sun has dropped low; ahead the mountains grow dark against a bright silvery sky. Jared, Robby, Tom, and Jane are small against the horizon. I pull my jacket collar up against the wind.

"Thank you for the Xanax," Charly says quietly.

"Oh, it's nothing." I'm worried she might start talking about babies again. "I hope it helps."

She takes my hand in hers and we walk in silence for a moment.

"I mean it," she says squeezing my hand. "I sometimes get so twisted I think I might really lose it. Today was the first time in a long time that I felt relaxed."

"You're welcome," I say, gently shaking my hand free.

17

The wedding reception has taken over the restaurant, so we eat burgers and drink Buffalo Milk cocktails in the bar.

"This is the best drink I think I've ever had," Jared says. He has whipped cream in the corners of his mouth. "I'm only sorry you can't try any of it." He looks sadly at Charly, who sips a Shirley Temple.

"Is it real buffalo milk?" Jane asks.

Tom gives her a sweet, pitying look. "No, doll, it's just the name. Should I order you one?"

"I can do that," Robby says. He's been in a mood since seeing the wedding party in the restaurant.

The bride and groom, both very young, are dancing awkwardly to Etta James's version of "At Last."

"That is so cliché," Robby sneers at them. "Can't young people do anything original?"

Tom puts an arm around him. "Look, kid, there's nothing original about love or weddings."

"Wow, what wonderful guys we've brought along with us," I say to Jane and Charly.

"Hey, what did I do?" Jared says. I expect him to hiccup.

Charly pats his arm. "Nothing, honey, you never do."

He smiles over his straw, gives her a wet kiss. "We should order more of these. Do you think they can make them bigger?"

A group from the wedding party comes into the bar. One of the women has dark hair, pulled back in an elaborate updo. There are little plastic pearls tucked into the knots. She has the kind of face that would be pretty—that *is* pretty—except she has spent a large amount of time outdoors, and she doesn't have the type of skin that tans well.

"You guys were great this afternoon," she says to us.

Charly, always eager to make friends, lightly touches the woman's arm. "It was so beautiful from the water."

"They deserve the best," the woman says. Smile lines gouge either side of her lips. "When they're done with school they want to join the Peace Corps together."

I want to ask if it's too late to talk them out of that, but then a mustached young man—her cousin, she tells us—offers to buy us drinks.

"Nothing for me, I have to get up early to sail back," she tells him.

"You sail?" Jane asks, interested.

"Does she sail?" the boy says with wide eyes. "Bridget's a champion sailboat racer!"

"Oh, don't start with that," Bridget says, blushing modestly.

He turns to Jared. "Hey, is that the Buffalo Milk cocktail? Any good?"

"I've already had three."

"Fuck yeah, I like your style. You guys wanna play pool?" He points to a good-looking boy his own age who has stripped off his suit jacket and is polishing a cue stick. "My buddy's fuckin' wasted and a terrible player—he's wagered money. Like some serious fuckin' cash."

"You shouldn't take his money," Bridget says, and she looks at me apologetically.

"How much is a lot?" Tom asks, amused.

The boy leans in. "Like fifty fuckin' bucks."

I can see the look on Tom's face. It says: *How cute.* I want to smack him.

"I'll match that," he says, reaching for his wallet.

"All right, man!" the boy says. "What's your name? You guys were so fuckin' cool this afternoon. Like seriously, thank you for doing that. It's my sister's wedding—and I'm just so happy for her, you know? So fuckin' happy." The boy grins but his mustache is slightly wet from his beer and it hangs over his top teeth, so it's possible I only think he grins, because his mustache tips up on either end.

"Jared, you coming? Robby? You want in on this?"

Jared and Robby slide off their stools and follow.

"Not really," Robby says under his breath.

Jared squeezes Charly's shoulders. "Babe, order me another Buffalo Milk."

"Like he needs another one," she says to me after they've gone.

"Sorry about that," Bridget says to us. "I don't think he's ever played pool in his life, but he gets that way around men."

"How old *is* he?" I ask.

"Oh, I don't mean he's a child, he's twenty-one, but his dad died a while back and he gets all puffed up around older guys. I think maybe he's trying to impress them. You should see him around my boyfriend."

"Which one's your boyfriend?" Jane asks. She's drinking a margarita and has licked all the salt off the rim.

"Oh, he couldn't come, he's on call. We both are. But I couldn't miss the wedding. She's the sweetest girl, studying child psychology at Chapman."

The bride has changed out of her wedding gown and into a

flouncy blush-colored dress that belts at the waist. I watch her pull something from her new husband's hair, adjust his tie; she's about to brush something from his sleeve but he catches her hand and pulls her onto the crowded dance floor.

"What do you do?" Charly asks.

Bridget looks embarrassed. "I'm a firefighter," she says.

Jane's eyes grow big. "Are you really? A firefighter?"

"And you race boats?" Charly adds.

She nods, grinning, and those lines on either side of her mouth deepen. "What do you ladies do?"

"Oh God, who cares?" Jane says, laughing. "You race boats and fight fires. That's amazing. Tom is teaching me how to sail— he's the one who so modestly pulled out a wad of cash in front of your cousin."

"Where have you sailed?" Charly asks.

Bridget pulls out a stool beside us. "All over, really, I've sailed almost every sea."

"What's your favorite place?" I ask her. She looks at me for so long that I wonder if I asked the question out loud.

"Probably . . ." She stalls. "Probably just on the other side of the island."

Jane looks disappointed. "I thought you'd say the Mediterranean, or Mexico—Tom says Mexico. What's so special about it?"

Bridget continues to look at me, or just behind me, where the isthmus lets out to the Pacific. She dips her chin to her chest, relaxes her eyes as if she is daydreaming.

"Have you seen the ocean on that side?" she asks us.

"We walked over the isthmus earlier," one of us says, but Bridget just shakes her head.

"Then you didn't see the *open* Pacific. Have you ever seen it?"

Jane laughs. "Of course we have."

"We're from Santa Monica," I tell her.

But Bridget shakes her head again. "Then you've seen the Santa Monica Bay."

"I've driven up and down the coast hundreds of times," I tell her.

Bridget sighs. "That isn't the same as what's out there." She jerks her head toward me, out beyond me. "It's wild *open* ocean. Nothing for miles. Nothing but you and the sea. The swells compete, the ocean really churns, and it feels—savage. The wind can change in an instant." She snaps her fingers. "And the sea can suddenly seem calm. But those currents are waiting just beneath. If you aren't experienced you can get overpowered. I've had friends lose boats."

"Wow," Charly says, a little alarmed.

"I think I'd prefer sailing the Gulf," Jane says, and she asks Bridget how the bride and groom met. The conversation changes then, taking a more traditional path of wedding talk, and giggling, and looking around the room to see who's watching. But I'm still lost in the open ocean—out there, calling. I steal away to the bathroom to take some medicine and fix my makeup. The mirror is dirty; someone has carved on it *Lisa was here*. I touch it lightly but still somehow manage to cut my finger. I wrap it in toilet paper. There's a knock on the bathroom door.

"Just a minute," I say. The doorknob jiggles. "Someone's in here," I shout. I wipe the blood from the sink and flush the toilet.

Outside is Bridget's mustached cousin. He's even drunker, his eyes heavy, lazy.

"Hey," he says, leaning into me. "You're so fuckin' hot."

"I'm taken."

"That's not what your friend Tom says," he whispers, backing me up against the wall.

I take his face in my hands so roughly that he whines. "Not for you," I say, pushing him away. He looks as if he might cry.

"You have a strong grip for a girl," he says, rubbing his jaw.

I suddenly feel bad for him. I can see how he'll look in ten, twenty years, after life teaches him a thing or two. Hunched over a desk like Robby—or maybe he'll be king of his own world like Jared, or Eric. How envious I am of this, of being trapped only by the bounds of ambition. But that isn't fair—poor boy has it rough. The weight of the world, of history too. I pull him closer. He smells yeasty, like warm beer, and something sharp and cheap, a drugstore body spray, probably. He flinches at first, and I feel a swell of pity for him again. *See, Elsa? He's already learning, you've already taught him things.*

I close my eyes and think of Eric and how when he kissed me the slightest pressure of his hand felt like he could hold me up forever, how with him, in New York, I felt sure of who I was and what I wanted. *Eric, Eric.* Could I conjure him? If I think of the vast Pacific just outside the bar, with its roaring, its dark tumultuous depths, would it be like having him here? Because yes, it was like that with him. The swelling of something—the almost violent crashing of pleasure—like drowning, like being weightless and heavy all at once. *Yes, yes. Let it consume you. Let it swallow you up, up, up—*

When I open my eyes the boy has his hands on my breasts, my hips, my ass. His mouth hot on my neck and I'm groaning—*groaning*—with pleasure.

Robby is there too—coming out of the other bathroom. I see his face and there is real hatred in it, disgust. This surprises me, the groan catches in my throat and I pull away. But then Robby isn't there and I wonder if I've imagined it.

"Hey," the boy pants. "Wait, where are you going? Fuck. Seriously?"

I find Charly and tell her I want to go back to the boat. I ask if she'll go with me. She nods, sadly, watching Jared, who has his arm around a bridesmaid.

18

Charly is quiet on the boat ride back. She doesn't even brighten when the coastguardsman flirts with her. He's in his sixties, weather-beaten, with white whiskers—a real seaman who motors us over the water, the restaurant lights reaching out across it, the water cracking and sending the light even farther.

Back on Tom's boat she presses her hands to her face, saying, "I cannot believe how tired I am."

I make a joke about the coast guard liking her, but she only looks at me blankly.

"Go to sleep," I say, directing her to her cabin. "Things will be better in the morning." But she hesitates, gnawing on her lip.

She asks where I disappeared to at the bar. I tell her there was a line at the bathroom, and suggest we make hot chocolate.

"I don't think I should," she says, screwing up her face. "I'm just so tired, but I don't think I can sleep. There's this vibrating . . ."

I should tell her I have the same feeling—a ringing that starts as a flutter in my heart, pulsing like hummingbird wings until I'm light-headed, until the buzzing is in my blood, bouncing around in my head so that my hands shake. I should tell her that it's a constant fight to keep it in check—that it's been this way since we were eight years old, sitting in front of her vanity, trying on lipsticks, but something knocked it loose and now it fucking rings all goddamn day. She should know it's a dangerous thing to be a woman. We want things, just like anyone else. Power, control, success— more than the world has to offer us. So we shove it down, hush it up, hope that it doesn't tear us apart. I should tell her this but I'm worried she might not feel the same—that she is cracking up from not being able to toe the line, whereas I want to destroy it entirely.

I produce the Altoids tin. "Take it," I tell her. "Take the whole thing."

And she does, slipping it into her pocket shyly as if she'd been waiting for it the whole time.

"Sweet dreams," I say, but she's already shut her cabin door with a polite click.

My bedroom is a thin mattress with a curtain to separate it from the rest of the boat. With the curtain closed I have only a tiny porthole window for light. But the moonless night is so dark, and the water in the harbor is so still, I can't get my bearings. It's like bathwater out there, tepid and stagnant.

For a while I drift in and out of sleep, imagining the roar of that open ocean just on the other side of the island, my heart thumping against my ribs. I think back to earlier that afternoon, when we were at the isthmus, when Robby hiked up the ridge, his profile light against mountain and sky, how he waved at me to follow him up. But I didn't want to go any farther; my feet hurt from hiking in sandals and it was growing dark—*and* it alarmed me how casually he called out to me, as if we were vacationing alone together, as if no time had passed at all. So I turned back to the bar. All the while the Pacific crashed just a half mile away, around a bend and up a small hill. It's eating at me still—being so close. I can imagine the swells in tune with my own heartbeat, and how being out there would be like looking at my true self. The wind churning white-caps into huge thrashing waves, large like nightmares, bulging and roiling over one another. But underneath, that vein of current, steady and strong, those black depths no one talks about, down below with the sharks and stingrays and eels.

Something knocks against the boat. The sound is gentle, like a stone plunking into a pool.

"Charly?" I pull back the curtain. The cherrywood cabinets are bluish in the moonlight. I can hear gentle snoring from her cabin.

The sound again and this time it's recognizable: the dinghy against the side of the boat. There is male laughter, female shushing. I let the curtain fall back.

"Grab his feet." Tom's voice, sober and direct.

"I got them, just worry about his head." Robby's growl and then Jane: "Robby, he's just trying to help."

There is grunting, swearing, and Tom saying, "He's heavy for a little guy," which makes Jane giggle. I can feel Robby tense up through the curtain.

They say their good-nights, and I can hear Tom climb up to the deck, his sandals flopping against his heels. I wait; I want to be sure Robby and Jane are asleep.

I find Tom pissing off the back of the boat. Out across the bay, Los Angeles twinkles in soft, smoky light.

"Morning, kid," Tom says when he's finished. "No sleeping beauty, are you?"

"You don't look so hot either."

He makes a sound of dismissal. "Please, I only need five hours of sleep." His attitude changes suddenly. He pulls down the collar of my sweater. "Come to get some?"

"No thanks," I say, pulling away.

He shrugs. "Not ripe yet, no problem. I can wait. What can I do for you?" He rolls out a sleeping bag. "I always sleep on deck.

Air's better up here. Doesn't matter if you have models or aristo-crats below deck, it'll smell like farts in the morning."

"Lovely," I say. "Listen, I was wondering which way we're tak-ing to Avalon in the morning."

He stretches out in his sleeping bag, arms propping up his head. "What do you mean? The only way. Suddenly interested in sailing?" He smirks. "Jane'll give you a run for your money."

"Do we go around the island, I mean."

"Ha! Hell, no. That would take an entire day, and that's with a light wind."

"Could we, though? I want to see it."

His eyes soften and I think he might be falling asleep. But then he tilts his head in an inviting sort of way and pats the seat beside him.

"Come here."

I sit down. His eyes are shut now, but he puts his hand in my hair.

"Your hair is soft," he says. "I thought from all that dye it'd feel like hay—but it's baby soft," he says sleepily.

I try again. "We could sail around and make it to Avalon in time for the jazz festival. I'll even help pilot or steer or whatever it is you do to make this thing move."

He sighs, looking tired and amused. Seals somewhere in the murky dawn begin to call to one another.

"Poor Elsa, come closer." He moves so he's lying on his side. I hesitate. He smells of whiskey and something faintly sour.

"Will you take me? Us, I mean. Will you take us?"

He sits up then and moves so close I recognize that smell. Bile. I turn my head away and he clicks his tongue.

"I don't think so. Better get some sleep, kid." He lies down and looks over my shoulder. "My, what a boat of light sleepers we have."

And there is Robby. He turns when I see him. His back's slightly hunched, a windbreaker taut across his shoulders, hair standing almost straight up. He doesn't say anything, just disappears back below deck. I follow him down only to find his curtain pulled closed, shifting a bit as if there were an indoor breeze.

I can suddenly smell the stink of Tom's breath, and still taste that drunk boy; it's up in my gums, settled in, tall and rank. I grab my robe and toiletries and head for the shower. The sound of water gurgling in the pipes is almost therapeutic, the sudden rush of spray. It thunders, vibrating the shower door. I am nearly undressed, nightgown around my ankles, when there's a soft brushing at the door.

"Elsa," I hear Robby whisper. He slides in. I watch his face take me in.

"What are you doing?" I ask, taking my nightgown from the floor and using it to cover myself. "If Jane wakes up . . ."

"She drank her weight in tequila. She'll sleep past ten—and that's late for Jane."

I reach around him to shut the water off.

His face strains. "No, keep it on, I don't want her to hear us."

"Then you probably shouldn't have come *in*." The water struggles to turn back on. "Can you hand me my robe, please?"

He could throw it to me. But he doesn't. He takes it slowly from the rack, grasping it with both hands, staring intensely at my face.

"Elsa, what are you doing?"

"*I'm* about to take a shower. What the hell are *you* doing? I like Jane, I like you guys together, I'm glad—happy for you two—really, I am."

The mirror is steaming up. I can see streaks from where someone tried to wipe it with a towel.

"I mean tonight. I don't like Tom. He's a rich prick—thinks he owns everyone. I don't want you to get wrapped up in his shit." He's still holding the robe. "Have you . . . ?"

"Oh Christ, Robby," I say, taking the robe and wrapping it tightly. "Don't do this."

"Jesus, Elsa, if you saw yourself at the bar, or up there—with him."

"I was there, thank you very much." Our whispering is louder now.

He leans in, pulling me closer by my robe belt. "You're out of control."

Just then Jane calls for Robby. We stand completely still, the steam clinging to us.

"I'm fine," I say, as quietly as I can. "Now get a towel and splash some water on your face, for fuck's sake. I'll hide in the shower. Get her to go back to sleep. Jesus Christ, Robby."

I shut the water off and climb into the shower. I hear Robby tell Jane he needed a shower. He woke up drunk and thought it would help.

She asks where I am. He says I slept on the deck with Tom. She wants to get up, go for a swim. He convinces her to lie down with him.

I wait. I lick at the salty mixture of sweat and water that's gathered above my lip and think how I should take Mother up on her offer. I should catch a plane with the last of my savings and move into the guest bedroom. She'll wake me up at dawn, offer freshly pressed juice the color of sludge, her face pulled back by a sweatband. *Let's jog together,* she'll say, or *How about a Pilates class?* And she'll cart me around to the salon where she works, showing me off. But oh, the effort she'll have to put into it now. How she'll need me to play up the role of beautiful, composed daughter, make it really sell. And she'll ask questions too: *Where did you run off to? How is Charly—still acting? Poor Robby—poor dear old Robby—still a lifeguard?* No, Mother, no. Nothing is the same.

I try to imagine Eric, but all I can picture is his hands. He's tracing the mouth of his wineglass, slowly, with his finger. I cannot picture his face, though, and panic, heavy and cold, settles in my chest. I focus instead on how I felt in his office while we reviewed

Picasso sketches, the moment just before he finally touched me. That swelling of electricity that crackled between the two of us. *It was like that, wasn't it? For us both?* It must have been.

I steal back to my berth. I try with great effort not to make too much noise, but when I roll onto my side the curtain gets stuck and suddenly Robby and I are looking at each other over Jane's sleeping body. His eyes are red rimmed. He looks old. He opens his mouth to speak, but something about his expression embarrasses me. I think he feels it too, because he just shuts his mouth and looks helplessly down at Jane.

19

On the way to Avalon we pass the same herd of buffalo on the ridge, but now they're facing in the opposite direction, like a weather vane that's shifted with the wind. The seals bellow when we coast by. A few splash into the water to play in the boat's wake. I point and call for Jane as she's taking out her camera.

"I see them," she says, her mouth thin. I try to read her expression, but she's too quick. Her smile is back up.

Charly does not make breakfast. We instead eat little boxed cereals and bananas. She isn't hungry—"Too tired," Jared says to me. "Poor old girl, sailing isn't your thing," he says to her. "When we get to Avalon I'll get you Dramamine."

As we round the last wild cliff, the grass jutting out, waving us on, we see a cruise ship on the horizon. It's ridiculously large, smoke billowing from its stacks, little orange boats gliding back and forth from it like ants on a log. And suddenly there are sailboats and yachts, people in caps and bikinis shouting "Ahoy!" Speedboats race by, a jazz band plays from a beach covered in white umbrellas, a helicopter whizzes overhead.

There are people everywhere too: on glass-bottom boats that

look like tiny cabooses, chugging along near the rocks; on Sea-Doos, teenagers in life vests, the fishing boats blaring their horns at them to get out of the way. There are scuba divers and snorkelers and, standing on the rocks and pier, fishermen fat and thin, playing hand radios. The Catalina Express sits in the harbor with its engine roaring, spewing exhaust.

Tom turns on the boat's radio. He seems indifferent to this sudden assault—they all do. Jane is peeling off her jacket, rubbing sunscreen into her shoulders. Charly has her eyes closed, tilting her head toward the music. Jared is at the bow with Robby, both perked up, their faces alight with excitement.

"It's gonna be fuckin' wild," Robby says.

Jared turns back to us and beams. "We should've been here the whole time. This is where the party's at."

Jane glances at Tom. "I liked Two Harbors."

"You and me, kid," Tom says, winking at her.

The boats and Sea-Doos create a nauseating artificial swell, and the boat lurches.

"Where are we mooring?" I ask.

Tom motions with his chin to a small cove, and we motor with care through the various boats already anchored.

"Look at the golf carts, how adorable!" Charly says, pointing to land. "Can we rent one, Jared?"

Jared nods. "Comes with the villa." He stretches so the sun hits his face. "Aw, fucking land, thank God. The boat's beautiful, Tom, but I'm looking forward to toilets with plumbing."

Tom shrugs. "Sailing life isn't for everyone."

Robby's holding Jane, his face bent down on her shoulder. "I for one am looking forward to some golf," he says, kissing her neck.

"I thought we'd do the spa together," she says.

"You can't get Robby into a spa," Jared says, looking at me as if I'll agree, but I know better. I just sit back and watch a group of children throwing pennies at the pelicans lined up on the dock.

Charly seems to have woken up a bit, and she smiles at Jane. "I'll come with you to the spa. That sounds like just the thing." Her voice is funny, though, sort of far off and dreamy. Jared puts his arm around her and squeezes.

"Wifey needs some pampering," he says so we can hear. "Some Dramamine and some pampering."

But Jane still waits for Robby to answer. He finally shrugs, laughing a little. "I'm not one for massages. It's not really my thing."

"I didn't know that," she says quietly.

The pelicans suddenly launch without making a sound and sweep off across the water. The children celebrate the birds fleeing, rushing to the end of the dock, their parents shouting, "Careful! Careful!"

We get the boat anchored and Tom radios the luxury rental villas to send us their water taxi. A young bleached blonde motors out to us. She's driving a flashy speedboat, painted navy with teak flooring and handrails. The side of it says *Hamilton Cove.* Two plump boys in white polo shirts take our bags.

"Welcome," the girl says. Her uniform is cut low, a polo with a matching short navy skirt. Her name tag says *Rachel.* When she smiles she looks right at Jared. I can see her feeling out who has the cash. "How was the trip over?" She's finally landed on Tom, who's hopped down from the wheel of his boat.

"Perfect weather," Tom says. He taps her name tag. "Rachel . . . means little lamb, doesn't it?"

She has enough sense to blush and take a step back. "Is this your boat?" she asks after we've settled into our seats on the taxi.

Tom makes a show of modesty. He breathes in long and hard, turns to look it over. It's shining under the summer sun, looking hand-polished and expensive.

"It's my baby. I've sailed it all over, down to Costa Rica, out to the Cape. Last year we took it to the Mediterranean." He says "we" as if he means all of us, so she looks at me, sitting closest.

"He doesn't mean me," I tell her. "I'd have drowned him if we sailed farther than the Santa Monica Bay."

Tom laughs. "And just this morning you were begging me to take the long way around the island."

"How long have you been married?" Rachel asks, smiling.

This thrills Tom. "Seems like forever," he says.

I shake my head at Rachel. "We're *not* married."

She looks at us, confused. "You're not Mr. and Mrs. Brownstone?"

"That's me," Jared says as we motor in. "And my wife, Charly," he adds, motioning to where Charly's sitting, eyes hooded again, a sweet sleepy smile on her face.

I can tell Rachel doesn't know what to make of us, so she just looks straight ahead and concentrates on getting us to the dock.

"Hamilton Cove is still new," she tells us when we've come ashore. "We've opened only a year ago."

You can tell this is true, everything's clean and a little plastic-looking. They've shipped real sand by the boatload to make the beach. Moms in floral cover-ups watch children with sand toys, digging away, while dads mingle at the tiki bar, watching the many flat-screen TVs. A fake parrot lords over them, and sitting on the bar is a large rum keg with *It's Island Time* in a distressed font.

Rachel leads us along a winding pathway, pointing out the tennis courts and swimming pools.

"We have a saline pool and a lap pool," she says, smiling her tour-guide smile.

Jane's stopped to look at where she's pointing. "I've read you have free transportation to the Zip Line Tour, is that right?"

Rachel nods enthusiastically. "Yep—just arrange it through the front desk."

"It's the longest zip line in the country," Jane tells us.

"And the spa?" Charly interrupts. Her cheeks are pink from climbing the steps to the clubhouse.

"Right across the lawn. There should be spa menus in your villa," Rachel says. "Try the papaya mango facial scrub." She touches her smooth young face, as if to show us it does wonders. "Makes your skin super soft."

"Oh, that sounds heavenly." Charly sighs. "It's so nice to be off that boat—oh!" She gets embarrassed and touches Tom's sleeve. "Don't pay any attention to me. I haven't been sleeping well."

Tom assures her he isn't offended, even gives her chin another tap, which deepens her blush.

After check-in, Rachel is there again, sitting in a golf cart, her hair pulled into a ponytail as if she might do some heavy lifting. One of the boys is behind the wheel. We climb in, teasing Rachel about how young she looks. Robby asks if she's even old enough to drive the golf cart. She's enjoying the attention, I can tell by how she's looking sideways at Jane and me. Charly has checked out, staring off toward the harbor where a group of children are playing volleyball.

The villa itself is large and high up on the cliff so there is a view of everything coming and going in the harbor. The cruise ship sits on the horizon; a helicopter whisks just above the sea; Sea-Doos and sailboats and yachts cut frothy, chalk-colored paths across the water. On our deck are sun chaises and a fire pit that lights with a key. Everything feels slightly forced—it smells of new paint and air freshener, and the floors are laminate meant to look like real wood.

But Jared is ecstatic. "Look at this kitchen," he says, running his hands across the counters. "Now I wish we'd gone for soapstone."

Robby comes out from one of the master bedrooms. He's rubbing his hands together. "Did you see the minibar?"

"Nothing mini about it," Jared says. "It's fully stocked."

"The prices are a bit much," I say, flipping over the menu. "Fifteen dollars for a bag of peanuts?"

"Says the girl staying at the Miramar." Tom comes out from his room. He takes the menu from me, studying it.

"It's not the prices." I frown. "It's the *quality*."

He taps the menu on my nose. "Gallo not good enough for you, is it?" His teeth seem very white indoors. His bald head is pink, the rest of him burnished that brown only white boys get when outside all the time, the color of a soft leather purse. "Come on, Jared, the ladies request better-quality wine. We'll go into town and stock up."

Jared's head is very close to Charly. They're having some private tiff. But when Tom says his name he looks up, all smiles.

"Perfect," he says. "The girls can check out the spa, and by the time they get back we'll have the barbeque ready." He kisses Charly on the cheek. "Treat them to anything they want," he tells her, and then smiles at Jane and me.

Charly's face is red when the boys walk out, her chest drawn up tight. "He's turned into a real ass, hasn't he?"

"I don't think Tom's the best influence," I tell her.

She touches the spa menu left open on the counter. "He's so impressed with himself since becoming an exec at the firm. I mean he was always into flashy things, but now everything has to impress." She sighs, wringing her hands together.

I touch her arm lightly. "Having nice things isn't that terrible."

"I know that," she says, pulling away. "It's just hard work being in a relationship—you wouldn't understand."

Jane puts her arm around Charly. "Robby's like that too. Get him around other guys and he's lord of his domain. Get him alone and he's a child."

I can't help but feel slightly protective of Robby, of Jared too. *Fine,* I think. *Let's play our roles.*

"Come on," I say, turning on my easy, breezy smile. "You'll feel better after a shower—then we'll go spend a shit ton of Jared's money at the spa."

"I'll buy us mango papaya facials," Charly says, and they laugh.

We wash up, each of us changing into fresh clothes. Charly is in a sweet cotton dress with little eyelets, her neck deeply sunburned. "I don't know how I missed that spot," she says, looking at it in the mirror. "I'll have to text Jared to get aloe vera."

Jane changes into Bermuda shorts and an oversized tank top— I can see her zebra-print sports bra underneath. "God, do I need a facial," she says, looking at her face in the vanity.

I look into the mirror too, at my bare shoulders, the white cotton top making them seem tanner than they really are. "Me too," I say. "I'm breaking out."

"Where?" Charly asks, turning from the mirror to look at me. "I don't see anything."

Jane rolls her eyes. "Your skin is perfect."

At the spa they have only two appointments available. The woman at the front desk looks apologetic, her lips knitted together in a grimace. She looks at me. "We can fit you in tomorrow morning."

Charly starts to complain but I shush her. She pouts alongside the woman. "It's okay," I tell them both. "I didn't really want a facial anyway." Which is true. I'm suddenly eager to be away from them.

"What about a massage appointment?" Charly says with urgency.

Jane is flipping through a magazine, her spa robe draped over her arm. I think she must be trying very hard not to tap her foot.

The woman at the desk shakes her head. It's the jazz festival, she tells us. "You're lucky two appointments canceled."

This settles it. I tell them I'll go into town and find the guys. I make a joke that they'll probably need supervision anyway, but only Charly laughs—a strained little sound, not really a laugh at all.

20

I make my way down to the sandy beach. The light out is bright and eager, sweeping over everything. I turn my face up to it. I imagine it's Eric's face—that intensity, that warmth, that goddamn smile.

A jazz trio performs on the grassy lawn, couples spread out on blankets and chairs; families play with a beach ball and Frisbees. A Boston terrier bounds past, his owner chasing after her, calling, "Lucy! Heel! Stop! Heel! Damn it." The man is red-faced and sweating, and when he runs past I catch an intimate whiff of him. The dog slows, then turns and bolts into a cluster of long dune grass.

I stop to look at the grass, which was clearly planted there to give the impression of rolling Cape Cod beaches. Last summer—has it already been a year?—we gathered at the head curator's house, a sprawling Provincetown estate, for the Fourth of July. The weather was warmer than this, wetter too, heavy with condensation from a tropical storm off the Atlantic.

I remember pulling up and thinking: *This is the type of house you always hope is your destination but never is.* This beautiful house with a circular drive made out of tiny pebbles the color of pearls. It could be in France—a château in miniature, small only by Marie Antoinette's standards.

Estelle, a robust woman with snow-white hair and tiny polished glasses, is standing on the front steps in a casual pale gray linen suit. Her wife, Bette, an artist and gallery owner, is in a Stella McCartney wrap dress, and has two chubby Cavalier spaniels in her arms. She hugs me over the black-and-white one she calls Poodle.

They take us through the high arched foyer, flanked on either side by Mark Manders sculptures, variations of *Girl Study*, and one that I do not recognize but is a tangle of man, animal, and nature. The main room is all reclaimed wood and white walls with crown molding, and on the far wall, large windows overlooking the ocean below. The side doors are thrown open so the sea air can roll in, and I can just make out various lawn sculptures, bright yellows and reds.

The house has eleven rooms, most with windows facing out to Cape Cod Bay. Together Estelle and Bette show us their Damien Hirst Kaleidoscope painting, made from hundreds of butterfly wings—a great burst of blues and golds. In the dining room, painted directly onto the wall, is a Swoon mural, a woman in dreamlike meditation. Among the fourteenth-century Chinese cabinets with jade inlay, and the collection of Tiffany art glass and transferware, hangs a collection of Louise Bourgeois drawings—of eyes and spiders, of grotesque womanly figures.

Outside on the patio are the rest of the curators and staff. Photography is drinking negronis with Illustrated Books. Both are fit older men who like to wear expertly tailored pinstriped suits, always with a pocket square. One sneaks me coffee-flavored candies in the afternoons, holding his hand out as if it were a surprise. The other leers at the research assistants—young girls still in graduate school, working on their dissertations—but he never does anything about it.

Architecture is the one I have to watch out for: new, young, with a raging God complex. I can hear him giving the bartender a hard time—*Too much vermouth, make me another*—before he turns away to continue his conversation with one of the curators from MoMA PS1.

We drove up from the airport with Eric at the wheel and three women from Painting and Sculpting in the back. He teased them about their husbands and grandchildren, complimented them on new haircuts and shoes, a particular scarf, a signature scent—he notices everything. And it doesn't hurt that he is handsome and boyish, and wants to see you smile and laugh. By the time we arrive the women are pink-cheeked and giggling like schoolgirls.

When we enter the backyard patio after the house tour, the partygoers visibly relax. Illustrated Books hands a drink to Eric, and they pose for the photographer, arm in arm, laughing easily. And those female curatorial assistants, they are *clamoring*. The exhibition isn't ready until Eric gives his approval, and it's not a party until he arrives. He is the bright center of their world, and when he turns that light on me, their world becomes *mine*.

Film and Drawings show up with their families, and Estelle brings out a tray of soda and peanut-butter-and-jelly sandwiches for the kids. She's even hired a lifeguard, a pimply teenager with a potbelly and two red spots on her cheeks, who ushers the kids to the pool.

The curators and their assistants mill about drinking cocktails and eating barbeque that I remember being not very good. The martinis were good, I remember that. And that I was the only administrative assistant there—the other curators did not invite their assistants. *Thank you, Eric.* And I remember he was in a good mood, all easy humor and charm. Even when Architecture, with his sullen young mouth, made a point of saying *It's a pity your wife couldn't make it*. Even then, Eric was all smiles.

At some point I wander off on my own, a little drunk and feeling awkward because I made the mistake of calling Poodle the Cavalier spaniel "Pancake the Pork Chop." The curator wives smirking at me over their drinks like *Uh-huh* and moving away from me. Eric oblivious, too busy making his rounds.

Inside the estate the windows are thrown wide and the wind off the sea sends the curtains billowing into the hall, filling the house with its briny scent. I'm studying the Louise Bourgeois prints, the dark mounds and valleys, the caves of the female body. Their blank, crooked faces stare back at me. The sun hangs low in the sky, putting the prints half in shadow, half in buttery light. They look strange, wanton—phantomlike.

Architecture is there now, wants to show me the library. He asks where I'm from and we talk about Los Angeles, and art, and nothing. I'm enjoying the attention, and if I blur my eyes he looks like a young Eric. I accept another drink. I'm very loose now, and since Eric hasn't come to find me, we snuggle up on a leather couch overlooking the great span of lawn below us. Sounds from the party on the patio carry in through the adjoining doors, and I hear Eric's openmouthed laugh.

At some point Architecture kisses my neck, making his way up to my ear. I can feel the tip of his tongue—hot and wet—and his teeth, very lightly on the lobe. I tilt my head toward him, as if he's telling me a secret, and that's what Eric must think when he walks in. His eyebrows go up and his mouth drops open. I can't hear what he says, but he puts up his hands as if to excuse himself and walks quickly away.

I find him later on the beach, skipping rocks. The rest of the party is still up on the patio, just out of sight. I can hear the music, though, the soft chatter and clinking of glasses and plates.

His shoes are off, pants rolled up above his ankles. He's standing with his feet in the wet, muddy sand. It's a beautiful beach, wide and curving with rippled tidal flats.

I tilt my head up at him, *Hello*.

He studies the rock in his hand, bottom lip pulled in, dimpling his cheeks.

I replay this moment often in my head, his expression that day. His hair wild from the onshore wind, his eyes narrowed. How he breathes out and chucks the rock so hard that I step back, afraid the swing of his arm might hit me.

The women from Painting and Sculpting come down the path that leads from the house to the beach, and Eric pushes past me, shouting *Hey there!*, leaving me alone in the cold, slapping surf.

Later the lifeguard brings the children down to the beach to play in the waves. I change into my bathing suit and join them because at this point the children and the lifeguard are the only friends I've got left. When one of the little boys is knocked down by a wave, he holds his arms out to me. Big fat tears roll down his grubby cheeks, but he stops crying when I pick him up. I put him on one of my hips like Bette did with her dog. He plays with the strap of my suit.

I can feel the adults watching me from the shore. They're in swimsuits and cover-ups with no real plans to go in. Someone yells *Get Elsa!* I see a little strawberry blonde girl holding a long strand of seaweed in her pudgy fist giggle and charge toward me, arm outstretched as if holding a sword. I laugh too and she chases after me through the surf. The little boy smiles, squirming in my arms and sticking his tongue out at the girl, who kicks water at us. We play this game, the other children taking turns with the seaweed, until the sun gets too low and our teeth chatter.

And then the parents are on the shore, holding towels and speaking over one another. *You're so good with children*, someone says. *You were wonderful, thank you, thank you*, they say.

And there is Eric with my towel. He folds me into it, smiling.

Now it's important to get this right. This is when it matters, this is proof. Eric there with my towel, wrapping me up tight, arms lingering for a moment—furtive glances to see if anyone is watching—then pulling me closer to him. Not so close that our bodies are touching, just close enough that I can feel the warmth coming from his skin, and then, and then—he takes my cheek in one warm hand and brushes his thumb over my lips. I look up at him, stare into those dark eyes, and tuck his thumb into my mouth. It tastes salty from the sea. Somewhere down the beach a bonfire is lit; the smell of wood is thick.

I knew he would be jealous. That he would not be able to help himself. That I could turn him away from his colleagues and coworkers—make a fat dent in that charming carefree exterior. I knew too that he could not stay mad for long, that he had watched me on the beach with the children—and that motherhood prompts forgiveness in men.

So we're not on the beach when the fireworks start. We find our way to one of the bedrooms on the second floor. It's dark until the fireworks BOOM and the room is filled with green and blue light. Hot breath in my ear. *Do you know that painting, Elsa?* I'm shaking my head no. Teach me, teach me. Hot hands groping; panting in my ear—*Turner's Hannibal Crossing the Alps.* How can he speak when his mouth is so full of me? *In the face of nature, man is powerless.* BOOM again, and the painting reigns over us both—that monstrous dark wave. His hand is half in my mouth now, trying to quiet me. *Hush, Elsa, hush.* BOOM. Gold. Purple. Blue. Gold again. He's hurrying now, before I give us away. Before I shriek this house down, before I grind everything, crushing it all, collapsing, falling, disintegrating into ash. Left smoldering still.

21

The dog's owner has caught up to her, and is working to get the leash back onto her collar. He is shiny with sweat and looks at me apologetically.

"Sorry, she's usually so good off leash," he says, and motions with his chin to the jazz band. "I think it's the music." The dog's tail wags manically, her head darting back and forth.

She pushes into my hand. "It's okay," I say, rubbing her face. I'm still thinking of Eric, so my voice cracks when I say "She's sweet."

I take one of the pink pills I brought with me from the villa and head into downtown. I pass the Casino, where the jazz festival will be held the next two nights. It's an impressive Art Deco–style building about twelve stories high.

There's a small museum on the bottom floor, and as I get closer I hear a commotion. A father is scolding his son in the gift shop, the boy, maybe six years old, turning and tugging on his mother's dress just as I see them. He's sobbing. "Daddy's mean. I hate him, I hate him." His mother is pretending to read her brochure, but when our eyes meet, I can't hide my embarrassment. She yanks the child's arm from her dress, chucking it off like a bug.

"God," she hisses as if to curse them both. She walks right past me, her face red.

I watch her join one of the cruise groups waiting for a tour of the Casino—one long line of sunburned calves and tired eyes, all looking at one another as if surprised to find themselves in such company. It's a different set than at Hamilton Cove, but both will come for a tour of the Casino. They'll stand in the same line, take photos with the same view, exit through the gift shop and buy the same key chains, and T-shirts, and postcards of Catalina. The attendant smiling brightly, asking over and over, *Would you like a bag?*

So obediently they wait in line to buy the things they're told to buy, with the babies they're supposed to have in tow. How are they not jumping out of their skin? I think about Jared and Charly endlessly remodeling, and Robby and Jane exercising obsessively, and me so desperate to move to New York—all things thrown into the pit, hoping to fill it up. It occurs to me suddenly, maybe learning to settle is part of adulthood. Maybe if you don't, it eats you up.

Too late for me, then, I've let it boil down until it's part of the fiber, until it's become that ringing center of my core, and watching these tourists wait in line has it blaring so loud that I want to scream, *What are you all waiting for?*

Instead, I interrupt one of the tour guides to ask where I can find the grocery store. He's telling the crowd how the Casino is the island's civil defense center—how it can house the entire year-round population in an emergency.

"It's a small island," he tells me, annoyed that I've interrupted him. "You can't miss it."

Before I can find the store I see them. Or rather I see Rachel; she's twisting her platinum ponytail around one of her fingers, shoulder to shoulder with a Latina around the same age, both drinking from straws as if practicing for a role much too old for them. Jared has pulled up a stool beside Rachel. Tom is sitting back, watching him with an amused expression.

Robby stands off to the side, awkwardly holding a drink garnished with a teal umbrella. When I'm closer I can make out a tiny plastic monkey too, neon green, hanging off the side. Robby raises his shoulders, helpless.

"We stopped for lunch," he says to me. "They happened to be here."

Jared pulls me into a long hug. I can smell the tequila and salsa on his breath—heavy on the lime and onions.

"Elsa!" he says. "Look who we found." Rachel thrusts her chin out as a greeting. She's in a pink strapless dress, the top low across her chest, the skin pinched and rough, the color and texture of a walnut. She's delighted by Jared's attention.

"Hi, Rachel," I say to her. "I hope they're behaving themselves."

"We bought them lunch," Jared says, beaming. They're seated on the patio, and there's a good breeze coming up from the harbor, but still, he's sweating through his shirt.

"And drinks," Tom adds.

"What gentlemen."

The girl in a skirt and tube top throws out her hand. "Marisol," she says. "They were telling us about your trip to Two Harbors. My family lives there in the off-season."

"Can you imagine *living* there?" Jared says. He runs a hand over his face.

I think of those modest tract homes in the isthmus, the swings underneath the eucalyptus, that wild open ocean during storms, watching it twist and churn, maybe even swimming out into it on calm days. The pill I took finally kicks in, making everything fluid and gentle. It's like I'm in the sea again, weightless and floating on my back, the lulling swells beneath me. I'm about to ask Marisol how to do it, how to live there too, but then Tom is talking and I realize I've missed the moment—I've missed several moments—and I work to catch up.

"How often do you get to the mainland?" Tom asks, leaning

into Marisol. He's watching her think about it, letting his eyes drop to her chest.

"I haven't been in almost two years," Marisol says proudly.

"I go over every month," Rachel says as if embarrassed by her friend's answer. "My dad works for Catalina Express. He's a captain."

That fluid feeling of weightlessness is gone too quickly. I'm checking in my pockets for another pill when something occurs to me. "Have you been on the open ocean?"

Rachel makes a face. "Well yeah, of course. He used to take me out on his fishing boat." She plays with her ponytail, smoothing it around her fingertip, and purses her lips. "I hated the smell and I always got sick. The swells are terrible."

"Does Hamilton Cove offer trips to that side of the island?" I can't find the other pill. Tom catches me checking my pockets a second time and grins.

Marisol is shaking her head, but it's Rachel who answers. "Nothing but wild cliffs and sea—there's nothing to do."

"I said I'd take them out on my boat." Tom's looking at me over their heads like a cat with a new toy.

"Did you, now."

Rachel's excited. "He's planning to sail to Tahiti next. God, what a dream." She bites her straw at him.

The waitress comes up, looking relieved to see me.

"Can I get you anything?"

Marisol takes the waitress's hand. "Miss Ballard was my teacher in Two Harbors. She used to take us to see the horses at El Rancho Escondido."

The waitress looks mortified. This could be Miss Sandy, no longer taking seventh graders to New York City—still plump and miserable and trying very hard not to be either.

"Bet you never thought you'd be serving us tequila," Marisol squeals.

134

I drop my purse hard onto the table, sending the empty salsa bowl spinning. Robby's sensed the party's over. He sets his drink down.

"Just the check, please," I tell the waitress, who has stepped back from us all. "And waters. Lots of waters."

"Jared." Robby motions with his head. "Let's go clean you up." Jared's shirt is see-through now; you can see his nipples, pink and nubby like pencil erasers. I help Robby get him to his feet as Tom looks on. He blows across the mouth of his beer bottle so that it hums.

"I'm surprised at you, Robby."

"Don't blame me for this," he says to me, but then Jared groans. "I don't feel too hot."

Robby hoists him up. "I got you, buddy, come on. You're fine."

Rachel takes the umbrella from Robby's drink, tucking it behind her ear.

"Marisol, take a picture," she says, holding out her phone. And they pose.

Tom takes my arm, drawing me close. "What if I stick around? What'd you think of that? That brunette could use some kicking in."

"They're *children*."

"And your bellboy at the Miramar, what's he?"

I'm breathing a little quickly because I don't remember Tom meeting Rex, or how he saw us together. Was it the night he tried to come up to my room? Had I introduced Rex? Had Tom seen the two of us together? I remember Eric's face when he saw me with that hot wet secret in my ear, and start digging around in my purse again.

"Do whatever you want, I'm checking on Jared."

I push past belligerent groups of tourists devouring burritos and enchiladas and screaming at the bartender to turn up the volume on some television show that they all seem to know.

I find two white pills, half crushed at the bottom of my purse. They leave an acrid aftertaste. I drink down half an empty bottle of beer someone left at the bar. It's warm and a little flat but I don't care. Someone's shouting at the back of my head. I think he must be shouting to someone on the other side of me because he keeps saying, "Susanna. *Hola*, Susanna. Hey!" And then all at once— almost the moment he touches my shoulder—it clicks.

22

It's like one dream being pulled into another. I feel light. So light I worry I might float right off over the ocean, joining those pelicans in the safety of the sea. The Latino producer is looking at me with expectant eyes, his mouth pulled up in a sly grin. He smooths his dark curls with one hand, points a beer bottle at me with the other. He's with a group, all of them looking at me with interest.

"There you are," he says. "*Susanna.*" He says this fake name with emphasis.

"Oh, hello," I say, taking his hand and looking past him, at Tom and the girls, who aren't paying any attention to me, but then Rachel turns to look over her shoulder. I step closer to him, which he takes as a sign of affection and folds me into his arms.

"Found you," he says, breathing me in. "You smell good."

"Rafa," his friends are saying to him. One in a tank top, a fat gold chain tumbling in his chest hair, clicks his tongue at me. "Rafa," he says. "Introduce us."

"What are you doing here?" I say, putting on my best smile.

"You said you'd be in Catalina over the weekend—so Rafael Ochoa came to find you."

I nod stupidly—had Susanna from San Diego told him that? The jolt of seeing him in my present has not completely worn off. I thought I had left him on his private beach, bodysurfing in tandem with the version of me that stayed behind. But here he is, hands on my hips, sashaying me toward him. I can feel his T-shirt, soft and moist from the heat. The smell of him comes back thick in my nose. He makes a *tut-tut* noise with his tongue. "If your friends are anything like mine, then you could use a dinner away from them," he says, pointing toward Tom and the girls.

Just then Tom catches sight of us from across the restaurant, tilts his chin at me. I have a distinct desire to flee.

"Come on, Mama, have dinner with me tonight," he urges.

"Rafa likes to keep the pretty ones for himself," his friend interjects. "Where'd he meet you? Some audition?"

"Does she look like an actress? No. Too sophisticated, too severe for that." I can't tell if he means this as a compliment or not. His expression is pleased, he's a little drunk, and the shadow that flickers over his eyes says he remembers the feel of me—the sounds I make.

I feel trapped, powerless, and turn as if in a hurry to meet someone. Tom watches on, clearly entertained by my discomfort.

"It's good to see you," I say. "But—"

"Aw, don't be like that, Mama, I came all the way over to find you."

"We just wrapped our show," his friend tells me. "And Doug's got a yacht." He flicks his head toward the others.

"Would you like to see it?" Rafa asks. He's very smooth; the cadence of his voice matches his eyes, almond-shaped, with long lashes and meticulously groomed eyebrows. If it weren't for that square jaw and faint beard he'd look like a schoolboy.

"Actually," I say, glancing quickly at Tom, "I've got to go."

He kisses me then, quick and right on the mouth. He motions to Tom and, laughing a little, says, "That your *novio*?"

"If he is, then kissing me wasn't a very nice thing to do."

He shrugs, a practiced gesture of humble conceit, letting me go in favor of his beer. His friends have lost interest too; they've turned back to the television.

Rafa catches me glancing at the bathroom. His face lights up. "Ah," he says. "*Novio*'s taking a piss."

I manage a carefree sound, something between a giggle and a sigh.

"I'm here with friends. The one in the bathroom is my ex-husband."

He wrinkles his nose at me, entertained, and tips the last of his beer into his mouth. It's funny, I'd started to forget what he looked like. No, that's not right; I didn't *forget*. It started to change, or morph, or whatever it is that time does to a moment after it's happened. I remembered his hands—large and skilled. How they felt rough on my hips, but in the water they were soft. Yet here they are, ordinary male hands with bony knuckles and too-large thumbs scooping chips and salsa into a mouth I remembered being tender. I had forgotten his dimples, too—how they add to the schoolboy effect. He is both handsome and pretty. I remembered the curls and his height and the wicked shape of his chin, like a stonecutting blade, but I misplaced the sound of his voice, how it's flat and practiced and when he speaks he looks right through you.

This startles me. How quick and easy it is to forget. How imagination can step in, fill those holes without you knowing.

I try to pull up Eric in Provincetown. His bottom lip sucked in, his eyes narrowed, almost steely. What am I forgetting? What am I changing? Did he have freckles? No. Just a mole near his temple. And his cheeks always pink. Bare arms, a tan stopping where his sleeves are cuffed. Delicate wrists, but wait, that's him holding a pen in his office, not standing on the beach with anger weighing him down, hands clenched into fists.

Tom lights a cigarette and leans back in his chair, legs casually crossed. When our eyes meet, one side of his mouth tilts up and he blows smoke toward Marisol, who playfully pushes it away.

"So what do you say? Dinner?" Rafa smiles, bats those heavy dark lashes.

Whatever show his friends are watching has gotten them into a heated debate. One says, "Let's settle it, then," and slams his fist onto the table. The one in the tank top looks at Rafa and me.

"Doug thinks I won't beat him at arm wrestling," his friend says.

"It's an ongoing argument," Rafa apologizes. "Please don't banish me to dinner with them."

Tom's alone now. I look around but don't see Rachel or Marisol. He points his cigarette at me, and like in some slow-motion scene from a telenovela, he gets up and crosses the patio, grinding the cigarette into a flower box.

I let out a strangled half laugh that surprises even me. "You win. But I can't come with you now."

Rafa strokes my bare arm with his thumb, his face soft. "Whatever works for you, Mama. What are you in the mood to eat?"

"Anything, just as long as the wine's good."

He rubs his lip with his thumb, the tip of his tongue darting out to meet it. Tom is there now, extending his hand to Rafa.

"Tom," he says with an impish smile.

"Hey, buddy." Rafa takes his hand. "Rafael."

"And how do you know our darling girl here?" Tom asks, putting an arm around me.

"Oh, we go way back," I say. "Old friends. We're going to catch up over dinner tonight. Isn't that right?"

Rafa taps his lip again. "Whatever you say, Mama."

I ignore the pleasure Tom is taking in this. He looks over at the bathrooms, waiting for Robby and Jared to emerge. Robby will see right through this, and he'll ask hard questions. He'll want to know the truth—that I arrived a few days early, that I met this man on a private beach and didn't care enough to give my real name or remember his, that I may or may not have invited him to this island—that I'm jobless and scared and taking various pills stolen from my mother.

"Should I check on them?" Tom says with mock concern, gesturing toward the bathrooms.

I ignore him, telling Rafa I'm free at eight.

The bathroom doors swing open then, and there is Robby, looking directly at us, followed by Jared, pink-faced and swaying.

"Oh, look." Tom smiles. "Here they come." He even waves.

Rafa seems just as entertained as Tom now. "Eight o'clock, Bistro de la Mer? It's the only decent restaurant in this amusement park."

"Sure. Perfect."

Rafa's pleased with himself, and sits back on his barstool just as Robby arrives.

"I sent Jared to the golf cart. Everything all right?" His shoulders are tight, thrown back a little. He's looking from Tom to Rafa. I can tell he thinks I need saving.

"Just making dinner plans with an old friend, apparently," Tom says, smiling at me.

Rafa looks Robby up and down, fingers his beer bottle. "See you tonight," he says to me, making a show of kissing my cheek.

"You know that guy?" Robby says when we make our way back to the golf cart. His voice is hesitant, tense.

Jared is in the backseat of the golf cart, half asleep. "Took long enough, jeez," he says. "I got churros for Charly; they'll be cold now."

We climb in on either side, with Tom at the wheel. Robby mumbles, "Nice fucking diamond earring. He a cocaine tycoon or something?"

I make my voice as steady and light as possible, which is easy now because the crisis is over. "Produces TV shows, makes a killing."

This I know will shut Robby up. Talking about money always does. He grows quiet and withdrawn.

Jared stirs. "Wait, what'd I miss?"

"Oh," Tom says cheerfully, "there was almost a second Alamo."

"Please shut up," I say. "Let's get to the market without running into anyone else."

"Any *old friends*, you mean." Tom gives me a look that says we're in cahoots now.

Jared rests his chin on my shoulder from the backseat. "Don't tell Charly about Rachel, 'kay?" The golf cart jerks forward, thrusting him back into his seat.

23

"Ohh, they have steamed mussels!" Charly says from the bedroom. She's looking at Bistro de la Mer on her tablet, her skin dewy from her facial. "Look at these prices. Who is this guy?"

"He produces television shows," I tell her from the bathroom.

"Really? Which show?"

My reflection is looking a little worn-out. Even after a second shower and a face scrub and a mask I still look weathered.

"I don't know, he might not have said."

Charly's glistening face pops into the bathroom. "How well do you know this guy? I mean, what if he stalked you here, have you thought of that?"

I'm using powder, and a great plume of beige has settled over the sink. I can't say that I don't remember whether I told Rafa to meet me here or not. It would mean I'd have to explain that the last time I saw him I was very high and very drunk—or, for that matter, the last time I saw him was the first time I met him, and that would be giving away too much.

"This is the modern dating world, darling. There's always *some* risk involved."

"Ohh, is this a date?" She bats her lashes. "Are you *dating* him?"

I plop some powder on her nose. "It's just dinner."

Up on the deck Robby and Jared have started the grill; the smell of oak and lighter fluid comes through the open window. Since our return from town Tom has been on a roll, making every effort to imply that he and I share some big secret, winking at me over Robby's head when he asks about my dinner plans, telling me I should wear something nice for my *old friend*. When we carried the groceries into the house from the golf cart he lingered beside me, whispering *Heartbreaker* in my ear.

"I wish you weren't going," Charly says, sitting on the edge of the bathtub. "But this is nice. It's like when we used to get ready before a junior high dance. Remember? It seems forever ago. I miss those days. We were so innocent. Do you remember my pink denim skirt? It had silver rhinestones on the pockets."

I'm working eyeliner onto my eyelid. I smile at her in the mirror.

"You'll have fun tonight, Robby says it's a good lineup at the Casino."

"I loved that skirt; it was my sister's." She watches me for a moment. "Who taught you to put makeup on like that?"

I examine the eyeliner. "A cousin, maybe. Or a friend in high school, I don't remember."

Charly lets her shoulders drop. She leans over and turns the water on in the tub.

"I learned all my makeup tips from you. Did you know that?" She turns the water off and watches the tub drain.

"God, I hope that isn't true." I laugh. "You know, I probably learned from the women at my mother's salon in Bakersfield."

"Jared likes it," she says, sighing a little. "And Robby. And Tom. I think I'll take a bath before dinner."

I turn to look at her. She was always a self-conscious girl, the

144

kind you want to make sure gets home okay. I suddenly remember a story she told me once. Charly is sixteen when her older sister, the one with the tendency to swim naked in their pool while Charly and her boyfriend study, calls from some Florida college to invite her for spring break in the Keys. So Charly kisses her boyfriend goodbye—a real good make-out session, because Charly's a very capable virgin—and heads to Florida. Her sister takes her to one of the islands and shows Charly how to snorkel. They hold hands and swim out past the seaweed, through the dark shadows, when sea snakes, hundreds of them, emerge from a boulder, their bodies moving with such grace that it's beautiful and terrifying all at once.

That image stays with me—the water warm and salty, soothing. How relaxed and free you'd feel. And then snakes, but your sister is there, taking your arm, looking at you from behind goggles—her eyes magnified. I can picture it perfectly: *Trust me,* she is saying. *I've got you.* It makes sense suddenly, why Charly is the way she is with me. Why she hasn't written me off. Sisterhood is something I don't understand, something I've always thought could bite back—like those sea snakes, beautiful, dangerous, a little mysterious. Best to get out of the water altogether.

But poor Charly, despite how the story ends, still has not learned that lesson. Her sister was a flirtatious drunk who thought it hilarious to finally admit to sleeping with Charly's boyfriend. *The way she laughed, Elsa,* Charly told me. *She laughed like we'd both think it was funny.*

"Do you want me to stay?" I ask Charly.

She's filling the tub, running her hand under the water. She shakes her head.

"Just make sure it doesn't take you five years to come back," she says with a little tilt of her head. That dizzy look is back. She looks pill drunk. I want to ask how many she's taken, but there's a knock at the door.

Robby sticks his head in. "Burger or dog?" he asks Charly.

"Hot diggity dog!" She giggles. "And have Jared toast the bun, too."

Robby looks at me. I can see his throat working. "You look nice," he manages.

24

I'm already loose from the Vicodin I took, and everything starts blurring together. Soft focus. Watching Charly shove hot dogs with mustard and relish into her face while Jared knocks back whiskey like it's the cheap stuff. Jane asking for a veggie burger without onions and taking it personally when Robby says, *I thought you liked onions?* Tom laughing, always. Robby growing fierce and defensive.

Robby's thinking of me, of course. I'm the one who likes onions, but I don't say anything. I let them go over it—and over and over—working it out as if onions were some vital detail.

Then Tom is there, taking me out to the deck. The light is blistery and golden, the cruise ship floats on the horizon like a large buoyant pearl. He makes as if to hand me my purse but then shakes it to hear the prescription bottle. My little tambourine. I snatch it from him, relieved he didn't go through it; the last of the Miramar coke is in the inside pocket.

He lights a joint and passes it to me. "Want to hear a story?" he asks, pushing my hair behind one of my ears.

"What about?" I blow smoke at him.

He licks his lips, making them glisten, and sits on one of the deck chairs. "The sexiest thing I've ever seen," he says, rubbing the seat next to him, so I sit too.

I take another drag from the joint and turn so I don't have to see the excitement in his eyes.

"I was visiting a cousin." His voice floats over to me. "In East Los Angeles. It was a real shithole neighborhood, lots of stucco and duplexes, small yappy dogs everywhere. You know the kind."

I nod my head yes.

"It was around Christmas. A single mom lived next door. She was in her early forties, possibly younger but life had hit her hard—you could tell. Her kid was young, cried all the damn time, a real brat. One night I hear fighting—her boyfriend was this big Salvadoran dude, tatted all over, wore a bandana. They were really going at each other, just screaming their heads off. I don't know where the kid was. They had gotten a Christmas tree earlier that day and I had watched the boyfriend sweating and swearing, trying to lug it into the duplex. Anyway, I hear a slap—a real good smack—and then the screen door bangs and the boyfriend's car peels out down the street. It's late, maybe one or two in the morning. So I go out, and I see her inside, the mom. She's in jeans, the top button undone, with no shirt on. She's wearing this flimsy bra. I can see her nipples through it. And she's crying, hanging Christmas ornaments on the tree by herself."

That's terrible, I say—but really I'm not sure I've said anything at all. My voice seems very far away, and I've missed something. We're no longer sitting, but standing very close together, near the end of the deck. And the view has changed. The light is nearly gone, almost dark. But I'm still partially in East Los Angeles, stuck with the smell of Christmas tree and scorched rubber.

"That's just how it is, baby," comes Tom's voice. "The worst kind of want is to survive, and we all have that."

"The joint is almost finished," I try to say.

"Come here," Tom says. His hands at my waist feel sudden but then I think maybe they've been there the whole time. His voice in my ear: *Take it easy, girl*, he breathes. *This weed's got bite.*

I make an effort to push him away but he asks if I'll blow the last of the smoke into his mouth. It's just us, out on the deck watching the darkening palms, the smoke curling up like a question mark between us, then blowing out toward the sea. I can feel the strength of his hands, his thumbs digging in. *Brute.* I'm imagining that hard slap, the sting of hand against cheek and a metallic taste of blood.

And then I'm pushing away, saying goodbye, relieved to get away for a bit. From Tom's jeering, Robby's uneasiness, that motion Jane does with her arms as she explains the various parts of a mango papaya facial. Charly walks me as far as the door, asks if I will meet them at the Casino. *You can bring Rafa, I'm sure we'd love to meet him. Just try, okay?*

And then thank God I'm down at the beach watching the older children ride bikes. Tom was right, the weed is strong—probably too strong. I try not to struggle against it. The sun has tipped behind the mountains and the jazz band on the lawn has picked up, the trumpet hopscotching with the drum kit, the piano following close behind. I tell my heartbeat to calm down.

A group of well-dressed black couples—all slacks and knee-length dresses and skirts—dance on the lawn. Someone has a bubble machine and the toddlers trip after the lopsided pearly spheres. I watch one float up toward the trees, the children jumping and stretching after it. I blow at it. *Get away, little bubble.*

Up ahead there's been a bike accident, two rentals have collided. Both parties are fine but traffic's stopped. The music from the lawn has stopped too—or at least I can't hear it over the noise. A line of golf carts stretches in both directions, their little horns going *meep-meep* while two men in cargo shorts and strappy sandals wave their bike helmets at each other. At the docks the cruisers are waiting for tugboats to take them back to steak dinners and ballroom drinks, the tugboat horns ringing off the mountains like thunder rolling in—*boom-boom*. A group of boys in basketball jerseys spray silly string at one another, the girls walking in front of them, smiling back over their shoulders. My skin feels too tight—I can suddenly feel the bones underneath. One of the boys turns. *Is he looking at me?* I jump when someone whistles, sharp and grating.

Rafa is waiting outside the restaurant. He's smoking a thin cigar, the smoke *putt-putting* out of his mouth. He smiles, such confidence, that diamond earring twinkling.

"Susanna," he says. He drops the cigar into a potted tree and kisses me on the corner of my mouth. I can taste his aftershave.

"Stunning." He sounds practiced, his voice strangely entrancing. Like being in the desert on a hot day with cicadas in the trees, their high-pitched buzzing a vibration through your skin.

"You stun me," he's saying. A shiver crawls up over me.

He holds open the restaurant door to a crowded small room made to look like a yacht club. Tan wood everywhere, knotted ropes, and a rusty anchor next to a fish tank. The bar has a mirrored back, so I can see Rafa and me enter. In this light, my hair is blazing red.

The maître d' must like what he sees too because he gets very eager and jolly. He seats us at a window table, telling Rafa he's glad to have him back. But the way the maître d's stomach brushes against everything—the chair he pulls out for me, the menu he takes from his side, my arm when he bends over to point out the specials—makes me jumpy. Reminds me of lunch at the Plaza, that waiter with the sagging cheeks—Mary in the bathroom, only a matter of minutes before she comes back.

"Would you mind if we didn't eat here?" I say after he leaves. Rafa looks surprised.

"I'm just not very hungry." He sees me eyeing the maître d'.

"Whatever you like," he says, folding his menu. "But this is the best restaurant on the island."

"Have you been to Two Harbors?" I'm thinking of the plain burger from the village's only grill, how it was dry and stuck in your throat but the lettuce was fresh and the beer was very cold.

"God, no. Hicksville," he says. "Why would I go there?"

"Where are your friends tonight?" I ask him, and ignore the flash in his eye.

He leans over the table, taking my hand. "At the Casino for the jazz show."

"And you're skipping it?"

He shrugs, taking his menu back up. "You are too."

I think about Charly back at the villa, probably getting ready with Jane. Charly putting on Bowie or Talking Heads, how she'll curl her hair and then give up, blow-drying it straight at the last minute. How Jared is probably whiskey drunk by now, telling Robby not to worry, he'd always give him a job, saying, *One day you'll make as much as me*, while Tom, dressed in an easy-money suit, snickers from the other side of the room. And poor Robby, just sitting there growing darker and darker.

"Do your friends know you, I mean really know you?" I ask Rafa because the carpet seems to be lunging up at me. I might be holding the edge of the table. "I mean do your friends like you?"

"What a question! Are you all right? You don't seem yourself." He looks concerned now. I can tell this isn't going the way he'd like it to.

"This is the first time I've seen these people in a long time."

"How long?" He waves an approaching waiter away.

"More than five years." I'm bunching the table linen between my knuckles.

He must have given the maître d' a look because he's back now, bending over as if he might eat right off the table.

"Sorry, Gus, not tonight," Rafa says, handing him the menus, and Gus, pink-faced but polite, pulls out my chair when I get up.

Outside, night's come on quickly. It's still warm, though. The humidity on the rise. Rafa takes me to the same quickie mart where Robby and Jared bought a handle of whiskey and Tom loaded up on hot dogs and hamburgers. It's even the same cashier. I think she recognizes me because she sort of half smiles—impressed with my stamina, I guess.

Rafa buys two bottles of wine and asks if I like sardines. When I don't answer he buys them anyway, along with crackers, sparkling water, lemons, and two candles. They're pine-tree scented, the candles, I can smell them even though they're at the bottom of the bag. He takes me to his friend's yacht. I can barely see it in the moonlight, large and looming, ghostly but beautiful.

On board he turns on some white lights and music. When he comes up from the kitchen he has two glasses of red wine. He lights the candles and sits beside me.

"Is this better?" he asks. "We can eat later."

I can barely see his eyes. I tell myself that's fine, one day you'll forget what color they are anyway. When he puts his hand between my legs, I feel the callus on his palm that I'd forgotten was there. I shut my eyes and let him work his way up, up—right on up till a moan works its way out of me.

I whimper into his mouth when I come.

"*Me encanta tu panocha*," he tells me, and smiles. "Do you feel better now?" I can see his teeth in the candlelight. I catch the scent of pines. It's strong and slightly nauseating.

"So what have you got?" When I blink at him he says, "You're high as a kite, what's in your purse?"

I pull out the plastic bag of coke, which he says isn't much, but he starts to rack lines on the cockpit table with a credit card.

And then we're talking about something—possibly everything.

He keeps trying to put my head in his lap, and finally I say, "Susanna isn't my real name."

He laughs, his mouth open so wide I can see gold fillings. "I know," he says. "You don't come off as the kind of girl who takes care of her grandparents."

This strikes me as cruel. I remember when my father got sick—I was there for him even though he hadn't really been there for me. I can still recall his hospital room in New Mexico, how it smelled of bleach and everything had that plastic taste you get when someone you love is dying. How I was there for almost three weeks, how my brothers showed up for a weekend, bringing bagels that sat in a brown paper bag turning to rocks.

"Not many women give me a fake name, and I don't think I've ever gotten a fake phone number." He looks deeply impressed by this. "So I thought I'd come find you, find out your real name." He regards me for a moment with a sardonic expression and then raps his knuckles on the table. "So what is it? What's your name?"

"Does it matter?"

He considers this for a moment. "No, I guess not." His hand goes up to my head again, fingertips pulling my face toward his crotch. They're saying, *Come here, Come here.*

I toss my head back and look across the bay, toward the Casino. I wonder if they're all there now. It's the first time I've missed them. I want to ask Rafa if he misses his friends, but when I turn back there's a cutting look about him. A slight sneer catches the upper part of his lip.

"What if I named you?" he asks.

"No, don't do that." I start to stand, but he catches me.

He holds me in place, tapping his lip with his thumb at each name—that too-pink tongue darting out to touch the tip.

"Michelle, Dorothy, Katie, Danielle."

I'm shaking my head. The coke is very bitter. I can taste it in the back of my throat.

"How about Lacy—I had a cocker spaniel named Lacy. A real bitch with bite."

"I think I want to go home," I say, standing up.

Rafa stands too, puts his arms around me. "Where's home, Mama?"

I shake him off. He catches my arm and I almost stumble on the gangplank.

"What about my turn?" he says lightly.

"Sorry, you'll have to take care of yourself."

"Is that so?" he says, but I'm already on the dock. He reaches out and I slap at his hand so he loses balance. He knocks his glass of wine off the galley table, and it crashes to the deck.

"Shit," he says, serious for the first time tonight. "Do you know how much this deck cost? You can go, whatever your name is." He waves me away as if I am dismissed.

I find his distress hilarious. I laugh at him until his face turns red. He moves as if to come after me, so I jet.

"Ha, ha," he calls. "Look at you, running. Run, *Susanna*, run."

25

I'm suddenly very thirsty. I could die of it. I wander along the waterfront, toward the shops and crowds.

Someone out on the water is lighting sparklers, I can see them shoot up green and yellow, bright and sharp in the darkness. There's laughter too, and shouting, and the smell of the sea and the chaparral coming down from the mountains. The walk back seems to take much longer. I stop at a candy shop, filled with tired kids and exhausted parents, everyone red-eyed and drooping.

In the bathroom I put my mouth right on the faucet. I drink like I'm in grade school, gulping it down. When I've had my fill, I look up, into the mirror. My makeup is smeared, the eyeliner over my right eye has wilted, and my left looks like I tried to wash it off completely.

It's terrible business being a girl. I remember when Mother first took me to the salon for an appointment. Up until then I hadn't been a customer. I used to help sweep piles of hair with a tiny broom they got just for me, and arrange the gossip magazines by who I thought was prettiest on the cover. For the longest time they had me convinced Cindy Crawford was a real-life princess. The salon owner would take me to pick out the candy we'd have for the kids who were getting their first haircut. I chose Tootsie Pops and sometimes gummy bears.

Before my first appointment the women at Mother's salon loved to play with my hair, styling it on slow days, when they would share avocado sandwiches, their pedometer clicks, newly discovered beauty tips. *Add baby powder and it won't burn your scalp.*

It was like having a whole army of mothers.

I remember Connie, who liked to give me giant beauty-pageant updos. Connie, divorced, had crazy black hair and lipsticks always the wrong shade, and a great gulping laugh, one that made the whole room tense. Wait—the woman with the big laugh wasn't divorced. She had an out-of-work husband at home with her kid, and at night after dinner, with the baby asleep, they'd crack open a bottle of vodka and sip until it was empty. Her breath would still be heavy with alcohol the next morning, filling the salon as she sat blowing out her blond curls before the salon opened.

Connie was the newly divorced one, I think. Just discovering pedometers and Jazzercise, only just developing her alcohol habit, hands all twitchy, so Mother never let her cut my hair. I remember seeing her slip once: an earlobe dark and gushing.

I feel terrible I can't remember any of them as individuals. They've congealed into one cautionary tale: a pile of yielding flesh, worn-out and softened by age and freckles and everything nice bubbled down into one big glob. Those sweet nobodies, probably blow-drying someone's hair right now, or checking a perm, the sour chemical smell filling up the room like cat piss.

But, my first appointment.

The salon is near the country club, but none of that business crosses over. They drive right past, windows rolled up, A/C blasting because it's one of those smoggy, foggy days when you know you probably shouldn't breathe a lot. Mother only works at the salon part-time, blowing out hair, doing nails, helping with shampoos.

My father wishes she wouldn't. *My wife, working in a strip mall,* he mutters. Reminding us again that we are descendants from Scottish kings—*From Vikings,* he says. And Mother corrects him, her lip curling: *Nothing but horse thieves and rapists.* My father would rather have made the money, but an out-of-work lawyer has little choice.

The girls at the salon hug and kiss me, leaving behind lipstick smears and the smell of cheap perfume that I've always liked—like new plastic Barbie dolls or the candle aisle in the grocery store. My appointment is with their new aesthetician, a sassy man named Luca. I can still remember him so clearly: a stocky guy in a tight T-shirt and distressed jeans, his hair slicked back so it shines like black linoleum.

And there's Mother telling him how she'd like my eyebrows to look. She probably holds up a picture of Michelle Pfeiffer or Jamie Lee Curtis or some other celebrity she admires. And Luca takes me into the back, a quiet room that smells like vanilla. He has me lie down while he babbles on and on about what a pretty girl I am, how much he loves Mother—whom he does not call Cynthia, but Cindy.

Cindy is the cat's cream. You're so, so lucky to have a mama like that. Uh-hmm.

And he touches my face with gloved fingers, pinching and pulling and rubbing lotions into my skin. *Baby girl's gonna glow.*

I imagine he's right, my ten-year-old face is on fire. There's astringent and mask and some instrument that blows steam right onto my face so hot that I'm scared to breathe in.

When he's done my eyes are watering and he's saying *One more thing, baby girl.* He dusts my eyebrows with his fingertips, which feels real nice. Then comes the hot wax, which is warm and feels good too. Then he pulls the wax off. The first one is very quick and I barely have time to gasp. It's the second one that gets stuck and he has to pull twice. That one fucking hurts. Then he does the same thing to my pubic hair.

Pain is beauty, Mother said, chuckling, when I complained afterward, handing me a present. It is a haul of makeup. More than you could ever need, especially at ten. Liquids for eye swelling; blush to enhance bloom; expensive lipsticks; lip gloss, dewy and thick; brow liner, lip liner, eyeliner; shadows and shimmers and shades of various colors.

That was when everything changed, I think, eyeing myself in the mirror. The Connies of the salon stopped kissing you soon after, and started to look at you sideways. Your father stopped hugging and tickling you. Your brothers looked away when you walked into a room, but their friends looked you up and down. And once you realized that walking this way, or tilting your head that way, got you things, you started to do it all the time. You learned to use your mother's present of brushes and makeup to get whatever you wanted. But with the perks came the catch—the guys in the liquor store follow you outside, want to know why you're in a rush; the barista thinks you owe him something and tries to get you alone in the back; the mechanic makes a show of watching you walk, *Ay, Mami*. You are a young, too-pretty girl in a bright, big world. One that can hurt.

And here I am, years later, coked-up and alone in a bathroom that smells like sugar and spice, a framed picture of a cupcake over the toilet, makeup dripping off me, eyes red, skin blotchy. It looks old—no, that isn't quite right, it looks aged. I feel it too: my back hurts from sleeping on the boat, my feet ache from these shoes. There's a rasp in my chest from the cool, damp air.

This stranger has aged.

26

I buy some banana saltwater taffy and walk back along the boardwalk, chomping and throwing the wrappers into the sand. There's a large group all done up in their best, smoking cigarettes and shuffling in the courtyard of the Casino. It's poorly lit, with Art Deco lamps and tea lights in the trees, but I can make out Robby leaning over the rail, staring out at the harbor. He's in a sport coat, and with his hair curling and wild, he looks exactly how he did ten years ago.

"Hey, sailor." He turns, his face knit with such concern that I falter.

I give him my best smile, but I must look bad, because it doesn't change him at all. The crease between his brows is like a canyon now. I lean over the railing just to get away from that sullen pout. The moored boats shift and move with the swells.

He turns back toward the water and we stay that way. An ex-married couple standing in dim moonlight, watching anchored boats slap against each other like lovers.

"How was dinner?" he says finally, putting out his cigarette.

I shrug. "We never ate."

He shakes his head and takes out another cigarette.

"I don't mean it like that," I say, even though that's exactly what I meant.

I might be breaking his heart, but I can't help it. I remember once he wanted to move to Buenos Aires. *We'll drink maté in the morning and swim in the Rio de la Plata where the fresh and salt water mix.* My first thought had been, *No, it's either fresh or salty.* One beats out the other. *They can't coexist.*

He offers me a cigarette. "No, thanks. I could use a drink, though." I motion to the Casino. "How's the party? Am I under-dressed?"

"It's all right. Buddy Guy didn't make it, though, had a bron-chial infection. Might have been the last time to see him too, the guy's in his eighties," he says, depressed. "Soon it'll just be Kenny G shit."

The cocaine has loosened its grip, and the nervous energy that was caught up in my head has moved to my chest. I take his ciga-rette. The smoke is steadying, heavy, the kind of inhale you want every time. I take another, but this one's sharper and it burns.

"When was the last time you ate?" he asks. I can't see his eyes; the lamp above us has sputtered and gone out. "Your hands are shaking."

I pass the cigarette back. "I wish I was hungry. The idea of a burger sounds fantastic. But I don't think I could stomach it."

His shadowed head nods. "Wait here." He hands me back the cigarette. I watch until the crowd's swallowed him up. My legs feel very heavy. They'd like to lie down right here and fall asleep. Or maybe they've got narcolepsy—can that happen to just your limbs? Because my arms are just as tired now.

The cigarette is almost done so I rub it out on a pile of rocks and plop on the ground. Everyone outside is drunk, their faces half in shadow. A girl in a short lace dress stands directly beneath one of the Art Deco lamps as if it were a spotlight, her dress so tight I can see the lines of her Spanx. She turns and flashes a smile at me. From here her face looks plastic—inflated upper lip, sculpted chin and cheeks—almost grotesque. Whoever she's with is off-stage, just outside the light. I can make out his loafers, hairy big hands gesturing. He must look over too, because she's smiling at me again, this time with her whole body. I smile too.

When she comes over she seems very tall, but then she helps me up and she's normal size. Short, even, and wearing steep stilettos.

"Hi," she says. "You look like hell."

"Nice to meet you too," I say.

"Marisol," she says. "We met this afternoon."

I struggle to see her more clearly. Could this be the same girl from the Mexican restaurant? The smooth chestnut-skinned kid? Her hair has been curled and teased out; she's wearing red lipstick and a push-up bra.

"Jesus, how old are you?"

She seems offended by this. Her bare shoulders pull back, thrusting her breasts at me. I can see a mole on the left one.

"Old enough," she says, tossing her hair. A man comes up and puts his arm around her waist, which is tiny and firmer than a tree trunk.

"Hey, babe," he says. He's got a yachtie look about him—polo shirt, pleated khakis. I think I can see gray at his temples. "Ready to get outta here?" In his right ear is a small hoop earring.

I have an urge to punch him in the face. I want to take that earring and use it to scratch his eyes out. Marisol doesn't feel this way. She picks up my purse from the ground and hands it to me. Then she kisses the guy right on the lips—a big wet smack.

"Just checking on my friend, I thought she'd passed out."

When they walk away I can see his hand on her ass.

And then Robby is there, holding a bottle of something and a bag of potato chips.

"It's all they had," he says sheepishly.

I'm almost in tears. "Thanks. I'm really tired."

He takes my purse and helps me away from the crowd. When we pass Marisol and her yachtie I press my face into Robby's warm chest. I can hear his heartbeat.

We stop at a bench halfway between the Casino and the villas. He hands me the bottle of sparkling water. It's a relief. And the potato chips taste amazing. They're greasy and salty and the crunch is violent.

"Oh my God," I say with my mouth full. "These chips are fucking amazing."

His face is very serious. "How is this going to end?"

I wipe my fingers on my dress. "I'm going to pass out."

"No," he says, sighing. "I mean this." He points to me.

"Can't I just enjoy these chips?"

"I know you, Elsa, you're on a bender. What happened in New York? You can tell me." He moves so there's less room between us.

"I'm fine, I told you—"

"A vacation, I know." He drops his head back, lets out a sigh. It would be wonderful to just curl up on his lap and go to sleep.

"Does it have anything to do with that guy? Did he follow you here from New York or something?"

I rub my face. "God. Robby, I'm tired."

"Elsa, tell me, please." He watches me and when I don't say anything he slumps and pats his lap for me to lie down. "Come here."

"No, thanks," I say. "I can make it to the villa."

The waves are gentle, they don't even crash against the rocks below, they sort of rub up against them. Every once in a while there's a good splash, sending sea spray up at us. From this side the Casino looks like a lit-up birthday cake, the Moorish windows casting domed yellow light across the water.

"I want to help you, but I can't if you won't talk to me."

"Did you know the Casino has enough food and water to house

the entire year-round population? I mean if there was a disaster on the island they'd get to live in that building. It's nicer than any house on the island."

"Elsa," he says.

I ignore him. "I went by the museum today. I didn't go in—too many tourists."

"*We're* tourists."

"You know what I mean. But I heard one of the tour guides talking about it."

"Did he mention it's enough food and water for only two weeks? It's not that much time."

"It's long enough," I say stubbornly. And then we're quiet.

An older couple walk by, arm in arm. They must be returning from the Casino. They look nice, both in suits—hers a little more feminine—and she has an ascot tied around her neck. They're deep in conversation. Whatever he says has her chortling, her head flying back.

Robby's sadness is palpable.

"I'm going back to the villa," I say, standing up.

He stands too. "I'll come with you."

"No," I say more forcefully than I mean. But he's standing there and he smells the same. The same Camel Lights, the same Banana Boat sunscreen. His hand on my upper arm—the way he used to hold me, as if I might fly away if he let go. I try to remember what it was like to kiss him, the taste of him. How it was comforting, how quickly comfortable became boring. *He likes you on top*—ah, there's the memory. Washing over like those waves on the rocks below. *His arms, his beautiful arms, flexed and urgent, holding you up.*

"Good night, Robby." And I make my way up to the villa alone.

27

Back at the villa, I try to pass out, to sink into that darkness. But my brain is buzzing, as if separated from my body. I go over things. I do it obsessively. I replay memories—the ones that have deepened and have needs of their own. You need to stoke them, like kindling. If you don't, they go out. So I tend to them. I play over the night, parts of it so crisp and others already changing. I remember Rafa's yacht being dark, when really it was lit up like a quaint corner café with tiny lights and those candles making everything smell like a camping trip. I'll try to remind myself of this fact, but it won't matter. It'll be his gold fillings I see, the smell of a warm salty ocean—jazz music not very far off—and the feeling of that calloused hand. I think back to Robby, how water beaded on his skin—those memories of beach days and swim meets. How during the summer his tan made his eyes spark, the blue like the bottom of the Miramar pool.

There are many. If you let one go it's impossible to find it again. So I think of Eric's hands polishing that stone while standing on the beach, and Rex—Rex looking me full in the face, that blemish just above his lip. I think of Charly and her sister surrounded by snakes, my brothers in their well-pressed Boy Scout uniforms. I think of Mother blow-drying hair at the salon, pulling a round brush through a client's hair as if it were a reflex. I think of my father in that New Mexico hospital—which is a bad thing to do. Alone in the villa, with the sound of the kitchen clock and the dull noise from the Casino, I am right back there, in that hospital corridor lined with colored-pencil prints of birds of paradise. The silent dripping of an IV, the *beep-beeping* of an EKG, watching his pulse—such a delicate flutter we boil down to.

But back, back, you must go back. To when you first found out, when you were with Eric. You'd gone to Brooklyn to see an artist about an upcoming show. Later to a hotel room, at the Wythe, just one of the many you'll explore with him. These are still early days. You will have two years to get to know these little boutique hotels intimately—which side of the hotel you prefer (east), which floor (fourth), which restaurant (rooftop), which drink (gin martini, because it makes you feel older). You will even learn to recognize which staff will smile at you and which will not. This kind of illicit knowledge will thrill you.

The meeting with the artist is a success and you're celebrating with a late lunch on the rooftop. The view is incredible. Across the river, silver in the late afternoon, the Empire State Building stands out against the rest of the Manhattan city skyline. On either side of the hotel, Brooklyn stretches out in lovely industrial rows. It is exactly the city you thought it would be, metallic and blushing in the setting sun. Somewhere sirens cry out, far enough away to sound muffled, there are car horns below, and music from the hotel bar floats out onto the patio. You are *in* it.

The salsa was better the last time we were here, Eric says, but you are distracted by the city.

Just look at that view.

And then your phone vibrates. You think it's his at first. But he shakes his head and then you recognize the New Mexico area code. You don't answer. But when it rings again, you pick up. It's your father's girlfriend, Nance, a tiny Asian woman he met at yoga.

I'll order for us—if you trust me, that is. God, that grin.

You're stepping away and Nance is saying something about stomachs. You think maybe she's dialed you by mistake. But then she says clear as the skyline across the river: *They've removed almost his whole stomach but they didn't get it all. They want me to call the hospice.*

Does time stop then? If it was fair it would. But it doesn't. You watch the waitress put your margaritas on the table. They look delicious, the salt dotting the rim like confetti.

Then you're flying to New Mexico. The flight attendants solemn as undertakers. One gives you a ginger ale you don't drink, another hands you a tiny bag of crackers you won't eat.

Nance is at the airport waiting for you. She's already crying, so you drive. Memories from the hospital are like those of the women at Mother's salon—they all conflate into one. Then there's Dad in the hospital bed. Everywhere that sterile cleaning fluid smell. He tries to hug you but his IV gets stuck and pulls, little drops of blood forming around the needle. You're looking at his hands now, they're big but thin, you can see the veins and bone and how they tremble when they reach out to you.

You take him home a few days later, after a visit from your brothers and their wives. Your oldest brother weeping in the hallway, saying, *I can't see him like this, I can't see him like this.* Messages from Mother, telling you to give him her love. *Tell him I forgive him for everything,* she writes. *Tell him it's all right.*

The hospice takes care of his diapers, feeds him through a tube until his body rejects it. Then they tell you to stop the feedings. They tell you there wouldn't be any use. His body is pale and thin, except for his abdomen, which is bloated from the tumor. Dim eyes, sunken now, but still asking when he can get another feeding, and you telling him, *Just wait, just wait.*

28

Jane says the next morning, "I thought we'd do the zip line today." Her voice is bright and grating, and her face is just as obnoxiously cheerful.

All of us are in the open kitchen, the deck doors thrown wide so the fresh breeze can fill the room. Out in the harbor there are already paragliders flying above the water.

"Fuck, yeah," Jared answers. He's making smoothies in the blender.

Charly slices bananas beside him, strawberries too. "I thought we were taking the golf cart out to explore," she says to him. "You said we would today."

Jared scoops more banana handfuls and pulses the blender.

"I'll rent a golf cart with you, Charly," I say from the couch. I slept poorly, woke just before sunrise with restless legs. I had gone out on the deck, everything so quiet I could almost make out the waves hitting the beach. Hardly a breeze until the sun rose and then it started to gust, blowing through the palms and sending leaf litter scampering across the deck. I sweated through my nightgown in the night, and I shivered as the patches of wet skin and fabric dried in the sudden wind. Now every part of my face hurts—my gums, the back of my throat, the cartilage in my nose. Doing the zip line with an enthusiastic Jane would make my pain double *everywhere*.

"I want to see the west side of the island anyway," I tell Charly.

Tom smirks. "There's no way to drive there."

Charly is frowning. "Jared, I don't want to do the zip line." She's a bit more animated this morning, waking up early and deciding we should all have smoothies. *Something healthy,* she said, *to counteract all that booze.* But there's still an edge to her appearance, the brightness in her eyes looks a bit frayed.

Jared adds ice and the noise is unbearable.

"You go up to forty-five miles per hour! And drop five hundred feet!" Jane is telling us over the roar. She's already putting her fanny pack together. "Tom, how long is it again? A mile?"

"Almost a mile; it's considered one of the best zip lines in the country." Tom has his sunglasses on inside. He's scrolling through his phone.

"You missed a good concert last night," he says to me. "But I'm sure you had fun too." I can't see his eyes—the sunglasses are too dark—but there's no concealing that smile.

Charly puts the knife in the sink with the food scraps. "Jared, I don't want to go on the zip line—let's rent a golf cart like we talked about."

Jane is checking the weight of her fanny pack and looking at Robby, who's still in his pajamas. "We should get there quick as we can, there'll probably be a line."

"I'm ready," Jared says.

"Babe," Robby says, running his hand through his hair. "You know I'm not one for heights."

"Jared," Charly says, hands clenched.

"You should've seen Robby on the rocks at Joshua Tree," Jared says to the rest of us as he mimes throwing his arms out as if the ground might give way, yelling for someone to help him.

"Jared!" Charly shouts. Her face is pink now. "I don't want to go on the *fucking* zip line!"

"Jesus, Charlotte. Elsa said she'd rent a golf cart with you, don't make a scene."

He takes her by the wrist, but she pulls away and slaps him. It's a light slap, laughable, really. It could have been a caress if you ignored the look on her face. Her face says, *I want blood.*

She runs into their bedroom, her sob, almost guttural, barely stifled by the slam of the door.

Jared stares after her for a moment, his back to us, arms at his sides. I picture his mouth agape, his face flushed, but when he turns his eyes are bright and he claps his hands together. I can see his throat working.

"Well, I need a drink. Jane? How about we stop at a bar on our way to the zip line." He pours us the smoothies and adds the little strawberry garnishes Charly sliced up.

"Jared," Robby says, as he gestures to where Charly's sobbing can be heard.

"Elsa will stay with her. Won't you? I think this trip has been hard on her. We probably shouldn't have come." For some reason he apologizes to Tom, who shakes his head and looks back at his phone.

Jared turns to me. "You remember that crack-up she had after she didn't get that part? A Crest commercial, wasn't it? She's a strong old girl—she'll be fine."

"It was a sitcom," I say quietly.

He adjusts himself, feet shuffling. He blushes a little. "Right, well, you remember how that was. Just needs a stiff drink and a nap. You'll take care of her, won't you?"

His hands are in his pockets now; he's a boy who's been naughty, trying to charm me.

"Sure, why not?" My headache pounds now. I think something must be trying to escape from behind my right eye, burst right on through.

"Maybe we should skip it," Jane says. "Robby, you wanted to go golfing anyway, right? And there's the final show tonight at the Casino."

"Yeah, but that's not till seven, and you've been talking about the zip line all week. You should go." He kisses her on the forehead.

"That was before I knew you didn't like heights. You never said." Her stare is steady. "What will you do instead?"

His gaze slips toward me, and her cheeks redden. "Fine, stay here. It's probably for the best anyway. Tom and I will do the zip line." She's furious; her nostrils quiver. "Tom, would you call the front desk, please? Get someone to pick us up."

"I'll come too," Jared says to them. "Elsa and Robby can handle things here."

"I bet they can," Jane says, and clips her fanny pack around her waist. She looks like an advertisement in an outdoor magazine: chino skort, pink muscle tee, fanny pack, hiking boots.

"Should we meet back here and go to the Casino together?" I ask.

"Nah, we'll meet you guys there," Tom says, painting his nose with zinc.

"Will Charly be up for it?" Jane asks.

"She'll be fine," Jared insists. "Won't she, Elsa? You'll get her right again, won't you?" His gaze is strained, searching.

"Elsa the nurse—that's rich," Tom scoffs.

Jared gives a forced laugh.

I ignore Tom. "When should we meet you?"

Jane answers me, looking me full in the face. "Eight. In front of will-call."

"Won't you want to come back and get ready?"

She holds up a small backpack and heads right out the door without looking back, Jared and Tom following after her.

"What should we do?" Robby asks once their golf cart is out of sight.

"I'm checking on Charly, you can do whatever you like."

I go right through their bedroom, where Charly is curled up facing the wall. In their bathroom there are still traces of beige powder on the sink. I try to wipe it up but it smears and turns thick and sticky. For some reason this turns the throbbing behind my eyes into stabbing. I dig around in my beauty bag for my pills, what I hope are the Percocet and Vicodin. The pain is so bad, I take three pills and drink a bottle of water. "I want to be pain-free," I say to myself in the mirror. The redhead who looks back wants this too. Her eyes are large, deeply set, the pupils big and startlingly black. You could fall right into them.

"Then let's make margaritas," Charly says from the bedroom. When I step into the room she rolls onto her side, her eyes shining. "We should make margaritas."

"I thought you were asleep," I lie.

"I'm not. Let's make margaritas, it'll be fun."

"You're in no condition to drink."

She sits up. "Did I ruin everything? Is everyone mad at me?"

"You didn't ruin anything," I tell her. "They went to the zip line and will have a marvelous time. We'll meet up later and dance the night away. It'll be great. Really, everything's fine."

She chews on her cuticles. "And Tom? Jared will hate it if I've embarrassed him."

"Please," I say, waving dismissively. "Do not worry about Tom. I think it takes a lot more to make him uncomfortable."

"Can we please make margaritas? I want to have fun."

"You should take a nap—here, I'll take one with you." I lie down beside her.

Charly rubs her face hard. "I can't sleep. As soon as I start to fall asleep I see a baby crying and I can't comfort it because it isn't mine. And I want to—you know? I really want to but I can't."

She chokes back a sob. *Hush*, I tell her. *Hush*.

"You don't understand," she says. "You don't want children. You probably think I'm such a cliché. I am! Sometimes I look at myself and I could die of shame. I just— I just want to be a mother. That's what I want. I want a family of my own—without a child I'm just a failed actress married to a frat boy."

"There's other things in life," I say.

"Like what? Don't you dare say a career or I'll scream."

"You and Jared could travel."

Her nose is red and snot runs over her lip. She laughs, a big swinging laugh. "I want a family, Elsa. I'm not like you. I don't *want* to be alone."

It hits me then how Charly must see me: frigid, uncaring, selfish. She sees my life in New York as self-centered. Not aspiring, or independent, but hardened and cold and careless. Never loving, never having loved.

Nothing ever touches you.

This startles me. I think over our friendship. Back in the beginning, in those dusty orchard days, I'd swear we were on the same page. Maybe it was later, on that field trip in New York, when one of the Jenner boys kissed me in a dark corner of a museum. Maybe that's when we started to grow apart. Or maybe it was when I divorced Robby. Maybe she felt abandoned too. I had, in a sense, divorced them all.

But I'm here now, I sigh to myself—chest wet from where her tears have soaked through near my breast, the nipple hard from the chill. Why won't these pills work faster? I want to put this sadness— Charly's heaviness and my own—far, far away.

"Okay, why not. Let's make margaritas."

"Oh yay! I can have one—one is allowed," she swears, holding up her hand. "I promise."

"All right, but let's get you showered first. I'll do your makeup like how we used to."

She is obedient and happy, stripping off her clothes, giddy from being naked in front of me.

"Robby," I call from the bedroom door. The shower clicks on, and I can hear Charly singing. Robby pops his head in from the deck.

"Charly is feeling better, will you make us margaritas?"

"Is that a good idea? Aren't they trying to get pregnant?"

"You know about that? Has Jared talked to you?"

"I know enough. I think it's driving them both insane."

The pills have kicked in finally, everything is warm, and I'm comforted that he's here, that he knows what's going on too. The feeling blooms in my belly when he smiles at me.

"Well, she's laughing and we should try to keep it that way. Make them weak."

"Weak margaritas coming up," he says, and I feel like we are finally on the same team.

We sit on the deck, Charly stretched out on a beach towel, her feet kicking back and forth. The sun is very bright and warm and the breeze carries music up from one of the neighboring villas. When she finishes her drink she makes loud sucking noises with her straw.

"Let's go swimming!" She has a dizzy, googly-eyed look to her.

"I don't know if that's a good idea," Robby says, a little buzzed but looking at her with real concern.

"Oh, I probably shouldn't go." Her laugh is high and nasal. "I want to watch you two swim."

"A swim does sound nice," I say.

We get our bathing suits and walk down to the pool, which is crowded and a little too warm.

"Feels like piss," Robby says, disappointed.

"Then let's go to the beach! I want to see you guys race. I used to love to watch you two race."

To please her we go down to the beach and wade out past the surf, Charly waving from the sand. A swell comes and Robby's arm slips around my waist and we duck under together. His hands are wonderfully familiar. There are no rough spots. I'm proud of myself for remembering them exactly right.

Try to keep a clear head, I tell myself. But then the sun is very warm, and that giddy sensation, that lightness, wants me to love everything.

We tread water with our shoulders just touching. His arms are warm and freckled and I want him to hold me—*Danger*, my mind is saying. *Watch yourself.*

"Ready?" Charly shouts from the shore, and she makes a sound like a gunshot.

Within five strokes, Robby's ahead and I'm choking on seawater. I think drowning might be the best way to go. I reach out and grab his leg, pulling him back so I come in first.

"Jerk!" Robby says, laughing.

I'm coughing and struggling with a swell that's determined to push me under.

"I told you I'd win."

"Come here, you're drowning, you idiot."

I push him off and swim back to shore, my legs shaking. I drop onto the sand beside Charly, who is clapping.

"You play dirty, Elsa."

A speedboat guns its engine in the harbor and somewhere a firecracker goes off. Children down the beach are screaming about sand crabs.

"Too much noise, too much, too much," I say, pushing my head into the beach towel.

Back in the villa I shower and notice my beauty bag is sitting on the vanity. There are only three orange pill bottles now, all half empty. I combine them into one. A handful left of the good white ones, some of the tiny pink ones that loosen up the dark matter behind the eyes, and several peach ones with the letter *K* stamped through the middle. The blue ones are gone. The light pink ones too. Luckily there's still plenty of Vicodin left—at least I think it's Vicodin—though their numbers have dwindled. It occurs to me suddenly that at some point I will run out of them all.

29

We decide we want fish tacos but Charly passes out, so it's just Robby and me. We leave her sleeping, sprawled on her villa bed, her pale yellow dress twisted, the curtain beside her blowing out like a sail, then deflating, showing the blueness of the bay against the pith-white sky. She murmurs a little in her sleep. *Gerber* or *Berber*. I can't tell which, but she quiets down when I shut the window.

In the hotel golf cart Robby holds on to me, his grip tightening when we hit a rough bit of road. The driver looks over at us. He smiles. "Good-looking couple." He nods and looks at me. "Lucky guy." Robby overtips and we walk along the shops without talking.

The sun has moved behind the mountains, but it will be light for another few hours. Already people are excited for the final jazz show. The yachties are all drunk, wearing straw "Island Style" hats. Robby asks where he can buy one, and a thick, sunburned man with white whiskers gives him the one from his head. We pass a group of girls on their way to the Casino, swinging their hips for the fishermen who are packing up their tackle. The fishermen whistle long and low. Along the shoreline the lamps switch on, and beneath them couples lounge hand in hand.

We look elsewhere.

"Elsa, why'd you leave?" Robby asks.

My headache has come back and there's a knot in my stomach. We've stopped at the same Mexican restaurant where Rafael and the girls from the hotel had been the day before. But it's later in the day, almost dusk. With the change in light it could be a different restaurant entirely. There's paint peeling on the Spanish fresco, a chip in the fake adobe. We order tacos that come in bland tortillas, the salsa thin and watery.

Robby sits with one hand on his head. He's taken the straw hat off; it rests beside him on the table. His other hand picks at the label on his beer.

"Robby, we were never going to work. Let's not do this."

He laughs, really more of a bark. "That's horseshit."

I put a chip in my mouth to hide that I'm taking another pill. "Come on. Jane is a firecracker," I say. "She reminds me of someone I knew in New York—the wife of someone I knew, actually. I bet she can keep up with you on your morning swims."

He huffs a little, a painful sound. "She drags me out of bed, if you can believe it."

"Good, then you've met your match."

"We're living together and everything," he says with that same pained tone, the beer label in pieces now. "She's one of the strongest women I know, a triathlete, for God's sake."

A small boy in the booth across from us turns to cough into his arm. It's a great big dramatic cough that children do for attention. Robby smiles at him. "Good manners. His parents taught him right," he says.

"I know you, though; you've got to be the hero. What's her story?"

He fidgets with his beer. "Her apartment burned down about a year ago."

"Ha." I watch his face. "Oh, you're serious. That's terrible."

"She lost everything."

I pat his arm. "And you swooped in. Ever the knight."

"I couldn't save *you*." His eyes have a watery sheen to them now. He brushes the pieces of beer label into his hand and throws them.

"I didn't *need* saving. That was our problem."

His head is back in his hands. "Why, though? Was our life that horrible?"

"Jesus, Robby, get a hold of yourself. We're still friends. We just didn't work."

The family with the coughing boy looks at us across their burritos. The mother has smile lines. She's younger than me.

"I would have moved to New York if you'd wanted me to."

"But I didn't want you to."

"Fuck, Elsa." He thumps the table with his labelless beer. "We could have had a family by now."

"I didn't realize how drunk you were."

"Don't pretend like none of this matters. I know you, Elsa." He reaches for my hand across the table.

I'm suddenly furious. "Stop saying you know me—you *don't* know me. I never wanted that, *never*."

"Jesus. What's happened to you?" He says this with such force it feels like the whole restaurant turns in their seats to see who this *you* person is—to wonder what exactly happened to her.

"I got fucking fired from my job, all right?" I nearly spit. "There were cutbacks and I got axed—is that what you wanted to hear? Good. You heard it."

His face flinches. "Elsa, I didn't . . . I'm sorry."

"I don't need your pity. Pity yourself. I am fine—*fine*."

The knot in my stomach jumps into my throat. I'm up and walking out, shaking Robby off me. I catch the mother looking away from us. She pulls her coughing boy into her lap and presses her mouth into his hair.

Then I'm outside, looking for a quiet place to vomit. The harbor is completely gray now, the skyline one bright white spot, pink-rimmed. On the other side, a city starts to shimmer—Los Angeles. The Vicodin punches now. I vomit behind the Albertson's Express.

30

Charly is awake. She's up and cleaning the villa when Robby and I get back. Her googly eyes are glassy from taking a nap, but she's in good spirits, humming as she washes dishes.

"Let's get ready together," she says to me after drying the last plate.

She requests smoky eyes. She tries on several dresses, rambling about the kids in her classroom and the hunky school vice principal. She examines herself in the mirror.

"Maybe I should dye it? Ooh, that's a good idea. What do you think?" She looks at her reflection. "Something darker—no, lighter. Maybe I'm a blonde and I just don't know it yet. What do you think?"

"I think we both should," I tell her. "Try something new."

I've ignored Robby since we left the restaurant. He pouts out on the deck, watching those far-reaching city lights across the water, all oily, slick-looking—smoking cigarette after cigarette, smoke trailing into the condo. Charly is oblivious. She calls out to him, "We're almost ready," and her giggle bounces off the sides of the tiled shower and claw-foot tub, tumbling out toward him. "Hold still,"

I scold her, and paint her lips with a tiny wand dipped in a color called Earth Red.

We meet the others outside the Casino. Something has happened on the zip-line trip. Everything feels charged. Gone are Jane's cargo shorts and fanny pack. Instead she's in a white dress, her trim waist wrapped in a thin turquoise belt. Her hair and makeup are immaculate. She's had a shower. So have Tom and Jared. Tom was tan before, but now his face is pinched pink. It's been well moisturized too, his bald head shining under the lamps and his teeth fluorescent against his skin. He stands a little behind Jane, reaches out to brush something from her dress. Her hand goes to the back of her bare neck, lingering there for a moment. She looks at Robby, then Charly and me, drawing herself up.

"Hiya, babe," Robby says, pulling her away from Tom. He makes a show of kissing her.

Charly fidgets with her navy shirtwaist dress. "It's riding up, do I look okay?" she whispers to me.

"You're beautiful," I tell her, and she is. Her eyes are dark, smudged in the corners with eye shadow and liner. The Xanax has relaxed her, smoothed her out. She looks breathless, flushed and glossy. She could be eighteen going to prom.

Jared sees Charly and his eyes go wide.

"Elsa." He looks at me and then back at Charly. "Charlotte, you've taken my breath away."

She blushes, starts to pull at the dress. "You don't think it's too much?"

"Not at all," he says, shaking his head. He looks back at me. "You've outdone yourself. I owe you a drink on this one."

Charly's face falls a little but then Jane takes her hand. "And I'll buy this lovely lady one," she says.

"I'll open a tab at the bar, would you like that?" Tom asks Jane with something like sincerity, but she ignores him.

Robby takes Jane by the arm. "I think I can buy my girlfriend a damn drink."

Tom shrugs, plucks two of the jazz tickets from Robby's hand. "Then I'll buy *Elsa's*."

My name is a snake in his mouth, the way it rolls off, nearly swiping across Robby's face.

Jane pulls her arm free. "Come on, Charly, let's go in."

"Tom can buy *my* martini," Charly says with a high-pitched giggle.

I take one of the pills from my purse and follow them in. The mob is fierce, everyone pushing at one another, and the smell of sunscreen, shampoo, and too many flowery lotions is suffocating. Then I'm in the rotunda and there's room to breathe. A blues band is playing and there's a line at the bar. Jared asks Charly to dance and they disappear into the crowd. I don't think I've seen her so happy.

Robby turns to Jane, but she shakes her head.

"No, I'm too tired from the zip line," she says, looking past him. "I'd like to sit down. But you have a good time, babe." She touches her bare neck again.

"I'll bring you a drink, then," he says.

She's studying the floor now. "Tom has already gone to the bar."

Just then Tom brings martinis and Robby's face goes tight.

"Extra cold," he says to Jane, handing her the drink. He gives Robby a knowing look and turns to me. "And extra dirty."

Robby makes a sound I haven't heard before, like a growl crossed with a moan, and then he's shoving Tom hard so that he falls against another couple, sending their drinks crashing. Jane's knocked back too, but she gets up quick and is between them again. Her hands splayed out on Robby's chest look surprisingly delicate.

"Which one are you fighting for, huh?" Tom sneers from the floor.

"Robby, please," Jane is saying. "Please." She looks at Tom. "Go, just go."

Tom looks momentarily hurt, his face strained. Then he pushes himself up and walks off.

Robby hasn't missed a thing; he's waiting for Jane to look at him, and when she does she starts to cry.

"I'll take her to the bathroom," I tell him.

"I'm sorry, Robby . . . ," Jane starts, as I steer her away.

We push through the crowd—it feels like everyone is pressed up dancing against one another. I think I catch Rafa talking to a made-up Marisol beneath a fan palm. She's in a lace dress similar to the one I saw her in last night, this one bright pink and just as tight. Then the light changes, one of the canned lights goes from blue to red, and the couple changes too. They're too short and squat to be Rafa and Marisol—or maybe I'm remembering them wrong and that really is them.

The bathroom is big and beautiful, built in the first half of the twentieth century, so it has a powder room and full-length mirrors and two settees and urns and vases and black-and-white photographs of Joan Crawford and Myrna Loy.

Jane's stopped crying but is still upset.

"How was the zip line?" I ask.

"It was beautiful. Really beautiful," she says, wiping at her eyes.

I help pin back her short hair. "I have lipstick in my purse—are you more of a pink or purple girl?" She sits like a doll while I trace her lips. "I wanted to tell you, Jane, I think you're really wonderful for Robby. He needs someone like you."

She hugs me suddenly. I think she might be crying again.

"It was just very hot out on the zip line," she says, straightening herself. "We rented a hotel room—they only had a double, so we got ready together. Have you ever done that? Rented a hotel room by the hour, I mean, I didn't know that was a real thing. But we were short on time and had to get ready." Her chest has red splotches across it. "We all got ready together—it only took a couple hours." She looks at me soberly in the mirror.

"Well, you look lovely," I say.

"Jared went out to get a six-pack and a pizza."

"Oh," I say. And her reflection stares hard at me.

"I like that dress, Elsa. You're very beautiful. But you know that, don't you? Beautiful women are always told how lovely they are." She looks at herself in the mirror, and her voice changes. "Such a *pretty* girl."

She touches her lips, which I've painted Posey Pink.

"But that never makes a difference, does it? You never get what you want in the end." Her face takes on a wry smile. "Sorry," she says, shaking her head. "I need a drink is all. Let's get good and drunk." She's pressing my hand, squeezing the bones together.

Robby is waiting outside the bathroom for us. Jane falls into his arms.

"Let's dance," she says.

He kisses her on the forehead. "Sure thing, babe."

At the bar I order a scotch neat and take another pill, which burns all the way down with the scotch. Then I'm imagining Jane and Tom in that hotel—with its slanting floors and crooked windows. The door closing behind Jared, the air crackling, and then Tom is there, whispering, everything soft and blistering until his mouth is everywhere and you let it happen because he smells so goddamn expensive and has the kind of authority that makes you tingle. You come louder and harder than you ever have in your sad little Jane life.

The scotch hits me hard. Tom is suddenly beside me. He looks older. His airs are sort of tired, as if his well-pressed Armani suit were wearing him.

"Everything all right?" I ask.

184

"Yeah, just a little sunstroke. There was a long wait at the zip line and no shade."

"You ought to buy it and plant some trees."

He laughs. He's watching Jane and Robby across the dance floor. "They make an attractive couple," he says.

"I heard you rented a hotel room by the hour. Classy."

He grits through his teeth. "You are such a bitch."

I correct him: "A bitch with bite."

31

In the rotunda an announcer is giving out raffle prizes and throwing beads into the crowd, who roar back with delight. The crush is maddening. I feel in my purse for another pill. I don't see Rafa or his friends but there's Jared talking to Rachel, her platinum hair curled and shining. Where is Charly? But then Robby finds me. He's holding a martini. His mood has changed considerably; he's practically beaming.

"I'm sorry about this afternoon. I was drunk—it's a bad excuse, I know, but I'm sorry anyway." He hands me the drink. "Things have been difficult with Jane since we moved in together. To tell you the truth I wasn't sure we'd make it—and then you showed up." He smiles a little. "Anyway, we're gonna be okay, me and Jane. We've talked it over. Tom's just an asshole, likes to push buttons. Forgive me?"

"Yes, of course."

"Let's talk more when we get the hell off this island, as friends, I mean. I want to help you get through this. Really, whatever I can do to help."

"Yes, fantastic. Help. Sounds lovely." My voice cracks a little. I think somewhere far off I must be crying.

"Friends?"

"Friends." I think, *You poor son of a bitch.*

We clink our glasses together.

The band rejoins the stage, their faces still sweaty from their last set. They look haggard and bleached-out under the spotlights. But then the music starts, and the singer changes. Eyes closed, holding the microphone like a lover—he is sensual now, handsome. He reminds me of Rafa, not the Rafa from last night, but the first one, the one from the beach. Funny how a person can be many things. Was that only five days ago? It seems so firmly set in the past. Like Robby in the desert. Years, eons ago. Back when that ocean first started to rage—when it became deep and vast and filled with mystery. And this trip—I can feel it slipping away already, shifting, changing into whatever is next. *God, I'm tired.* How exhausting it is to be alive.

We watch for a moment, until Jared lumbers up like a drunken puppy.

"Have you guys seen Charly?"

"Maybe by the band," Robby suggests.

Jared makes us do shots of whiskey. We toast *To good times* or something. I'm only half here now. The other half is quite worn-out—it's slipped out to sea. Everything shiny, like those tinsel palms in Santa Monica. It's warm too, the balmy kind of heat you find in the tropics. I could sleep right here in a hammock, yes, that sounds nice—a hammock in warm salty air.

When I open my eyes everything is spinning. Tom is there now, saying something to Robby that makes him tense.

"I think I'm going to be sick," I say, but no one is listening. Jared asks again about Charly, but Robby and Tom are locked in a primal stare-down. Jane walks up then, and Tom moves so that they are shoulder to shoulder, like lieutenants, like a united front. I can barely make out Tom's face in the blue light, smirking at Robby, self-satisfied and contemptuous.

And for a moment Robby surveys them both, his head dragging back and forth. Jane looks at me.

"I think I'm going to be sick," I tell her, but she looks away.

She tries to apologize to Robby. I watch her hands turn up as if in surrender—they move toward him, coaxing. I see Robby's wide swimmer shoulders contract and then expand, his arm pulling back. All he says is *Jane* and then he backhands her across the face. I feel bile, thin and acidic, at the back of my throat. I reach out. *No, no,* I think. *Stop.* Jane melts down to the floor. Tom grabs Robby by his jacket, Robby takes a swing. I'm knocked back by one of them. The room is really spinning now—the band, the lights— I'm having trouble keeping my eyes open. Women nearby have knelt beside Jane, staring daggers at Robby, whose face is twisted in a snarl. Spit flying from his mouth. *Bitch,* I hear, and flinch, the nausea amplified. *Motherfucker.* One of their shoes squeals against the tiled floor. Tom is red-faced and grunting, attempting to throw Robby to the floor. Jane is crying, but I can't hear her—the music is too loud. She has one hand against her cheek, eyes wide, hysterical. Jared's voice, whiny and frightened, *Where's Charly? Charly! Has anyone seen Charlotte?* Security guards show up and get in on the action. The lights change from blue to red again and it's like the floor beneath me drops. The vomit is nearly here. I push my way to the bathroom.

There's no line, I'm able to stumble right in. It is beautifully calm and cool here with the tall ceilings and wide marble stalls. And so quiet. The nausea passes. I rest my forehead against one of the walls and take deep, steadying breaths. I must have a fever. Maybe I'll end up in the hospital after all.

There's a floor-length mirror and I can see my full reflection in it. *Pretty girl,* Jane's voice is saying. I can hear Robby and Jane and

Jared and Eric and Mother and the golf-cart driver and everyone, all at once: *Such a pretty girl.* I hear that and the sound of Robby's hand against Jane's face—*smack*—louder than the music.

I push open the handicap stall and there's Charly, sitting on the toilet, face pressed against the little metal shelf meant for purses. Her dress floating about her, heels peeking out. The handicap stall is the place you go to hook up. It's the place to rack a line of blow. There's a good amount of elbow room; we could fit a third, maybe a fourth. It should be a blonde, I think—that would make a nice set of three. I should call Rachel in here. But then what to do with Marisol and lovely Jane?

"Hey, wake up," I say. Something ugly settles in my stomach. I step closer. "Charlotte?" Blood, dark red and shining. It seeps out from beneath her navy dress—a study in color juxtaposition, like a painting Eric showed me. *Rothko wants you saturated in color until there's no difference between where you begin and his color red ends.*

I squat down so Charly and I are face to face. I say her name again. I shout her full name. She's not moving. The red has reached past her black heel, pooled in the seams of the chicken-wire floor. I can feel it now, some of her blood has smeared onto my bare leg, still warm.

Charly, Charly, Charlotte—is that my voice? High-pitched and grating, bouncing off the white tiled walls. I do not want to leave her alone. Someone is screaming—is it me? A pale woman, older, with pearls in her ears and around her throat—her mouth open wide—such a wide red mouth. Then she is gone too. I can hear the band. Someone should tell them to stop playing. Shouldn't they stop playing? I can feel the bass through the walls, the ceiling, my skin, it's in my blood too, back behind the skull, tight along the jaw—my teeth are *grinding.* And then Charly is pulled away, someone is working right on top of her. All that dark hair, matted and twisted, black eyeliner and eye shadow smeared and running down her pallid face.

Outside I push through a crowd to find Robby, who is standing close to a security guard, his head in his hands. I think about how in college he thought about becoming a doctor, then maybe a paramedic, then a firefighter. I was with him through all of it. He settled for lifeguard. I remember when he decided, and I thought, *How can you be a lifeguard in New York City?* But it was already over by then. Any one of those careers would be more useful right now than UX designer.

I'm already crying, and I shrug him off when he tries to calm me. *Charly,* I am trying to tell him. *Charly.* No one knows where Jared is.

The ambulance is quick. Or at least I think it is. Time seems to go very fast suddenly. Robby is holding himself now, arms across his chest, and then Jane starts to cry and I watch him slide closer to her, watch her accept his arm around her—her head falling softly, her hands covering her face so that she can cry harder. Tom watches them too, hands in his pockets. Jared is there now, following the stretcher into the back of the ambulance. For some reason the crowd continues to dance, the band playing on.

32

You remember a day but only in moments, and it's always in a dream so that when you wake all that's left is the awareness of how hot the day was, how the air at the orchard was so humid and heavy you thought that if you just clenched your fists hard enough, shook them at the sky, maybe you'd produce water in your hands.

Do you want to see if Jack can take us out? You remember how Charly's eyes narrowed when she said it, as if you had said something in your sleep about the oldest Drucker boy, and now she was going to make you pay for it.

The Drucker brothers are one of the best things about sleeping over at Charly's. The boys out on the farm are something to giggle over, to talk about in whispers, to make you feel your friendship is a heavy, serious thing that you share, perfectly, with only each other.

It's summer, and Charly's sister is in Paris with their mother and cousins. Charly telling you, *I didn't do well enough in math this year.* But it's okay because her sister will bring back chocolates and they'll plan a trip together when they are older. *Somewhere more exotic than Paris*, she'll say with a shrug. For now she's stuck at home with just her dad and the Drucker boys, so you spend the night often.

Sometimes you'll remember exactly how the oldest Drucker boy's face felt that day, pressed against yours. Rough because he had a beard, and the weight of him—how the dry earth chafed your butt, and how the dappled sunlight came through the branches of the old oak, which kept changing and shifting in a breeze that didn't make it down to where you lay, skirt off, tank top pushed up, exposing a training bra and pitifully small breasts. This you'll always remember with rushing shame at how ridiculous you must have seemed to him at thirteen.

Everything comes back in lush detail like that.

In this dream-memory Charly's dad is a flirt. He lets you decide what's for breakfast, ignoring Charly's request for scrambled eggs. You choose pancakes and then change your mind to waffles, and then back again to pancakes. Charly's dad laughing and saying, *No man can refuse you, he'd be a fool.* This idea pleases you because at home your brothers never let you do anything, and your father is just beginning to stay away.

After breakfast you and Charly will take the old airsoft gun, and shoot at cans and fence posts. There's a strong smell of eucalyptus trees and Charly's lotion, which is cucumber melon, and those smells will permeate your clothing so that days after, you'll push your face into them and be right back there again and again—listening to the sound of cicadas, feeling that sense of lawlessness because the town and your school and your house—most importantly, your house—are very far off and cannot touch you.

The citrus orchard is a few miles away, but you want to pick the wildflowers that grow near the fruit trees. Charly's dad radios the Drucker boys to pick you up—*No man can refuse you.*

Jack, the oldest at twenty, is driving, his shirt already soaked through from sweat, a cigarette tucked between his lips. His younger brothers, Ryan and Justin, are in the bed of the truck. They call out for you to ride with them. Dust, lots of dust clouds up at you, and Ryan, the youngest and the only Drucker boy still in school, ties a bandana around your face. Charly ties her own.

In the orchards, endless beneath a cloudless sky, the citrus trees with their gnarled trunks like old witch hands, you and Charly giggle when Jack yells to the workers to take their lunches. His Spanish is spot-on. When he turns you'll catch him looking at you from beneath his baseball cap.

Justin, the middle brother, nineteen, has a laugh like a bird in the middle of the night. It makes you cold to remember it—and you will, often, because it seems there are just so many Justins in the world.

He teases you, always teases Charly too, but with you there is a sense of malice. On this day he looks from his brother to you and then back at his brother—you could rest an arm on that sneer. He produces a brown whiskey bottle from his pack, insists it's a lunchtime tradition.

When you tire of picking flowers, there is whiskey and Coca-Cola and turkey sandwiches and potato salad. Charly has brought the airsoft gun and she shoots soda cans—the empty ones from lunch—and you both drink whiskey out of paper cups, giggling and smiling at each other. You feel so grown-up.

Charly's a good shot and Justin challenges her to shoot a grapefruit from a tree. This becomes a game. With every grapefruit Charly hits, you run with Ryan to gather the evidence. You glance back at the group on the blanket, at Jack watching you from under his hat, but then Charly is shooting another and there is Justin beside her, glaring.

You and Ryan pause beneath the canopy. He's out of breath, his face full and freckled. At school his nickname is Tub.

And there's the smell of citrus, like sunshine, a tightening in your chest, it's juicy—getting *everywhere*—and the buds on the branches are the color of seashells, and the bees sound like butterflies, and you are not scared, the whiskey making your chest warm; then Ryan tries to kiss you, smelling like fried food and the erasers at school.

When you come back to the blanket, arms full with grapefruit, you pretend you've hurt your ankle and don't want to play anymore. Ryan is sweaty and pink, looking like he might cry.

Justin says something like, *Well, God forbid Elsa gets hurt, I guess we all have to play something else.*

Charly glares at you, you've ruined her day. But then Ryan suggests everyone play tag. When Jack refuses, Ryan rubs his knuckles against his head, making Jack jump up and give chase. You watch him: the narrow spot at his waist, his broad shoulders and chest, his muscles flexing beneath his T-shirt. Then Charly is up, kicking Justin in the foot—getting him to rally too. You watch from the blanket, your friend enjoying the attention, shrieking as the three brothers chase after her. It's a pretty picture to remember: the gnats and dust like light rainfall.

You're flipping through a men's fitness magazine from one of the boys' backpacks, and pretending not to blush at all that bare skin, when suddenly Justin is there. He's looking down at you, his body blocking the sun, saying, *That's my magazine.*

You try to sound nice, polite. You think of Charly's dad and how he let you choose breakfast—how something about you makes grown men want to be kind. So you smile up at him, hoping this shows.

Justin has taken out his pocketknife. He kneels down so you are at eye level.

Do you trust me?

The knife has a bone handle; sun glints off the blade.

You try to smile or laugh but neither of those things happens.

Do you trust me? He makes slow, slashing motions, up and down.

You look for the others. They're chasing one another around the stump of an old tree.

Say it. He inches closer. *Say you trust me.*

And you can't help it, you instinctively throw up your hand because the knife is too close, and it cuts perfectly across the fold between your thumb and forefinger.

His eyes fall to your hand and then to his knife, and you'll want to remember fear or pity or some emotion flit across his face before Jack is there, punching Justin hard, in the head. Then you are crying because seeing your own blood and hearing the sound of bone against bone and the thud of body to earth is too much.

Then Jack takes you off to get bandaged. Charly is left behind with Justin and Ryan to clean up the mess, to wait for you. You hang your head half out the truck window—the beating wind, the choking of it, this is the only way you will stop crying.

Jack takes you to a small shed near the orchard with supplies and pulls down a first-aid kit. The shed is dark and damp, lit by only one overhead bulb that he has to twist to turn on. He's good with your hand, though, his face worried, tense. A bit of your blood stains his pants.

You'll remember his forehead being very close to yours, just touching, and you rest that way, with him holding your bandaged hand, your foreheads bent as if in prayer. You are sitting on a folding table, knees together, but then they're not. He's standing between them now, still holding your hand, your heads bent and touching. You watch his breath slow, how the lace on the bottom of your tank top barely flutters now.

He tells you, *You smell like grapefruit,* and then kisses you lightly on the lips. You let this happen. Even close your eyes and open your mouth to him. When he pulls away, you're too desperate to be embarrassed. You're holding him with your legs.

Have you ever been with anyone?

Your face is flushed and hot, and you hesitate but he won't contradict you when you lie. *Yes,* you say. *Oh, yes, yes, yes.*

He takes you outside then, leading you by your uninjured hand to an oak tree where the ground isn't as hard or as dry as the orchard's. You lie down, terrified he won't have sex with you, almost shaking from it. But he does. He isn't slow about it either. He licks his fingers and touches you. His body is heavy, and you think of Charly's sister in Paris, could Paris be this heady? Perfumed with citrus blossoms and something foreign, your own sex—a wet, earthy smell that slightly embarrasses you.

There's no pain, only wetness and his face scrunched up as if in deep concentration. When it's over, he helps you with your underwear and you lie back down beside each other, his arm across you as if you are now his. And you watch the patches of grass, how they wave up toward the sky, taller than you, and you feel warmth in your underwear, the thumping of your heartbeat, hear the buzz of flies—the big ones you find outside of town—and you shiver at the coolness seeping out from the musty shed.

This is what you'll be left with once the sun is up and the drugs have worn off. You're left thinking back to that day, remembering how it ended. Charly's curiosity, her suspicion. *Where'd you go? Why were you gone for so long?* You were reserved, nonchalant even. *I was with Jack.* You answered how you thought an adult would, because now you were one. No more sleepovers and lizard hunting for you. Charly resented it, was jealous, and began hanging out with other girls at school. Soon she would move with her mother to Simi Valley, in the same state but a world away, and you would lose touch completely. She won't be there when Jack enlists and leaves town, or when, years later, Justin corners you at a high school graduation party and puts his hand down your pants. How you let him.

I wish it was easy to pin down a timeline: this is when you and Charly will stop being childhood friends, when the oldest Drucker boy lays you down in the soft earth; this is when the ocean was created, the clusters of stars exploded to form Hydra—when you realized beauty was a dark and dangerous thing, getting you what you want, but always with a catch. You get Jack, you lose Charly.

In the present everything feels chronological but later everything becomes jumbled, abstract. You can't say for sure when anything happened. Like Charly's dad saying to you once while he sectioned a grapefruit from his orchard, *It's perfect, like your beauty, any longer on the branch, any earlier picked—ruined.*

33

Every way back to the mainland is booked from the festival—it seems everyone wants to leave today—so our only option is sailing with Tom. We don't waste any time. We wake when the world is still pale and everyone from the party the night before is asleep or just getting to bed. The ravens from the other side of the island have shown up to pick through the leftover garbage. Out in the harbor the cruise ship is gone. Without it the horizon looks endless.

Rachel brings complimentary tea and coffee to our room. She hugs Jane, who has a purple bruise across her cheekbone, and we file from the villa, leaving the keys on the soapstone countertop.

At the hospital Jane worries over which flower bouquet to get—lilies or roses?

"Roses aren't very appropriate but they look healthier than the lilies," she tells Robby, who, without saying anything, buys the lilies. They lead the way, with Tom not too far behind.

"We should really get going," Tom says. This is the second time he's mentioned leaving for the mainland.

The waiting room, called the Family Lobby, is staffed by a handful of volunteers wearing washed-out white button-ups. It's a narrow room, painted soft mint green with framed photographs of sailboats. There is an old boxy television in the corner, next to the brochures for the zip line and golf course.

When Jared emerges he looks horrible. No way could he pass for college-aged now. His hair is disheveled and, I can see now, his stubble is coming in gray. His shoulders are slumped, an upside-down U. He's wearing the same clothes from last night. Robby hugs him. Jane does too. Even Tom puts a hand on his shoulder. I restack a messy pile of mammogram pamphlets.

"I'm just glad she's okay," Robby says, still embracing him.

"We'll fly back to LA when Charly's stronger. Maybe a day or two." Jared's voice catches, he gathers himself but still there are tears.

"God, man, I'm so sorry," Robby says.

"Is she allowed visitors?" Jane asks, getting choked up. She's fondling her bouquet, which makes the small room smell like a funeral home.

Jared shakes his head, turns his back to me, says something softly to them all. I take this moment to walk down the long corridor. A couple of nurses come out from behind heavy automatic doors. I can make out Charly in a room just beyond them. I recognize the tangle of dark hair, fanned out across the pillow. She looks like a tiny lump, white linens pulled up to her shoulders.

Just before the doors shut I slide through, into the hallway. She's facing away from me, toward the window. It's a too-bright silver morning; the room feels whitewashed and sharply focused. Charly shifts, looks over her shoulder at me. She's paler than I thought her face could look.

I wave, try to smile. She motions for me to come in.

"Elsa," she says, sitting up. There is too much room around her. She looks shrunken, small.

"How are you?" I sit on the edge of her bed. She looks away from me, out toward that bright window. "We're all here. Jane brought flowers."

She presses her lips together. Her eyes are wide and glossy, eerily dark against her pale face.

"Want me to shut those blinds?"

She looks at me without blinking.

There's faint chatter coming from the nurses' station. I wonder which is Charly's nurse. There's a whiteboard indicating pain level with the number 6 circled. Someone's drawn a sad face next to it and written her doctors' names.

"Why did you come back?" Charly asks.

"To see you, and everyone else," I say.

She looks at me then. "They said I lost three pints of blood."

"You're going to be all right," I start, but she shakes her head.

"It was a baby," she says, her voice quivering. "That's what I lost. A baby."

I try to say something. To stop her from telling me she was almost four weeks pregnant.

"She was a miracle baby," Charly's saying, rubbing her abdomen. "I went into cardiac arrest and *she* died."

My mouth is incredibly dry. I look around the room for water, juice, anything. But there's only Charly, words tumbling out of her mouth, over those chapped lips, pale and trembling—pointed words, the kind that can't be unheard. *Do I have a funeral for her? Do I buy a park bench, put her name on a plaque? Tell me how to mourn her, Elsa.*

I'm sorry, I want to say, but my mouth won't work right.

"Samantha," she's saying now. "Sam for short. We'd be Charly and Sam. Wouldn't that have been the cutest?"

Her face crumbles and she kicks her feet so hard I have to stand. I ask the wrong question: "How?"

She laughs, a bark, really, and throws her head back. "Did Jared tell you they found opiates in my blood?" She points to the pain chart. "That I'm talking to a therapist because they think I'm an *addict*, Elsa. *Me*." She wipes viciously at her face. "I can't seem to stop crying."

I think about the collection of pills in my beauty bag, their many shapes. I can feel them in my purse. My whole body can feel them. It's like they're radiating their own heat. Why didn't I think to take one before we left the villa?

"I would have asked you to be her godmother," she says.

This is the moment I should say something, anything, but my mouth is just so goddamn dry. I stand there dumbly, feeling the weight of my own body. Then the moment passes and she asks again, "Why did you come back?"

"Charly," I try. "They all look the same. The pills, I mean, I didn't know."

She ignores me, makes that terrifying bark again.

"I can see it in your face. Even now, none of this touches you." And then she says calmly, "You're an awful, awful person."

"Charly, please," I start to say, but then she's crying, really sobbing and saying Go *away, go away, just please leave me alone*.

A round nurse in pink scrubs comes in and I'm able to tell her that I'm sorry. I even say it twice before backing out of the room. I leave the nurse holding Charly like an infant with a fever, shushing and rocking.

Back in the waiting room the drinking fountain is out of order. I work the handle and then spit at it with the saliva I have left. The few elderly people, who cradle their injured limbs, some hooked up to oxygen tanks, stare at me.

So I kick the water fountain too. I keep kicking it, hard. I put small dents in the metal. I think of Charly, her soft pale face—that look she gave me. *Awful, awful person*. I think of the baby—tiny embryo, a slick sack of cells—how it was probably on the Casino bathroom floor. I kick until a volunteer comes running out shouting at me. But I'm thinking of Eric now, how he isn't here to comfort me, how he hasn't called, and when the volunteer reaches me I'm shouting too—thinking of that last meeting in Eric's office, when the human resource woman coughed politely, when Eric's hand was beside mine but not touching. Why won't he comfort me? The volunteer has gotten between me and the fountain. He is middle-aged with a kind, drooping face. His arms are up as if to calm me, fear in his eyes. *Please*, he's saying. *Please*.

I howl again, because he's gotten between me and the water fountain and I can't kick him, can't hit him. And I want to. I want to push right through his saggy middle section, put his whole face in my mouth and go *crunch*. Instead, I scream, just to see everyone in the waiting room jump, and swipe those pamphlets off the table as I leave.

Outside Robby and Tom are smoking. Jane isn't holding her bouquet anymore; she's standing beside Robby, head down, arms heavy on either side. I don't see Jared.

"Where'd you go?" Robby says, looking somewhere beyond me.

"Why didn't you tell me?" He just looks down at his shoes. My limbs feel rubbery now, spent. I've sweated through my shirt.

"Tell you what?" Tom asks from behind his cigarette.

"That Charly was pregnant," Jane says, and she starts to cry again.

I think about that sound Charly made in the room, that shrill sobbing. How the nurse rushed in to help.

Why did you come back? My tongue sticks to the sides of my mouth. I want to kick something again.

"Where's Jared?"

Robby shrugs, rubs his face.

"A baby," Jane repeats, looking at us all for a reaction.

Tom offers me his cigarette.

I shake my head. "I need water. Can we go? I want to get out of here."

"Don't you think we should stay and help out?" Jane asks, looking at Robby, who starts to cough, snubs out his cigarette, and spits into a bush.

"We should really get going," Tom says, squinting. He uses one cigarette to light another. Smoke billows from his nose. "I don't like the look of those clouds."

34

Down at the harbor the dock is littered with cigarette butts and, sitting atop a fence post, one lone beer bottle. The beachfront is almost empty except for the fishermen on the pier. A few families eat breakfast at the oceanfront diner, waiting for the morning Catalina Express. Many of the shops are empty, seemingly more so with a vacant boardwalk. There are rental signs and for-sale signs, and through the windows I can make out tarp-covered stools, floors caked with dust except for the odd footprint of a workman's boot.

The water taxi appears and the same plump boys from when we arrived help with our luggage. One of the boys is peppy, asks Robby how our stay was, his narrow chest pushed out, shoulders relaxed. It's Tom who answers. Robby just lights another cigarette and goes to the bow of the boat.

"Thankfully short," Tom says, pushing a twenty into the boy's hand.

The boys motor us out to our slip, the wind gentle, the flashy speedboat at a dim roar. No one speaks. Even the proud boy has taken the hint; he steers now looking straight ahead.

We climb aboard Tom's boat and there's only the sound of the anchor raising, loud as it bounces off the quiet harbor. Then the sailboat's engine, turning over and gunning, startling seals and scaring seagulls from the top of a buoy, the spurting of water as we motor out of the harbor.

I go below deck because the morning air is too cold, the noise from the boat's engine too grating. Jane is there. She blames me. Not just for Charly but for whatever is going on between her and Tom and Robby. She's huddled up, knees to chest, windbreaker pulled tight.

"Should I make coffee?" I ask, opening the fridge. My headache is fierce. I find a bottle of water and drink it down, crushing the plastic in my hand.

Jane doesn't answer. She seems relieved since getting backhanded, which can't be right. But there she is, staring out the port window—cold and silent, with a thin, satisfied look, that purple bruise like a dark spot of blush across her cheek.

Then we are out at sea. Far, far out. Right in the middle between Catalina and the California coastline. I can't see either. The sky is soft white, iridescent and eerie. The wind and swells have not been kind. It's taken hours just to reach the center of the bay, Tom cursing and the boat listing left and right. The gusts are unpredictable, strong one moment, gone another. Then it's calm except for a thin breeze that whistles high up, spinning the wind indicator.

Robby is beside me above deck. Jane comes up and he lets her climb onto his lap.

I keep saying—sometimes aloud, sometimes to myself—"Charly is going to be fine. She's all right. Jared's with her, she's all right."

Tom is turning the engine just as rain begins to fall on the *Liquid Asset* with its varnished teak deck and cherrywood trim. The swells become dizzying suddenly, sending the boat up, up, and then dipping down as if it were one of the rides on the Santa Monica Pier. Then Tom is in full rain gear; we could be in a Turner painting.

The cold rain pelts us. Robby holds Jane tighter. She's holding her legs, like she's trying to curl up inside herself. And I'm grasping the railing, knuckles white. The ocean is a monster, large and black and roiling. Capable of destruction, everyone at her mercy. *I take it back*, I'm thinking. *I take it back. I don't want to see your mysteries. I do not want to know your power.* My arms ache from holding the rail, my teeth chattering.

The boat lurches and slaps hard against a swell. This wakes Jane up. She's beautiful in a crisis. Moving swiftly and with purpose back and forth across the deck as if in an urgent dance with Tom, who shouts at Robby and me to go below deck. He's scowling and firm. Jane calls the Coast Guard using the boat's radio. How does she know how to do this? But there she is, dialing the Coast Guard and *maydaying* as if she'd been doing it every day of her life.

The boat pulls into Marina Del Rey just after sunset. Each of us is a little shaky and seasick; Jane is crying and hugging Robby, who has not looked me in the eye until now, which he does solemnly.

"Can we give you a ride?"

"No, I'll be fine," I lie.

Jane throws herself on him.

"Poor Charly!" she cries. "Please, let's go." And he's forced to lug her like an exhausted kid toward their car.

"I'll call you tomorrow and we'll talk," he tells me, and waves from behind the wheel. It's a funny romantic gesture that gets a snort out of Tom.

"I suppose he thinks you two will get back together now."

"Shut up." I watch Robby and Jane's car until it's out of sight.

"What a fucked-up love story," he says, and something in his voice makes me turn.

He makes a show of looking me up and down. "You just radiate it, don't you?" When I step back he smiles and reaches out for me. "Poor Elsa, was the ride back too bumpy? Do you need comforting? Why didn't you let your ex do the job? Is it because you want me to?"

"Fuck you, Tom."

"You can't help that pout, can you? That vicious bottom lip." He bends his face toward mine, holding me in place.

"At least I didn't fuck Jane in a by-the-hour hotel."

He lunges and bites my lip, hard. I kick him, landing just between his shin and knee. He lets out a howl.

I jump onto the dock before he can come after me again.

"Where are *you* going?" he asks, still holding his leg.

"Staying with a friend."

His snarl is perfect. It's everywhere in his face. "What friends have you got left? I don't think Charly will be sending any Christmas cards."

When I turn away, I can hear the venom in his voice.

"You know, when they asked, she didn't tell them where the pills came from."

That ugly feeling in my stomach punches into a sob, but I manage to walk up the dock, away from him, head straight, shoulders thrown back, only a slight wobble in my legs.

"You have nowhere to go, Elsa!" he calls after me.

35

There's a big hotel on Admiralty Way that wasn't there six years ago—windows lit up, a party going off around the pool. People laughing, clinking plates and glasses, the sounds of silverware. I cut across to the greenbelt as the lamps click on. Bicyclists race past on the bike path, their headlights glaring in the fading twilight. I'm thirsty again, my head and lip throb, and I'm frightened Tom might be following me—I jump when a bike passes from behind, its tinny bell sounding in the dark.

So I keep walking, past the new hotel, down into a neighborhood of beach bungalows—the kind with old wood windows that stick in their frames, air-conditioning units hanging from them like planter boxes. A tiny dog with a bark like a chirp runs alongside me, attacking the gate that separates us. I can still hear it at the end of the block, howling now. Despite the antiqued signs that say "Beach Life" or "Pug Love," I don't feel safe here either.

A group of teenagers drinking beer from brown bags catcall me from inside their garage. I cut back out to the main street and head toward the beach. It feels less threatening down where the homeless are getting high for the night. Small tents and sleeping bags between palm trees, reggae music coming from somewhere.

I make my way toward the surf and plop down on the sand. There's a Miramar Hotel napkin in my purse. Rex's number is written on it, and his writing looks so hopeful, with sloped letters and plump eights. He's written them how you aren't supposed to: with two big Os stacked on top of each other.

I think of what his apartment must look like, the posters on his walls, the bong on the table, the curtains his parents sent him. I think about what would happen if I showed up there for the night. My clothes would end up smelling like boy. And how that scent would haunt me forever, for infinity, like one of Rex's hopeful looped eights on its side. Much too long a time. I fold the napkin and tuck it back into my purse.

It occurs to me suddenly that there is someone I could call. I take out my phone. The alligator-skin case has frayed, the bottom corner stitching unraveling. I look up Eric's number and hit CALL. *Connecting, calling*—then I hang up, my heart beating violently.

The fog has settled over the water. It's completely dark now. I can't see Catalina but I know it's there. I think of Charly. That heaviness returns to my stomach. I think of her lying in a hospital bed, the open ocean just beyond her. This is when I cry—thinking about that great big ocean of dark, how Charly fell into it, and how when she came out, her womb was empty. Because this is the real moment we are no longer friends. Not that day in the orchards, over a boy, not when I divorced Robby and left for New York. It is right now—when I comforted her with pills instead of friendship. I can feel it being carved into my timeline: *This is when you lost your friend.*

My phone vibrates and I fumble for it.

"Hello? Eric?"

Her voice is thick and rich and I place it immediately.

"No, my dear, this is Eric's wife, Mary—we've met previously. I think you might have tried to call my husband just now?"

I look around, thinking she might be nearby in the dark, but there's nothing except the crashing of waves. I try to sound casual, *Oh, hello* . . . but she sighs over me and I'm reminded of how she looked staring out the Plaza window, watching the clouds, one hand propped under her petite chin.

"I have his phone, I've been waiting for your call. What time is it there? Never mind, it doesn't matter."

I can hear her breathing.

"I really don't have a lot of time, I was just about to go out," she says with a touch of impatience. "You understand why you were offered such a generous severance package, don't you?"

"Yes," I say, unsure. "There were cutbacks. I took the buyout offer."

"Oh, then you didn't, you really didn't. You're all the same—pretty and silly."

Could this be the same woman I watched that day? I remember how she stood on her upmost tiptoe to reach Eric's cheek, such tenderness.

"Did anyone else get let go? No. Have you ever heard of such a large severance package? No."

"I've never been fired before," I say sharply, which only makes her laugh.

"Look, I'm on your side, I think the way they let my husband scamper about with his pants around his ankles is quite—*revolting*."

I reach out for a handful of sand, which is cold and wet, and rub it between my fingers. I realize the wet is seeping into my clothes, the coldness too.

"Are you there or did I lose you?" she says.

There's a sea lion now, I can hear it calling. I make some excuse. "I have to go," I say, but don't hang up. I'm thinking about when I was called into Eric's office—to be *let go*. That human resources woman with her polite cough.

"I'll just cut to the chase," comes Mary's faraway voice. "I've been building a divorce case, can my lawyers contact you? I know several galleries in Europe—Paris, Prague, Lisbon. I'll put in a good word, wherever you'd like to go."

My hands are shaking. I've gotten it wrong. This is not the unwitting Mrs. Reinhardt I imagined—with her big museum jewelry and posh bright scarves that never wrinkle.

"Hello? Elsa, dear, you're a capable assistant—I can help you. Here, I'll text you my number, think about it. Don't get hung up on some *aging prick*." Then she adds coolly, "I'm going to bankrupt the bastard."

I hang up and when I feel the phone vibrate with her text, I shut it off and lie back in the sand. *You will not cry.* I close my eyes and try to focus on the crashing surf, the lulling repetition. That sea lion cries out again, and somewhere in the dark another answers. I shiver, exhausted, and sick to my stomach. *You're all the same, pretty and silly.* I think of those young curatorial assistants, the even younger research assistants—how they giggled, ate it up, whenever Eric, with that damn smile, walked into the room. The whole world wanted him and he chose me.

Why hasn't he called? It was real. It had to be. I could not have imagined it all. I curl up on my side, burrow into the sand, and try to picture him: *Eric Reinhardt,* with his silver hair and dark, serious eyes. Looking at me from behind his coffee, a martini, across a hotel bedroom. The man who threw a stone so far into the ocean that I did not see it splash—only watched that twisted expression on his face, his breathing long and low. But then I think about his wedding ring—and it hits all at once. I can see him now, in every instance, in the vaults, his office, each and every hotel room—that band always on, even when the rest of him was naked.

36

Let the dull roar of the ocean, several feet away, become the freeway—the 405. That soft sand, a well-worn bench seat in Rex's truck. You're bouncing along with Rex at the wheel, driving up, up. Every gear change over the Sepulveda Pass you can feel his triceps flex and jerk forward against your thighs, back, flick, switch.

Austin is with you too, the waiter from the hotel with the good coke. He's taller than you remember and several years older than Rex. He wears shorts and has a ridiculous amount of blond leg hair. When he smiles his eyes get a sharp glint.

What brought you to LA? Austin is asking.

I missed the sun, you're saying. You're between them both, sitting at an angle so Rex has to reach down beneath your skirt to change gears.

Well, let's have some sun, then, Austin is saying. And just like that there's a sunroof, and Austin pushes it open and turns up the radio. Hello, bright blue sky. Large cumulus clouds tumble overhead like an approaching wave.

The small truck climbs the canyon, and you can feel the change, it's in your nose, a pinching—everywhere that high, dry scent of eucalyptus and chaparral.

The Valley rarely gets rain, Austin is telling you, his blond leg hair tickling your thighs. It should rain, you think, why doesn't it rain? You can feel the drought suddenly, the parched earth waiting for water.

And then you're at a house party in the dry hills above the valley. There's a pool with a diving board and hot tub and there are young people, all swimming and drinking and looking like fourteen-year-olds with boobs and defined abs. The lights flash from blue to red and—is that Robby? Tom is there too. They have each other by the lapels again. But when you're closer they aren't fighting, only waiting for you to walk by, giving you matching judgy looks.

Enough of this, you think, and shiver because a little wind has picked up and the sea lions are crying out again.

Inside Rex is spinning records. Had he said he was a DJ? You can't remember, but there he is, sweet boy with neck acne and a grown-up's jaw, lips big like a woman's, smiling shyly, asking if you have any requests.

I need a drink, you're saying, and then you're wandering the house. It's ranch-style, so you can walk in a circle forever. Around the hall, down the corridor, into the living room, the kitchen, the dining room, and back out to the hall. Again, again. You float in loops until you're in a bedroom.

Austin is there too, only now he looks more like Justin. Tall and thin, hooked nose, shaded eyes. Flat wide hands. He's talking to a girl not yet twenty years old. The girl looks at you. She looks *like* you, with that wild-eyed marbled look young girls get when they're very drunk for the first time. She's wearing a blue dress, short and tight at the waist, flaring out over her hips. Then Justin is asking you, annoyed, *Can I help you with something, chica?*

But you cannot look away from the girl, who giggles and puts her hands over her eyes. You show him a twenty-dollar bill. His demeanor changes then—he smiles, waves you into the room. *There's some lines in the bathroom, they're yours.*

She's pretty, the girl in blue says. Her voice is light and familiar and feels like a hand squeezing inside your chest. She looks at you between her fingers.

Not as pretty as you, chica, he's saying. *How you doing? You feeling good? Did you miss me? Come here, baby girl, yeah.*

You can smell his breath even though you're only watching in the bathroom mirror. Stale and dusty. You want to do something, stop it from happening, but your limbs are heavy and helpless because this is history and there is no stopping it. So you watch him stand between the girl's bruised bare knees, watch him push her back onto the bed, his mouth near her face. You can see where his hand is. She's making little gasps, saying, *I can't, Justin, I can't. I'm on my period.* You're embarrassed for her, ashamed even. You know why she's letting it happen—you can feel his brusque maleness, his desire. It is bigger than her. Best to just go with it. Don't get hurt.

Justin, I can't, she's saying over and over, and when she stands up he does too, saying *Prove it,* and she does a feeble little shrug and without pulling up her dress his hand disappears underneath it. Then his voice is so brutal that you both flinch: *Fucking cock tease.* And he's suddenly Austin again, walking out with swagger, sunglasses on the back of his head, blond leg hair thick and coarse-looking.

The girl falls onto the bed and you think she must have passed out. She's just lying there, on top of the covers, penetrable in every way. But when you're about to leave, she turns her head and says, *Don't tell Julia.*

She's very young, this girl in blue, younger than Rex even. She has big hazel eyes, her curls messy, matted, not yet dyed. When she breathes her whole tiny caged chest rattles. She looks miserably drunk. You go to the kitchen to find water and Advil. When you return she is sitting up in bed.

Oh, get me the trash can, she moans.

You bring her the one from the bathroom. She vomits almost immediately. When she's done she lies down, exhausted.

You touch her back; it's very warm.

This dress, she's saying, pulling at the zipper.

Okay, you tell her, your hand still on her back. *It's okay. Hold on, I'll help you*. And you do. You help her out of her dress—she has very small breasts in a white cotton bra, no underwire and no padding. You can see her brown nipples, too large for a girl so young. She has on floral panties, not one curve to her body other than her ass.

She climbs back into bed, moaning and saying, *Oh, don't tell Julia, don't tell Julia*.

You tell her hush, you won't tell Julia a thing.

Austin is her man, hers, she says, her eyes bright, feverish.

You tell her not to worry, here is water and Advil. *Take three when you wake up*, you're saying. *Then go back to sleep. You'll feel better in the morning.*

She nods, her lips pucker and you think she might cry, but then she points cartoon-like to her lips, her eyes pressed tight. You know instinctively what it is she wants, a kiss good night—a token paid for sweet dreams. She smells a little rancid from throwing up, but you kiss her anyway, lightly on the lips, and she says, *Thank you*, as if you paid the toll and may cross the bridge.

Then Rex and you are alone in his truck. The radio is turned low, a small amount of fuzz, just for atmosphere. The windows are rolled down. He's taking the canyon rather than the freeway. There's the light rain you wanted. You want more. You want the dry canyon earth to be fragrant. You want to smell wet sage, licorice, eucalyptus. You want to quench this damn thirst.

You also want to tell someone the truth. So if Rex asks, *Did you have fun tonight, Ingrid?* you'll sit up so you can look at him straight on, and tell him. That you're not a wine rep from Portland, that your name isn't Ingrid. *It's Elsa*, you'll say. And you'll tell him how you were fired from the Museum of Modern Art for having an affair with your boss. That you have nowhere to go, that your childhood friend had a miscarriage because of you, that she is your friend no longer, that your ex-husband has left his girlfriend and wants you back in spite of it all. And you still do not love him. Because you're tired of being someone's prize, tired of the compromise. Womanhood has such a shitty exchange rate. You just want what you want. You don't want to have to pay more. You don't want to have to justify it, or feel ashamed.

And sweet young Rex will blink and you'll be struck again by how childlike he is. Maybe you'll cry. You'll get his sleeve wet with tears. *Fuck*, he'll say. *Are you okay?* And that will make you laugh, and you'll put your head back on his shoulder, saying, *I hope so.*

You'll be quiet then, Rex working the gearshift, the sunroof pushed open because now you want to catch various star formations through it. Goodbye rain, hello Hydra, with its orange and yellow giants—that solitary serpent in the sky.

Maybe everything will be okay. You'll go back to Bakersfield and live with Mother for a little while. Start things over. You'll write for one of those slick art magazines, work in the salon for some quick cash. Mother can teach you to blow out hair. *It's all in the wrist, Elsa.*

But then a breeze picks up, a cold, crashing sea air that starts my teeth chattering. No more Rex, no more stars. And somewhere nearby, seagulls, shrieking.

37

I wake up blindingly sober, the ocean just ten feet from me. I have sand pressed into the side of my face, inside my clothes, knotted in my hair. I roll over so that I can push myself up, but this is the kind of sober that hits back, and pain is everywhere: behind my eyes, between my toes, up and down my back. My brain swollen, my tongue swollen—I'm fairly sure the roots of my hair are swollen—with pain.

I try to focus but I can still feel the jerking of Rex's truck, smell the newly washed scent of the canyons, even Austin's stale breath.

And that girl in blue. I touch my lips, still tender from when Tom bit me. I realize then that I left my duffel bag on his boat.

A surfer pads out a few steps from me, gives me a quick once-over from the corner of his eye. I must look pathetic. I pat at my hair, brush off my bare legs, and stumble across the sand, back up to the boardwalk. The streets are empty except for a street cleaner and pigeons pecking at an overturned trash can. I catch a bus to the Santa Monica Pier. There's only me and the older Latina women on the bus; they're holding their lunches on their laps, on their way to work. They talk in happy animation—the ones that are awake—and do not look at me when I climb aboard. But when I reach my stop one of them calls out, *Buenos días*, just before the doors close.

At a corn-dog stand my card is declined. I think, *So this is it, finally.* I pull out cash but the pimple-faced teen insists I take it for free. I drink down the lemonade, which is too cold and sweet but helps ease the headache.

In the beach bathroom I try to wash up. The stalls are concrete and open at the top, so it smells like piss and the ocean. I think about my dream and how I thought of going back to Bakersfield, and laugh out loud. Working in the salon with Mother—what a riot.

I decide I want to ride the Santa Monica Ferris wheel at the end of the pier. Its lights are still on from the night before. It isn't the same Ferris wheel that was installed after the storm destroyed the original. They auctioned that one off on eBay to the highest bidder earlier this year. I remember reading about it while sitting in my MoMA cubicle, Eric bringing us our morning coffee. Me thinking, *So what if they got rid of the Ferris wheel? What happens in Los Angeles can't touch me. I've climbed out of Bakersfield, moved to New York City, to the Museum of Modern Art. I've reached the top.*

This new Ferris wheel is solar-powered and very shiny. The attendant, mid-yawn, locks me into one of the buckets. He waits awhile, plays with his phone. No one else is around, the park having just opened. Finally, he starts the ride.

There's an awkward moment on any Ferris wheel—when you circle back around and come up from the inside, facing the other buckets. Usually they're filled with riders, but at this hour they're empty, and it's just the lone attendant, scrolling through his phone, scratching at his stomach. Then suddenly he's gone, and it's just you thrust into the open sky, out over the silver curve of the ocean.

I can almost make out Catalina through the fog, those high-ridged mountains where the bison live. How their fur ruffled in the wind. But that's not right. I was too far away to see that kind of detail. Why not remember it that way? Their ragged fur, molting from the winter, moving like long grass on cliffs.

I turn my phone on. There's a missed call from Robby and a brief but silent voicemail. The corn dog threatens to come up, but then the ride peaks again and I gulp down the fresh air. I can see Catalina's mountains now. I think of Charly, about those orchard sleepovers, her childish laugh, bubbly and catching, a little bit mischievous. I can't imagine her laughing like that now. The weight of that threatens to make me cry again. It would be nice to talk to her, to tell her that in my dream everything turns out all right.

When the ride ends I find change in the bottom of my purse and use it to get a bag of hot nuts. I'm reminded of Central Park, those winters when everything seems like it's just waiting for that first snow, the one that will blanket the city. Maybe there isn't a version of myself still there, walking Central Park or haunting the halls of MoMA. But if things were fair, I must have left *some* imprint there, the way it's imprinted itself onto me.

On the pier I watch a gull peck at a fisherman's bait when he isn't looking. The phone vibrates in my pocket and I know it's Eric. But just in case, I stay silent until he speaks.

"Elsa."

I cry out *I miss you* and startle even myself. The fisherman looks over, pretends to be interested in the view behind me.

"Your wife called," I say, trying to control my voice. "But I don't care. I still miss you."

"This won't work," he says. "Not at all."

The gull has flown off, the fisherman throwing garbage after it. We speak over each other.

"Did she offer you a job?"

"Will you get a divorce?"

"Elsa," he says, sighing. "I've told you—it's complicated. You don't know what it's like to be with someone for twenty-eight years.

She'll never go through with a divorce—never. She always comes back."

That *always* hangs in the static between us. Twenty-eight years is a long time. When their son died there had been an extended bereavement period; two weeks turned into four. I imagine the funeral arrangements: the phone calls, the florist preparations—the cards with embossed calla lilies and letterpressed sentiments, *Sorry for Your Loss*, Mary and Eric opening them together. I picture Mary displaying them on a mantel in their living room. Had their dead son been good-looking? I never asked to see a photo. Why hadn't I?

"Yes, she offered me a job," I tell him.

"What? Oh, she did." He sounds worried. "Did you take it?"

"No," I say, and when he sounds relieved, lets out a puff of air, I say, "I told her I'd think about it."

I hear papers shuffling, what might be the coffeepot brewing in his office.

"That's not funny."

"I'm not laughing. I'll need a job eventually." I want to hear his voice catch, feel him squirm, so I say, "Paris is tempting."

He laughs, a light, nervous sound. "Sweetheart, darling, I don't think it would be a good idea—for anyone. It's best you stay in Los Angeles. Or maybe take time off, rest up in Bakersfield with your mom . . . Elsa, are you there?"

I hear his voice, but I'm thinking about his son's death, how it was then that our lines first converged, and how it was only after his bereavement that things ramped up—when the hotel rooms started, when his hand began to creep up my thigh at lunch or a meeting, when his mouth—when *everything* became filled with urgency. And I'd thought it had more to do with love.

That heaviness returns to my stomach, it smacks of mourning.

"I don't want to rest up, I'm fine," I tell him. "And I miss you."

"Elsa," he says. "Please . . ."

"Can't I come back?"

I want to hear him say my name again. Because that last time was not at all how I remembered it. I need him to say *Elsa* like he's tasting it. I want him to say it over and over until it permeates his clothes, saturates the room he's in, until it sounds right.

"I'm starting to think I imagined it all," I tell him. There are tears now.

The fisherman has reeled in his line. I watch him rip a piece of sandwich and push it on the hook, the fluorescent orange of American cheese between slices of brown bread.

"Look, it just won't work . . ." He pauses. "I mean, you freaked out when you left. You smashed an exhibition book through my table. You terrified poor Nancy."

"Who's Nancy?"

"From Human Resources. I had to talk her down."

"I bet you did."

"Don't be like that. It was frightening—you scared even me." He laughs again, that irritating light laughter that makes me want to kick through the pier. "My little firecracker."

I think back to that moment, to when Nancy from Human Resources asked me to sign severance paperwork. How she was a small woman, with a sharp nose and hawkish eyes. She kept using the word *generous*, and when Eric put his hand beside mine they shared a look above me—a look that said *Poor girl*. Had I started to cry? Probably, yes. I'm sure I did. I mean, I'm crying now, it doesn't seem to take much. And then there was the Picasso book, the exhibition that started it all. The last two years of research, of us entangled in each other. How appropriate that I would be let go when the exhibition was finally on display, the book we had labored over together currently for sale in the museum gift shop. And here it is, in my hands. I can feel the weight of it, the taut shrink-wrap, the embossed letters—M-o-M-A. I'm thinking of how I researched with him, *for* him. I'm thinking of those sketches, how those lines turned into sexual pleasure, how they built a kind of primal love on the page. A *gift*, Eric is saying. A *goodbye gift from the curators*. I hadn't thrown it, I let it drop—slammed it, maybe—just to get them to understand.

I hear myself saying *Goodbye*. I tell him, "Maybe I'll see you in Paris or Lisbon."

He says, "Let's not end things like this."

"Goodbye," I repeat, then add his name for finality. "Goodbye, Eric."

"Shit. Fine. Shit," he says. "You've put me in a hell of a situation."

"I have to go."

He's quiet. I can tell he's trying to think of how to ask me nicely. Finally he huffs into the phone, "You won't talk to Mary's lawyers, will you?"

I'm thinking about how eager I was for every part of him. My stomach turns. I belch and taste my fried breakfast again.

"Elsa, for fuck's sake," he says, and all I can think of to say is *Thanks for everything* or *Good knowing you, it's been a real pleasure*, so I hang up without saying a word. Later, I'll pretend I said something clever.

My phone does not vibrate again. The pier is quiet, except for the seagulls and the fisherman casting his line.

I stare at my phone for a long time, thinking about that first interview, years ago. I remember that it was fall, that it was early and even though the sky was overcast the museum was filled with natural light, that it was spilling into every corner. And coming in from the street, where it had been a dark city morning, all that light overwhelmed you. Gone were the smells of the city—the car exhaust, and the trash, the stench of human piss. It was like that whenever you walked into a museum. You left the ugly outside.

MoMA, that great institutional tomb where there is only the quiet *click-clack* of heels or that polished squeak of a good pair of boots—that rare air telling you *It's okay, you are surrounded by beauty, everything sterile, everything exactly in its place. Nothing bad can happen here.*

And then Eric. How at first he walked right past, but saw you just the same. A quick look that gave it away from the start. *Oh, hello, beautiful stranger,* it said, casually, with a slight smile, a glance thrown over his shoulder as he left the building.

The interview was short, or would have been if Eric had not shown up. At first it was just you and two women from the curatorial administration department—who you did not see much after you were hired. One was named Ruby or Debbie, with short, frizzy hair and bright plastic rings on her fingers. They asked you questions about your degree, about working for the UCLA campus museum. *What prepared you for a museum like MoMA?* You had arrived so confident, so eager, your boss at the campus museum having helped secure the interview. You tried to be light, tried to joke, telling them how funny it was that you were a terrible artist, but wanted above all else to be surrounded by beauty, that a museum was just the place. *Either that or a salon,* you said, but they did not laugh, only sat there with their legs and arms crossed, the austere conference room clock ticking. There is a sneer women give each other—it isn't in their face, so much. It's beneath the skin, a tilt of a chin, a long breath. Maybe they will look behind you, sometimes right through you. If you studied it closely you would catch a slight frown, a narrowing of brows—the contemptuous pout of female distrust.

At that moment you touched your hands together and watched them take in your manicured nails, your exquisite blazer, your blond hair bobbed at your shoulders, your skin dewy, Smoky Rose lipstick just right—how you were perfectly, expertly put together— and you wanted to apologize. To tell them this wasn't really you, that you could be whoever they wanted, if only they would hire you.

But then Eric was walking by in the hall, head down. He looked up just as he neared the door and smiled at all three of you. The interview changed when he joined, the women became softer, warmer. He filled the already glimmering room with more light. Suddenly we all talked like old friends. He asked, *Why New York?* Because New York was the pinnacle, the highest rung on the ladder. Because going from Bakersfield to Los Angeles to New York City to the Museum of Modern Art would mean you'd be untouchable, unreachable.

It was during that interview that I realized, without shame, that I would do whatever it took to make my escape. That I had seen my future at Charly and Jared's wedding and said *No, thank you.* From the moment I shared a look with the beaming bride across the room, I'd wanted to leave, to molt, to shed them all. And I would.

Goodbye, I could feel myself saying during the interview—*Goodbye, Robby; goodbye, Charly; goodbye, Jared; goodbye, life in Los Angeles.* I'm meant for more. No one can touch me now. Except maybe this man, with his laughing green eyes.

Stupid, stupid girl, I tell myself, wiping my cheeks.

The fisherman has packed up his tackle, shifts his rod to his shoulder and moves farther down the pier.

I scroll through my contacts, thinking, *You need a plan.* Robby will take you back, but he'll use that phrase, *Make love.* And you'll have to be okay with it—maybe call it that too. *Make love to me, Robby,* you'll say.

I can't get myself to do it. And there's no calling Charly either. She's lost the one thing she's wanted, and I've lost the right to call her about anything ever again. I am untouchable finally. Free from everything because nothing will have me.

There is no going back. Not to a dusty grapefruit orchard in Bakersfield, not to a New Mexico hospital, or a mansion in Provincetown where an influential man held my face in his hands and said *God help me, I love you.* Eric *had* said that, hadn't he? Everything about the moment suggested it—the way he wrapped me in a towel, pulled me into a spare bedroom, covered every part of me. It doesn't matter, because I can't go back. Too bad nothing gets left behind. You have to carry it with you into the future.

I think about Tom then, how he spat a little when he said *You have nowhere to go, Elsa*. I touch my lips, still slightly swollen and throbbing, more sore than injured. There will be no going back to New York. Or to Bakersfield.

It's too late to save that girl in blue.

38

The sun has come out and the peaceful morning is filled with cars and pedestrians all going somewhere important. My phone is off, shoved to the bottom of my purse. I found the napkin with Rex's phone number written on it, but it's slightly smeared now, enough so that I can't read it.

It's a short walk from the pier, so I make my way back, back over the palm-tree-lined bluff to the bougainvillea-and-jasmine-covered gate, the golden light spilling over the Miramar's circular drive, the red-vested valets huddled at the door. Only this time, the valets move away when I approach, so that I have to open the door myself. I look around the lobby for Rex but don't see him, only other hotel boys just as young, just as helpless. In the bathroom the attendant watches me. I can see her in the mirror straightening the bright packs of gum on the counter, looking at me from the corner of her eye.

I ignore her and wash my face, taking one of the tiny mouth-washes she offers without tipping, and carefully apply lipstick and mascara. I pinch my cheeks, do the mouth exercises Mother taught me—*You don't want jowls, young lady.*

Just then a manager comes in, dressed in a sharp black pantsuit.

"Hello," she says, and smiles at the bathroom attendant, who nods. I hear their little walkie-talkies hiss.

I smile brightly, wonder if she recognizes me from when I checked in. She had given me my room keys, written down my driver's license info, called Rex over to help with my bags. But now she washes her hands five feet away hardly seeing me, saying something that makes the attendant laugh.

"I'm looking for one of your employees," I say, but it's like I haven't said anything at all. They just go on chatting lightly.

I swallow a few times, my throat suddenly tight. I take one of the packs of gum and head for the front desk. At the counter a girl I haven't seen before, dressed in a crisp white blouse and a delicate neckerchief, smiles at me.

"Can I help you, miss?" she asks, beaming.

"I'm looking for one of your employees, Rex." I falter. "I don't know his last name."

She folds her hands, the fingers long, the nails manicured and painted a bright coral. "I'm sorry, ma'am, but we can't give out employees' last names."

"I'm a 'ma'am' now? You called me 'miss' a second ago."

The other employees look over; the hotel boys that could be Rex but aren't fidget with their shirts. I flash my smile so they know everything is all right.

"I only want to know if he's working." My throat gets tighter, I'm grasping the counter between us.

The girl grimaces and turns away to use her walkie-talkie. Then we're both waiting, watching the giant palm-frond fans circle above. One of the young hotel boys gives me a pitying sort of smile.

"He gave me his number." I struggle with my bag, pulling out the crumpled Miramar napkin. "See?"

A voice comes over her radio, says something I can't make out.

This girl is younger than me, probably five or six years, but she already has little forehead lines. They're caked with powder, and she's wearing two giant silver hoops in each ear. When she shakes her head they swing and hit her cheeks. "I'm sorry," she says, that head shaking, the earrings flapping. "But he isn't here." She looks sorry too—sorry for me.

I pull myself together. "Thanks anyway," I say.

Outside the air is too hot, too thin and too hot. I don't think I'm breathing right. I find the last of the pills at the bottom of my purse and take them without water. They snag somewhere in the back of my throat like sharp, jagged things, and I dry-heave until I'm vomiting a thin acidic liquid, the pills smashed up and half melted on the sidewalk. I spit, my stomach squeezing so hard I start gagging again. Beside me the valets have stopped talking; one has paused while retrieving keys from some hotel guests, all of them looking at this girl, broken and puking beside the bright hydrangeas and palm fronds.

I pick up and eat the pills from the ground in one quick motion, pausing only to look one of the valets square in the face.

At the bus stop I use the last of the mouthwash, chew the gum I took from the bathroom. It's minty and calming and for a moment I feel fine.

I ride back toward the marina, my hot forehead against the cool glass, the bus air-conditioning on full blast. It's marvelous to be cold on such a hot day. I watch a hawk soaring high above Ocean Avenue, almost in line with the bus. Its great wingspan shadows the walkers and joggers and cyclists below. The pills aren't working fast enough and I wipe at my eyes. It would be irrational to be angry with Rex. I tell myself this over and over but still I feel abandoned.

A child sitting with an older woman points at the bird, his little finger smearing the bus window.

"A hawk," I say, smiling. "Isn't it beautiful?"

The boy looks at me, the grandmother too, and then she looks to see where the child's pointing.

"That's a turkey vulture," she tells the boy. "They feed on carrion, dead things." She sniffs and turns the child away from the window.

Fine, all right, I think. *You win.*

I take out my compact. Mascara under the eyes, one a bit more smeared than the other. Lipstick gone. Hello there, *old* friend. The word beats like that, like the hum and thrust of the bus engine, like the toy the woman has given the boy to play with: *Old, old, old.*

But don't worry, it's easily fixed. I take out my beauty bag, empty now except for makeup, and begin. First, makeup-removal towelettes, lavender-scented. The grandmother watches me wipe away that old messy face. Next, foundation. You have to go in layers. Blur the lines, smear it up into the hairline, under the jawline too. Hide those dark circles. Make your fingers cold by holding them against the bus window. Press them lightly under your puffy eyes.

The grandmother watches, her lips pressed together. I almost can't see them at all, she's got them shut so tight. So I do my lips next. I purse them in her direction—*kiss, kiss*—and spread the lipstick color Lickable across them, smacking them together so that the child looks again. Hello, I smile that brilliant smile, the one I can feel in my cheeks, behind the eyes. *Hello.* The boy blushes and squirms in the old woman's arms. Then it's time for mascara: black, noir, negro. Enough so that they really pop. A little brow liner, some blush. How sweet am I now? *Such a pretty girl.*

At the marina bus stop I get up and walk past the grandmother and child with such ferocity she moves her bags out of my way and looks after me with her mouth a little open. *It's like that,* I tell myself. When you witness a transformation—a *metamorphosis*—you're left in awe. At the bottom of the bus stairs I slip off my panties, folding them neatly in my purse.

After the bus roars off I can see Tom washing down his boat, shirtless. I can make out his shoulder muscles, every muscle in his back and torso. I misstep then, some break in the pavement, a loose bit of asphalt, something. I bite the inside of my lip accidentally. I can taste blood, cold and metallic.

I think of that story Tom told me—that woman hanging Christmas ornaments alone. I think of Tom seeing her, watching her misery—how that was enough for him. I spit blood into the dry gutter.

"Tom!" I shout. My voice does not waver at all.

He drops the hose and walks over.

"You have my duffel," I say when he reaches me.

He holds open the gate without saying anything. I walk past him, down the dock. I make that short distance work. I walk like my hips are chewing, like every woman with a good ass and an agenda does. I walk and he watches—I know he watches, there's nowhere else to look.

"Where are we headed?" I ask, smiling.

When he looks at me, seething, a little turned on, I look away. I can't help it.

"Does it matter?" he says.

I shake my head. No, it doesn't matter at all.

Acknowledgments

To the following people and institutions, without whose support and guidance there would be no book: Mark Haskell Smith, Tod Goldberg, Mary Otis, David Ulin, Dara Hyde, Daphne Durham, Sean McDonald, Sara Birmingham, Jeff Seroy, Sarah Scire, John McGhee, Corinna Barsan, Jamison Stoltz, Olivia Taylor Smith; the University of California, Riverside–Palm Desert, staff, faculty, and students; the Getty Research Institute, The Last Bookstore, Mary Clare Stevens and the Mike Kelley Foundation, my family, my friends, and of course my husband (who has been my rock), as well as all the coffee shops and museum cafés I've haunted for the last four years—you have my eternal gratitude.

"*Catalina* is an extraordinarily engaging study in the tension of opposing forces: youth and world-weariness, beauty and unreliability, good intentions and roads to hell. The backbone of the novel is its relentless unwillingness to apologize for its main character—not for her faults, not for her complexities. Hot damn, and about time. Liska Jacobs writes with teeth; this book's got bite."
—**JILL ALEXANDER ESSBAUM**, *New York Times* bestselling author of *Hausfrau*

Elsa Fisher is headed for rock bottom. At least, that's her plan. She has just been fired from MoMA on the heels of an affair with her married boss, and she retreats to Los Angeles to blow her severance package on whatever it takes to numb the pain. Her abandoned crew of college friends receives Elsa with open arms and a plan to celebrate their reunion on a booze-soaked sailing trip to Catalina Island.

But Elsa doesn't want to celebrate. She is lost, lonely, and full of rage, and wants only to sink as low as the drugs and alcohol will take her. On Catalina, her determined unraveling and recklessness expose painful memories and dark desires, putting everyone in the group at risk.

Its every page taut with a creeping menace, Liska Jacobs's *Catalina* is a deliciously dark exploration of beauty, love, and friendship, and the toxic impulses that compel us.

Daisy Buchanan and the inscrutable seductiveness of Carmen Sternwood in *The Big Sleep*. Liska Jacobs writes crystal-clear, hypnotically sensual prose, and *Catalina* is California noir at its darkest and sharpest."
—**KATE CHRISTENSEN**, author of *The Great Man* and *In the Drink*

"In her propulsive debut, Liska Jacobs tells the story of a beautiful young woman's downward spiral with precision and insight. *Catalina* deftly explores the desperate social frontiers where the morals of the privileged class dissolve. You won't be able to look away."
—**J. RYAN STRADAL**, *New York Times* bestselling author of *Kitchens of the Great Midwest*

LISKA JACOBS is a Los Angeles native. She holds an MFA from the University of California, Riverside–Palm Desert. Her essays and short fiction have appeared in *The Rumpus*, *The Los Angeles Review of Books*, *Literary Hub*, *The Millions*, and *The Hairpin*, among other publications. *Catalina* is her first novel.

MCD

COVER DESIGN AND PHOTOGRAPH
BY TYLER COMRIE
AUTHOR PHOTOGRAPH BY JORDAN BRYANT

FARRAR, STRAUS AND GIROUX
WWW.FSGORIGINALS.COM